CARTEL BOMBSHELL

DIDI POUNDER

Cover Art by Ryan Gajda

@ryangajda

Printed in the USA

First edition, 2025.

ISBN - 978-1-968357-06-1

For you.
Buckle up.

A WORD ON TRIGGER WARNINGS

Listen, I know what this looks like, but keep your wits about you. You're telling yourself this is romance. Because it follows the romance topes. But don't be fooled.

This is smut.

And smut is the Wild West, my friends. Take note of the *Trigger Warnings*, and proceed accordingly. Nobody would blame you for bagging out now, but you'd be missing out.

— Sharp Levarius

Head of Trashcan Publishing

Triggers:

Non-Monogamy, Non-Consent (Not involving main characters), Physical Abuse, Drug Abuse, Urination, Sex Work, Murder, Bondage, Imprisonment, and more.

CARTEL BOMBSHELL
STARRING LYDIA SLICK

International Mistress of Danger

By
Didi Pounder

SNAP SHOT

<u>*Lydia*</u>

I'm going to drown!

My lungs blaze as I launch myself towards the surface.

Calm down, I tell my panicking body. *You're not going to fucking drown.*

Yes, I am!

The sun shimmers through the crystal water, and I kick my feet even harder.

Thirty feet.

I'm not going to make it!

Twenty.

Yes, you are.

Ten.

The final push.

This is always when my lungs hurt the most. I'm so close to breathing again, my whole body is ready to revolt and suck in seawater.

Patience.

I intentionally slow down, forcing myself to confront

terror like a former lover. Look him square in the eye and let him know who's boss bitch around here.

Now!

I shatter the top of the water like a glass ceiling and gasp in my reward.

Goddamnit.

Air tastes so much sweeter when you've been under water. Tempting as it is to heave chestful after chestful, I keep my head straight. Deep and slow. Discipline is about sublimating your impulses to your will.

And right now, my body really needs to calm her tits. Aw, who am I kidding? This rack is incapable of calming down. That's part of my charm.

Are there times when I lose my head? Damn straight. But never when it comes to keeping my functions in check.

How long was I down? Just shy of six minutes. That's chicken feed compared to the times I used to pull back when I did this shit for real.

What the hell was all the fuss about? I've been down twice as long as this and my lungs weren't such pussies about it.

Still, after a whole morning in the water, I'm ready for a break. What I need is some sun and an ice cold beer. Good news is I've got plenty of both on my speedboat just a dozen yards away.

Biser. It's Hrvatski for pearl, and the perfect name for my little water rocket. That girl has gotten me out of plenty of tight spots. She's also perfect for skipping like a stone across the Adriatic.

Sleek and black, like an unsheathed dagger riding low in the water. As lovely and lethal as anything I've ever laid out hard cash for, and worth every razor thin dime. She bobs on top of the clear, salty sea at perfect ease, but once her inboard thunders to life, it's a different story. No cutesy little kitten purrs for this jungle cat. It's tiger screams or nothing.

The law around here says you can't go faster than 8 knots

within 300 meters of the coast. As if there's anybody out here to enforce it. If there's one thing Croatians are famous for, it's rolling their eyes at the law.

I may only be an adopted Croatian, but that doesn't mean I give a hoot in hell about speed limits on the open sea. If the fuckers can catch me, we'll sort it out then.

But I can say right now—the man hasn't been born who can catch Lydia Slick.

Hauling myself onto the stern, I wipe saltwater from my eyes and slick my hair back from my forehead. If there weren't other boats nearby, I'd strip off my suit and lay out on the front hatch to dry out.

But nobody gets a free show.

Grabbing my towel, I glimpse a notification on my phone screen. Without even having to look, I know who it is.

Zero.

Sure as shit, her name glares up at me, already scolding me for not being at the ready. Her text is a masterclass in restraint.

Call.

Terse as ever. To her credit, the head of GSIA knows how to get to the fucking point. Even when it makes her sound like a bitch. Don't get me wrong, Zero is a cast iron bitch in her stocking feet, but I wouldn't say it to her face.

Following orders like the good little agent I am, I respond immediately. True to form, she picks up before the first ring.

"Where were you?"

"Hello to you too," I reply, and she tsks.

"Answer the question."

"I went for a swim."

"You didn't come up for over an hour?"

"Eight minute dives. I'm trying to get my free diving endurance back up to its peak."

"It isn't important," she cuts me off.

Not to you.

"I take it you're in Split?" she asks.

I shield my eyes and squint towards the coast. Technically I can't see the mainland between the islands shielding the city itself, but I've made this little jaunt often enough to know the score.

"About thirty kilometers out."

"We need you."

"Copy that." I smirk, getting my jollies by needling her *just a bit*. "Do I have time to pack a bag?"

She tsks again.

"If you must. The jet will be waiting for you at the airfield."

"Roger. Over and out."

Zero hangs up before I've even said it.

God, she reminds me of my mother.

Nice as it would be to stretch out and let the sun crisp me up, duty calls. Turning the key, Biser rumbles to life and we point for land.

Trees and scrub pock the sunburnt faces of Hvar and Vis. Part of the fun of coming all the way out here is shooting the moon between islands on the way home. If I were a good girl and toed the legal line, it'd take me a bit shy of two hours to put-put my way back to my marina.

Fortunately, I'm nobody's good girl.

I romp on the throttle so hard Biser's nose is in the air like a shark fin. The wind whips my hair into a chestnut auburn mane, and the sea salt crusts on my tanned skin until I'm about as tasty a snack as any man could desire. Careful though – this snack bites back.

Back in my bright little stone house off the marina, I fling together a kit bag of essentials. Headquarters is going to load me up with goodies for whatever mission this is, but a girl has a penchant for her own underwear.

A cold shower knocks off most of the sea, but I can still taste her on my fingertips when I step off my motorcycle at Split's quaint little podunk airport. Two terminals of nothing in particular, but it's hard to beat the view of Kozjak mountain just beyond the landing strip.

The beefy security guys scowl at me as I strut past. Every time I show up, it means a lousy day for them. If GSIA sends a jet, they have to shut down all air traffic until our wheels are up. International security comes with perks. These vest wearing flunkies get their perks too. I know how they look at me when I walk by. Having eyes in the back of my head is my literal job description.

Well, let them look. Christmas comes early this year, boys.

The engine's already running on the sleek, unmarked Cessna waiting for me, and we're in the air before I can sit down. Buckling into the plush leather seat, I run my finger along the sandalwood scented upholstery. GSIA is many things, but cheap ain't one of them.

The concierge comes over to deliver my cocktail without even needing to be told.

"Your Sazerac, Miss Slick."

Apart from the sparkling glass, she's empty handed. I narrow my eyes at her.

"Where's my dossier, Federica?" Protocol says it should be in my hand at takeoff so I'm fully briefed by the time we reach headquarters.

"Delivery on arrival, Miss Slick. Intelligence is still compiling."

"I see."

This must really be an emergency.

Zero never calls agents until all the pins are in place. Taking a sip of my perfectly balanced cocktail, I look out the window at the pristine coastline skating by below.

I don't have the faintest idea what I'm walking into, and I can already smell danger all over this mission.

Just the way I like it.

CHAPTER ONE

Londoon used to be one of my favorite cities. The history, the arts, the theatre, all that good gravy. When I was a backpacking college student, The Old Smoke was the most romantic city I had ever seen. Paris could suck a dick—it was full of goddamn Parisians. But London?

Swoon.

A decade and a half later, the shine has worn off.

It's dirty, dangerous, expensive (not that that matters when the government is picking up the tab), and worst of all, Global Secret Intelligence Agency is headquartered here.

Not that anybody would know it.

Secrets, amiright?

There's a little pub on Tavistock Road, spitting distance from the Portobello Road Market. The Gateway. It's old, and the barman Nigel has been pulling taps since St. George was in short pants. Give him a hey-how's-your-family, ask for a pint of the 'queen's bitters', and the tattooed bar back will show you the way.

Unless you're one of 'the regulars.'

Nigel's face lights up every time I walk through the door, but this time there's a special twinkle.

"Hallo, Lydia, darling." Cheek kisses. "You're looking well. Getting some sunshine?"

"As much as I can, Nigel." I look past him to the surly red mohawk idling behind him. "Rebecca." She only half looks at me.

"Plenty of time to work on your tan where you're going." If she wasn't studiously pale herself, I'd swear she was jealous.

"Oh? And where's that?"

She shrugs and nods me towards barrel storage.

"They're waiting for you, miss." Nigel lays an avuncular hand on my back. "Best run along."

"Yeah, well…" I sigh. "Wouldn't want mama getting angry. Good to see you, Nigel." I plant one more kiss on his scruffy cheek and duck behind the bar.

Now, when we say 'barrel storage', people imagine a dark room lined with casks of ale. Which is the whole idea. In truth, it's the light armory. A few dozen standard issue pistols and other goodies in case an agent needs to snag something on the run.

And we run a lot.

Beyond that is a set of steel doors and a security scanner. I pass muster, and the doors slide open to an elevator. The Gateway is quaint, but the massive underground complex it hides is anything but. Headquarters runs under a healthy chunk of Notting Hill almost all the way up to College Park.

If you've ever taken the Piccadilly Line, you've been right through the beating heart of GSIA and didn't even know it.

"Have a nice chat?" Zero asks as soon as the doors open.

Of course she's waiting at the elevator.

"All I said was hello," I protest.

"Save your breath, save the world." Her motto. I can't

help rolling my eyes, even if it's good advice. "Here." She hands over a tablet with the dossier and heads straight for briefing.

To say Zero is no nonsense would be like saying fire is hot. Her code name is more than her rank number, it's how much time she has for bullshit. A five-foot nothing woman of Indian descent with a spine of wrought iron. It would have to be for her to climb this high in a world dominated by men. One thing is for sure, no man has *ever* had the balls or the strength to dominate Zero.

She strides right down the center of GSIA, and I'm behind her every step of the way, scrolling through info on the hoof.

The Osorio Cartel. Interesting.

Zero pushes back the glass doors, and we walk into briefing. Most of the chairs around the long mahogany table are empty. A secretary is in the midst of turning on the banks of flatscreens lining the walls, while another closes the blinds on banks of windows facing the rest of the hive.

One chair is very much occupied, however. A lean, handsome man whose mere presence demands attention, and I glue my eyes to the pad in my hand to keep from giving it to him too soon.

"Matamoros, huh?" I ask as Zero takes charge of the remote control and waves off the underlings.

"Los Paramos, actually," she says. "It's just outside."

"Is that a town?"

"More like a kingdom." I can hear the smirk on Sir John's face without even having to look at him. Not that I can resist looking at him for long. The man is a feast for the eyes, and I'm just about ready to tie a napkin around my neck.

"Hello, Lydia." He gets to his feet, that slight catch in his hip from the injury that took him out of the field.

Sir John Fullstaff.

Once the most respected operative in secret intelligence. But don't let the glimmering eyes and ready smile fool you.

This man has slit more throats than he's had hot breakfasts, and he's got scars of his own to prove it. Most of them hide beneath his immaculately tailored suit, but a single thin line runs from his jawline up his left cheek. It's all I can do not to reach up and run a finger over it.

"Good to see you, Sir."

"Chit chat later." Zero flicks off the lights, ready for business. "Have you finished reading?"

"I'm fast, but I'm not that fast."

Sir John stifles a snicker, but Zero cracks off one of her signature tight sighs.

"Jacinto Osorio," she announces, and his face flashes up on the main monitor. Dark eyes, dark hair, dark soul. "Leader of the Osorio Cartel. In the past five years, they've monopolized the illicit substance trade along the Mexican gulf coast, running up to the Texas border."

"I see." I'm scanning the pad as she talks, and she's not kidding.

Decapitations, car bombs, public executions, good old-fashioned disembowelment, this guy has done it all. "He rode to power on a river of blood, didn't he?"

"Connections," Zero corrects me, and my eyes flash up from the screen.

"What kind?"

"Keep reading." She clicks through a range of documents and photos on the large screens. "If the organization was merely a guerrilla dictatorship, we would simply go in and eliminate them. But Jacinto hasn't just been manufacturing narcotics, he's been forming alliances with American citizens of significant interest."

"Such as?"

Something dangerously close to a smile flits across Zero's granite face. "That's what we need you to find out."

Sir John weighs in, all rakish charm. "An informant hinted towards a whole network of law enforcement, politicians, titans of industry, people of that ilk. Intelligence shows evidence of Osorio's products in every state of the union and even up into Canada."

"It's an empire."

"Of the first order," he nods.

"Where is this informant?" I ask. "I can get the names." And everyone in the room knows how.

"Lost cause, I'm afraid." Zero clicks a button and images of a bloodied corpse plaster all the screens. I've seen more than my share of dead bodies, but this one is something else.

"Jesus. They really wanted to make a point, didn't they?"

Zero shakes her head. "This is routine Jacinto." I can't hide my surprise.

"You mean, Jacinto did this himself? Not one of his men?"

"It seems he has a taste for it," Sir John says with a twist of dark admiration. "The man likes blood on his hands."

"And everything else." I take one last look at the picture, steeling myself for what I'm up against. "Alright. Walk me through the players."

Images of Jacinto blink to life. The physique of a body-builder, stout but powerful. Handsome in a cruel way, from his piercing eyes to his wolfish mouth. There are pictures of him next to others, and I note the lifts in his shoes.

He's not tall, and he's vain about it.

"Who else?"

"Diego Alamar." A new face flashes up, taking my breath away. "Jacinto's cousin and right hand man. There's nobody closer."

Hell, *I'd* like to get close to him. Taller than Jacinto, but no less impressive. He's all broad shoulders and narrow waist. Five o'clock shadow and sly eyes. If I met him in a bar, we'd be going at it in the bathroom before the second round.

Why do I always have a thing for the dangerous ones?

"Any chance we could flip him?"

"I admire your eagerness, but no," Zero frowns. Sir John

and I share a knowing look, and I can tell he's been reading my mind. "When it comes to Jacinto's inside circle, he's the most loyal."

Pity.

"Got it." I make a mental note to keep tabs on the handsome devil all the same.

"There's more information on him in the dossier. Next up." She flicks ahead, and I have to admit, I'm a little disappointed that the next guy has a face like a busted knee. For a second, I thought I was being shipped to the Oasis of Hot Drug Lords. "Lope Ortega, head of security."

I earmark details as we rattle along, building my cheat sheet to study on the flight down. It's a tight roster of heavy hitters, which lets me breathe a little easier. Zero never gets into the foot soldiers unless there's a potential mutinous recruit. One thing about Jacinto Osorio, he commands respect.

Having seen what happens when you cross him, I can understand why.

"What about the compound?" I ask when we finish rolling through the rogues' gallery. "What's the layout?"

"Unclear," Zero says. "Either Osorio or his government connections have jammed the area against surveillance, so there's a scarcity of bird's eye visuals. We have a rough perimeter, but that's it. So it's up to you to get a lay of the land and report back."

"Check." The screen rolls back to Jacinto himself, pistol in hand. "So. I presume this is a honeypot?"

"Precisely." Zero doesn't bat an eye, switching the lights back on. "Seduce him, get into his bed, bring back the names."

My specialty.

"Can do."

"And Lydia?" She sets the remote on the table—symmetrically as always—and waits for my full attention. "I want the whole network. Without that, it will just grow back under someone else. Plant doubts about Osorio if possible and see what rises. Gain access to his compound and get as much information as you can."

"So this is purely a fact finding mission?"

"Poor girl," Sir John purrs. "Were you hoping you could blow something up?" I look him directly in the eye and arch my brow.

"Always."

"Names first," Zero says. "Once we have the intelligence we need, you can blow up anything you want. When the time comes you can burn the whole place to the ground—just not before we know every link in the chain."

"Now you're talking! Let's get me geared up."

"Nine is expecting you in ballistics and technology." She raps twice on the door and her minions slink in to raise the blinds and gear up for the next briefing. "You fly out in four hours. Sir John, would you walk with Agent Slick and bring her up to speed on her contact in Matamoros? She needs intel on the first encounter."

"With pleasure." He catches my eye with a crafty smile. It's not just Zero he's looking to please.

She walks out without so much as a goodbye or good luck. Just like always.

"It's nice to see her so chipper," I quip.

"Isn't it just? Come on. We'll walk and talk." There's only a slight hitch in his stride as we wind over to the lab. I've never asked how many bullets he took, but I've had opportunities to count the holes. It's just that whenever I have access, there are always other things on my mind.

"Four hours isn't a long time," he muses.

"No." I shoot him a heated glance. "We'll have to make the most of it."

CHAPTER
TWO

G SIA headquarters is so squeaky clean, you could eat a five star dinner off any floor in the complex. That is, until you get to Nine's workshop. It's what would happen if a technology lab had sex with a landfill and gave birth in an auto body shop. Everything has a thin sheen of grease, and the acrid whiff of open electricity hangs in the air.

It's carefully orchestrated chaos, and the maestro Nine is the beating Frankensteinian heart at the center of it all.

"Is that Lydia?" he calls from behind a heap of detritus on one of the work stations.

"In the *flesh*." I put a little extra spice on the word, just to get Sir John thinking about everything my flesh is capable of. Not that he needs much prompting.

"Delightful." Nine shambles away from his project, his perpetual befuddled grin widening with affection. "Lovely to see you, my dear."

"And you," I reply with genuine warmth. Paunchy, wire-rimmed glasses ever askew, Nine is every inch the eccentric granddad all kids dream of. But one would be a fool to be taken in by his absent minded exterior. Beneath that thinning bramble of grey hair is one of the most formidable inventive minds in the civilized world.

"Why not give her the tour?" Sir John suggests, mouth curling because he knows what's in store.

"Yes, why don't I?" Nine beckons us to follow, using his arm to push aside a scattering of half-finished projects so he can lay out a covered tray. Plucking off the surgical towel like a birthday party magician, he beams at me with undisguised pride.

His Cheshire cat smile is well earned. The tray is immaculate, the few items arranged neat as a piece of modernist art.

"What am I looking at?"

"Well, for openers..." he lifts what looks like a seam ripper from a sewing kit, only smaller. "This is a syringe. If I were you, I'd keep one on me at all times. Here." Nine flicks off the cap and pinches the base. A tiny stream of milky liquid shoots out, splattering a day old buttered roll on a napkin.

"Looks familiar," I snip under my breath.

"Steady on," Sir John whispers back.

Nine looks at us perplexed. "Hm?"

"What's it for?" I ask, steering him back to the demonstration.

"This is an amalgam I've been working on for some time." He swabs through the fluid, rubbing it between fingertips. "A paralytic activated by contact with the blood. I'll spare you the science, but once injected, the party would be indisposed in five seconds. Or thereabout."

"Dead?"

"No, no. More of a coma, I should think?"

"I see. How long does it last?"

"Oh." Nine gives an ambiguous shrug. "A while."

"Fair enough. And these?" I pick up one of an array of pellets the size and color of aspirin.

"Careful!" Nine picks up a half empty glass of water and moves it to the far end of the bench. "Concentrated caesium tablets. I've fortified them with magnesium, lithium, and other accelerants to increase the strength of the reaction."

My mouth falls open.

"This is a water bomb?"

"Essentially."

I marvel at the pellet in my hand. Just add a splash of water, and this thing could set the whole room on fire. Marble floors and all.

"Not bad, eh?" Nine bobs his bushy eyebrows, a schoolboy giggle reddening his face.

"You never fail to impress, Nine." I put a hand on his arm, and the guy damn near wags his tail he's so pleased.

"There's also this." He pinches what might be a stray piece of string and presents it to me. "Audio recorder and transmitter." I can't hide my amazement.

"In *this*?"

"I thought you'd like it."

I take it from him and roll it between my thumb and forefinger. It's astonishing. Any tech company in the world would piss their pants for something like this. And Nine treats it like he just whipped it up over the weekend.

"How do I turn it on?"

"Oh, it's always on. But unlike his friends here," he nods at the explosives, "water is the enemy. One drop and the system shorts."

"Noted." Three items for my kit, each one indispensable. In less than five minutes, he's completely revolutionized the secret intelligence world.

"I almost forgot." Nine rummages for a second and comes up with a small sphere with an adapter on it, along with a flat black pad. He hands me the sphere first. "This is the receiver for the listening device. Plug it into your phone and it plays and records automatically."

"Perfect.

"And here's your ripper." The black pad thumps into my palm.

"My what?"

"Hm?" He's already distracted, fiddling with something else close to hand. "Oh, your ripper. Lay a cell phone on it and it duplicates the phone."

My jaw hits my chest while Sir John snickers into his handkerchief. No plugs, no connections. Just touch it with a phone and you've got every sext some poor dickhead ever sent behind his wife's back.

"Nine, I…" What the hell can I say? I couldn't fathom *beginning* to conceive of any of these, and he rattles them off with grocery list calm. "Thank you," is all I can manage.

"Just come back alive, my dear." Nine disappears into his work, leaving Sir John and I to wander out of his workshop in a daze.

"I second him on that sentiment," Sir John says.

"Which one?" I look up into his eyes, and there's a wistful tenderness peeking out from behind his patented devil-may-care glint.

"Come back alive, will you?"

He always knows how to soften my edges.

"I'll do what I can."

We linger close to each other, and for a second, I wonder if he's going to kiss me right here in headquarters. Then the rakish façade smooths back into place and he checks his watch.

"Just over three hours to takeoff." His eyes meet mine again, the tiger in him on full display. "Fancy a drink?"

When it comes to code, the question doesn't amount to much. But then, it doesn't have to.

We're not in his apartment ten seconds before we're ripping at each other's clothes. I don't know what it is about risking death that makes one feel so goddamn *alive.*

I can't get enough of his fucking mouth. I want it everywhere at once. Nobody kisses like Sir John Fullstaff. Gentle and ruthless, he plunders my lips like they're a Viking hoard.

"I've missed you," I whisper into his open mouth. He replies by slamming me against the wall and pinning me there with his body. I grapple at his back, ready to rip his jacket to shreds. He shrugs it off, and my greedy hands paw at his torso.

Retired from the field or not, Sir John hasn't lost a step. His shoulders are thick with muscle, tapering down to a trim, sculpted waist. I scour my hands over all of it, memorizing him.

Because every time could be the last time.

"I've needed you," he growls, eating his way down the line of my neck. "So badly."

"Take me." I knot my fingers in his hair, holding tight and pushing him lower. If he doesn't lick my nipple soon, I'll explode.

I've always had sensitive nipples, but Sir John is a poet with them. He trails his mouth over my collarbone as he fiddles with the buttons on my blouse.

"Rip it," I hiss. He tips his head back, peering up at me.

"What?"

"*Rip it!*"

"Lydia..."

"Ugh." I shove him off and tear my shirt open. Buttons skitter off across his floor never to be seen again. Fuck 'em. The world's got plenty of buttons. The fabric is in tatters as I strip it back and let it fall, then whip my bra over my head.

"Jesus Christ," he gasps hungrily the instant my breasts are free. He latches on without needing to be told, savaging my nipple with his tongue. I grab his hair again, more to keep from collapsing on the floor than anything else.

Stars shoot behind my eyelids as he toys with me. Nipping. Teasing. Suckling until I'm so tender I want to start wailing and never stop. He works my other peak between his fingers, rolling it to a sizzling pebble. A groan rumbles up from my core, and I tip my head back to the wall and give it full throat.

I don't give a damn if the whole building hears me. Let the fuckers be jealous for the rest of their lives. They could never dream of what he's doing to me, and we haven't even started.

He takes me between his teeth just right, and my thighs scorch to life. I slam them together, the tingling in my cleft spilling like wildfire. My panties are soaked, and the juice is even starting to run down my legs, dampening my trousers.

I need them off.

Now.

Thank God, Sir John is way ahead of me. He tugs at my fly with expert skill, and in an instant, my pants are sliding down. They pool up around my feet, and I kick them across the room.

I'm in nothing but my panties, and I pry his mouth off my breast to look him in the face.

"No fair."

"What?"

"You're still dressed." Seizing his shirt just below the collar, I gear up to set him free.

"Lydia, this shirt cost a thousand pounds."

I lean in so that my nose brushes his, my eyes glittering with unbridled lust.

"Am I worth it?" The question detonates behind his pupils, and the devil in him rages free.

"Yes."

I rip the shirt to ribbons. Scars from past battles crisscross his marbled chest, and I taste each one with an eager tongue. My fingers wage a furious war with his belt, finally whipping it out like a lash. His trousers are no match for me, and in seconds, his cock is in my hands.

As glorious as the first time I saw it, I can't help marveling at the sheer, rigid size of him. But looking isn't enough. I take him into my mouth as deep as I can, and he grabs a fistful of my hair.

"Jesus, Lydia. Easy." That only makes me suck him harder. Hearing him hissing between his teeth as I bathe him with my tongue sends a new flood between my legs. I grip him by the base with one hand, and work my clit with the other.

The sodden fabric of my panties offers exquisite friction, and I'm throbbing instantly. The closer I get, the more eagerly I devour his cock. Cries wash out of me, vibrating the dick stifling them in my throat.

My knees tingle, then my thighs combust on the spot. Molten gold bursts from my clit and suffuses through my whole body. I'm a sailboat, tossed on a raging sea of sensuality.

Suddenly, my mouth is empty and air rushes into my lungs. I didn't even realize I was drowning until Sir John saved me. Then he pushes me under again, covering my mouth with his, claiming me.

Melting onto my back, Sir John covers me with his body. I'm still trembling from the tail end of an orgasm when he puts my knees over his shoulders and presses into me.

I go blind.

And deaf.

My mouth locks open, but I don't have breath to make a sound.

Sir John sinks deeper with merciless deliberation. A lesser man would plunge in to the hilt—and I've been with lesser men—but Sir John is another species. He knows I'm lost in the wilderness, and he's intent to keep me that way.

Every time I run out of room inside me, he nudges a fresh door open.

"Please," I gasp. "Sir John, please."

"Please what?" He stops moving, and I go to pieces. Grabbing his ass and reaching up with my hips, I'm desperate for the rest of him. But he just laughs gently and pulses closer. "Is this what you want?"

"Fuck you," I grunt.

Just fucking give it to me.

"I am fucking you." The smug smile in his voice makes me want to slap him. Instead, I dig my nails into his ass and yank him into me. His hips clap against my ass, and his cock jabs so deep, I shatter. My back slides across the floor in a pool of my own sweat as I writhe under him. Kicking my heels at the ceiling, I howl so hard my lungs ache.

And that's just his first thrust.

We fuck the way only longtime lovers can. Giving and taking. Knowing each other's limits and testing them anyway. He knows all the spots and how to hit them, and I know how tight to grip him to make him beg me not to make him come yet.

Of course, I won't let him. Sir John is ever the gentleman, and I know I'm going to lose myself to him over and over again before he finally releases.

Now that the seal is broken, he drives me across the floor with thrust after glorious thrust. He wedges me into a corner and doubles me up, thundering into me until I'm a quivering, sex dumb mess.

When the spell passes, he rolls onto his back, bringing me along for the ride. And ride it is. He spreads his legs so I can sit sidesaddle between them straddling his thigh. His shaft is deliciously deep, and I hug his knee to grind my clit on his leg. He locks me in place with the other, and the divine pressure has me gasping at the ceiling.

"God fucking damnit," he grunts. "You're so fucking beautiful."

We got to it before hitting the light switch, and a loose chuckle scatters out of me.

"It's dark," I pant. "You can't see me."

"I don't have to."

Sly son of a bitch. He always knows what to say.

His hand cradles my breast, working my nipple again. A bolt of lightning shoots between my tit and my clit, and my hips take on a life of their own. They go frantic, fucking him like the building is burning down.

Hot as the two of us are together, it just might.

CHAPTER THREE

Eventually, I get to make good on the offered drink. After the evening we've had, we've more than earned it.

Though I'm not sure it's the most hydrating option. Still, what kind of host would I be if I left such a beautiful lady thirsty? A promise is a promise, after all.

"Here we are," I say, stepping naked from the kitchen. "Iced tequila, fresh lime, and a sliver of jalapeño."

Lydia wrinkles up her nose.

"You know I'm not a tequila girl. Whiskey for me, please."

"Tequila for you." I reach over the back of the couch and hand her the glass. "You're going to have to get used to it. Can't have your target thinking you're going to Mexico for the view."

"Ugh." She sits up just enough to take a sip. "Why is intelligence work so hard?"

"You know you love it." I come around to take a seat, and she lifts her shoulders for me so she can lie in my lap. Her body still shines with sweat, glistening in the moonlight spilling through my windows.

It's a delicious view—and I don't mean St. Paul's Cathedral. In this light, Lydia's skin is almost blue, and I lay my arm over her, dabbling my fingertips on her taut stomach. Every bit of her is lean and toned for combat. Making love to her can be like a battle sometimes—the kind where both sides win. It's just a matter of how many times I can make her win before my own victory.

Lydia gazes out the window, musing at the London skyline and sipping her drink.

She's nervous.

She'd die before she ever admitted it, and would choke the life out of me if she knew I suspected, but I know. We've been intimate a long time, sharing secrets we keep even from ourselves.

There's a twinge in my chest whenever I see her like this. Lydia is fearless in the face of so many things. It's her greatest strength, but also puts her at continual risk. That sort of thing takes a toll, no matter how inured one may be. Or pretend to be.

"What are you thinking?" I ask into the stillness.

"I should be looking at the dossier."

"Well, thank you very much. Glad to know you're satisfied."

She chuckles and raps my thigh with her knuckles.

"Oh, shut up. You know I'm satisfied."

"Do I?"

Lydia looks up into my face, that cocky, sideways smile of hers mingled with genuine vulnerability behind her eyes.

"I never scream like that for anybody else."

"Nor should you." We clink glasses and she cozies into my lap even more. I can't ask if she's afraid, but I can tell she needs to unburden herself. "You're not looking forward to this one, are you?"

Her answer is immediate.

"No."

The word hovers in the air like a ghost, and I give it space to say boo.

"It's just…" She sighs.

"Zero only calls when she needs a honeypot," I offer.

"Right?" Lydia sits bolt upright and faces me. "Was it like that when you were in the field?"

"Sometimes. We all have our skills."

"I have *lots* of skills!" Vehement injustice radiates from her finely hewn features. "You know it, she knows it, everyone in the goddamn agency knows it. But every fucking assignment I get is another goddamn honeypot."

"Itching for a little gunplay, are we?"

"Oh, there'll be gunplay," she assures me. "I just wish Zero wasn't throwing my pussy around like it's hers."

"Can you imagine?" I chuckle into my glass. "I'm sure Zero's never so much as tossed hers, let alone *thrown* it." That cracks Lydia's shell of indignation. She giggles, covering her mouth as they spread into guffaws.

After another drink, she flops back against the cushions and we stare out the window together.

"What we do isn't for the faint of heart," I offer. She snorts.

"No shit." Lydia rests her glass on my thigh. The sting of the sudden cold makes me flinch, as does the bead of condensation rolling down my skin. She loves inflicting little shocks on me like that. "Seriously." Her voice is hushed. "Was it like that for you?"

I take a deep breath as I consider it. She's not jealous. Neither of us have an aptitude for it, and one would never survive in our line of work if they did. But one can't help curiosity, I suppose. No matter how many cats have died from it.

"You could say I did more than my share. There were other agents who had the capacity, but lacked the…"

"Good looks?"

"I was going to say charm."

"And did you hate it?"

"That's a complicated question. Our bodies are hard wired for certain responses. If you fuck someone enough, feelings are bound to grow. It's chemical."

"Gee, thanks." Lydia elbows me in the ribs, then nestles under my arm.

"I'm not talking about you, of course." Planting a kiss on the top of her head, I give her shoulders a light squeeze. "You know what the worst is? When it was a chore. Some bloated dowager or dreadful, grasping harpy. I shudder just to think of it."

"No," she muses. "You're wrong."

"Am I?"

She takes a long breath, narrowing her eyes to study the air.

"You want to know what the worst really is? When there's a genuine connection. When you actually enjoy it. Part of you knows it's just a mission, but when there's a *spark*? When it's more than just a job? It blurs the lines."

"And you prefer black and white."

"There's no room for grey."

Then what are we, I want to ask.

We've been lovers from the day we met, but never breathed a word of commitment. We can't. Because there's always the chance an agent won't come back, and heartbreak isn't an option.

Most of us have pieced our hearts back together so many times, we wouldn't dare risking it again. There's that one big heartbreak in all of our pasts – the one that left holes behind from the shards we couldn't find. The bits someone else took with them when they left.

Or died.

Half-people like us are a different breed. As close as Lydia and I are, there's an uncrossable gulf between us—by design. Even if I wanted to keep her, she's not mine to keep. None of us are.

As if we're both thinking the same thing, we lift our glasses in unison and take long sips. I sigh with satisfaction, but Lydia is less impressed.

"Fuck," she winces after swallowing. "Goddamn tequila."

"This mission is going to be a trial to you, I'm afraid."

"It really is." She shifts to sit on her knees, facing me with a wicked, shit eating grin. "May I have some bourbon instead? Please?"

"I'm in management now, my dear. Your preparation is key."

"Please?" She perches her fingertips on my shoulder, bringing her nose mere inches from mine. "*Pleeeease*, Sir John?" Between the absurdity of her childish begging and my formal title, I can't keep from laughing.

"You know I can't refuse you." Mustering all the chivalry my sex drained body can muster, I collect her glass and heave myself up. Maintaining dignity while starkies is perilously difficult, but somehow I manage.

My heaviest tumbler, and two cubes of ice – cracked. I could fix her drink with my eyes closed. A generous slosh of my finest bourbon, shipped from America every quarter just in case Lydia deigns to darken my door. A gentleman must be ever ready to please a lady's palate as well as her other senses.

A gentleman.

All I can think of is my wretched, pesky title. And her insistence on using it.

"You don't have to, you know," I say as if we're already mid-conversation.

"Hm?" She lifts her voice from the other room. "I don't have to what?"

"You can call me John."

A glacier of silence slides through my flat.

"You know I can't do that."

"I do."

I've come to stand in the doorway, bourbon in hand, enraptured by her profile silvered by the moon.

There are so many things to say. Too many.

Fortunately my phone rings. It's Zero, of course.

"What may I do for you?"

"Give the phone to Lydia. She isn't answering hers."

Naturally Zero knows where to find her. No secrets in this world of ours.

"My dear," I purr, handing over the phone. Lydia straightens her spine, the spy in her taking over despite her nakedness.

"Yeah? Alright."

That's it. Two words, and she ends the call and gives me back my phone.

"The flight is ready." She looks up at me, her eyes all business. Lydia the Killer has returned. "I'm late."

"I see. You'll be wanting to go to the airstrip then." I lean low and whisper in her ear as I deliver her bourbon. "Fancy a ride?"

That deliciously coy shimmer dances back into her eyes.

"Another one? I'm afraid we haven't the time."

Lydia knocks back the expensive liquor in a single swallow.

CHAPTER FOUR

It's wheels down in Matamoros, and I know the dossier cold. All the faces, all the names, their habits, predilections, right down to what they like to have for breakfast and how many times a day they take a shit.

You never know what's gonna come in handy.

Getting all that stuff crammed in my skull is a brass tacks necessity because the GSIA pad is already on its way back to London. Along with everything but the barest essentials. A couple of bathing suits, party-girl clothes, and a king's ransom in sunglasses. I have to look like a tourist influencer of the first stripe.

Top all that off with a chic little clutch. The kind of thing no hardened macho man would ever dare to peek into. Their loss because this one is positively brimming with Nine's world shaking technology.

Skidding across the lone runway in a sleek Cessna would do fuckall for my cover, so we pulled a switcheroo in Brownsville.

Wave bye bye to the luxury jet and climb onto a commercial sky jalopy for the final leg. Sweating humanity packed like sardines into a two propeller death trap, visions of cheap beer and hundred peso hookers dancing in their heads.

Not that I'm one to throw stones at sex workers. The only difference between me and them is the pay and how influential our pimps are.

Jesus, I'm in a mood, huh?

We taxi to the gate, and I shrug off the world weary spy in favor of a glitter girl with a million followers. It's showtime.

"Oh, my God, you guys," I chirp into my phone's camera as I disembark. "This airport is just *ugh*!" Is that a good or a bad thing? Who cares? Nobody's really watching.

Passport control is a joke, and customs just waves me through. Nobody's worried about anybody sneaking drugs *into* Mexico. Not around here, anyway. From what I read about the Osorio boys, if you even dreamed of bringing your own blow to the party, you'd wake up with a slit throat.

Naturally, I let the cab driver fleece me. A six minute ride for sixty dollars? I get all distressed, holding out a handful of pesos.

"How do these work?"

The son of a bitch can't grab them fast enough. My bags and I are on the sidewalk lickety split, and I look up at a garish neon sign bolted to the facade of a glass fronted building. Smoke and house music spill through the tinted doors like the devil's breath.

Here goes nothing.

A line of hoochied up chicas runs down the side of the building, each one shooting daggers as I approach the beefy pair of sunglasses next to the door.

"Um… Por favor?"

He raises an eyebrow at my lousy Spanish.

"Can I help you?"

"Oh, thank God! You speak English." The girls in line look

ready to spit. In fact, a couple of them do. "Can I take a look inside?"

"You see the line." For fuck's sake. The smaller the kingdom, the bigger the tyrant.

My tits are already on full display, but maybe he hasn't noticed. Pressing the girls together with my upper arms, I lean forward to crane my neck around him to look inside.

"Sorry, it's just… My friend told me he was already here?"

My bouncer buddy gets an eyeful, and doesn't give a damn in hell who sees him do it. He doesn't even look me in the face when I turn back to him.

"Hey!" The gal at the front of the line has had enough of my little song and dance. "You heard him. Back of the line!"

"Aw." I pout my lips for the bouncer, plumping my tits even more. It's one of Christ's own miracles a nipple doesn't pop out. But maybe one should. That'd get me in for sure.

Just when I'm on the point of pulling the trigger, my salvation arrives.

"There you are!" Nando Rivera. My contact. Shirt open down to his belly button and pants so tight they squeak when he walks. "I tell you, Chewy," Nando claps a hand on the bouncer's shoulder—and with it a wad of bills, "it's a good thing my Alana is so pretty because she can't be on time to save her life."

The bouncer looks back and forth between us for a second, then takes the cash and lets me through.

Hurdle one jumped.

Walk into any club in the world and you can guarantee two things—dark and noise. They've never been my scene, but I've found myself in plenty. Dens like this are always the unofficial lair of criminal dirtbags, and even I have to admit there's nothing like cracking skulls with a thumping soundtrack.

Bars line two full walls, thronged by people shouting for drinks. The dance floor is no less jammed. Sweaty bodies gyrate against each other, and I gird my loins for combat. Chances are I'll be wading into the mayhem in due time.

A towering DJ platform sits in the middle of everything, crowned by the lowest form of life next to cockroaches—the spin doctor. Every one is exactly the same. Sunglasses, massive headphones, and a burning desire to render everyone within a square mile deaf. Dealing out tinnitus like pushers do pills.

Fuckers.

Nando sticks a glass in my hand and winks. "Drink up," he shouts, but good luck hearing him.

Tequila. Of course.

I knock back a healthy slug and smile as big as I can. Nando leans close, pretending to kiss my neck so he can speak directly into my ear.

"You spotted him yet?"

Eyes heavy lidded with mock ecstasy are perfect for scanning any room. Only the perviest lowlifes stand around watching a couple make out, so while Nando applies himself to my throat, I scope the place.

Jacinto isn't easy to miss.

He's roosted in the raised VIP section directly opposite us, rolling a fat cigar between his fingers. Even at this distance, an air of danger clings to him like a robe. Those cruel eyes flash everywhere he looks, starving for any excuse for a bit of bloodletting.

Digging my fingers into Nando's hair, I bite his earlobe.

"Target identified."

He grabs my tit.

"Accomplices at your three o'clock. Let's make our way over."

Peeling back from him, I lock Nando with a pair of bedroom eyes so sultry the whole club threatens to melt.

Act or not, his dick gets hard. Not that I'm looking, there's just no hiding it in those pants. Arms over my head, I sway into the crowd. Suddenly, I'm all hips and supple spine, carving a path directly for a pair of seedy fuckers in gaudy suits. When I look back, Nando is in hot pursuit.

The son of a bitch knows everybody. Every step he takes comes with a back slap or a handshake. The guy flashes smiles like he bought stock in the company that makes them.

I don't know where Zero found him, but she better pray she can keep him on our side. If he is on our side. Men like Nando play both sides against the middle every chance they get. Loyalty only lasts as long as the wallet is out.

It's a familiar type, and I know him to the marrow of his bones. If I weren't dancing, I wouldn't turn my back on him for a second.

At last I make it to the two sharks he pointed out. I do a spin, catching their eyes. All it takes is one complicit flash to tell me they're in on the game.

Let's do this.

Shifting my weight, I snap the heel clean off my right pump. My balance thrown, I flail for anything to keep from cratering to the floor. My hand snags the lapel of one of the two accomplices, and I hang from him like wet laundry.

"Hey!" He spills his beer all over himself, leaping back in outrage. I keep my grip and get dragged behind, struggling to get my footing.

The commotion chases folks back a bit, clearing a patch of floor to be our stage.

"The fuck are you trying to do," he shouts.

"I'm sorry! I broke my shoe."

"You got beer all over my suit, you whore!"

I wail in wounded protest, staggering back directly into his companion. His glass hits the floor and shatters, and he catches me under the arms – helping himself to a generous portion of tit in each hand.

"Get your fucking hands off me," I scream, wrenching

myself free. Wheeling around, I slash a stinging slap across his face. "Pig!"

His eyes burst into flames. If he's not one of our guys, he's in the mix now. He rears back to slap me back and I recoil, breaking the heel off my other shoe. That sends me crashing right into Nando, who arrives incensed.

"What the hell's going on, baby?"

"That one grabbed my boobs," I shout so everyone can hear. "I feel so *violated*!"

Nando drops me like a hot potato and squares up against goon number two.

"The fuck are you trying to pull, huh?"

"Listen, asshole," the guy says with his hands in the air. It's a gesture of placation, but there's no question he's ready to scrap. "You don't want any piece of this."

"Yeah, dude." My first target is still swatting at the beer stains on his jacket. "Control your fucking bitch, man."

My turn. I grab Nando by the shoulder and go ballistic.

"Who are you calling a bitch, *bitch*? Do you see your mama around here somewhere?"

The music stops and everyone draws back in anticipation. If I had a lick of sense I'd start selling tickets for what's about to go down.

"Motherfucker," Beer Stain yells, taking a wild grab for my hair. Nando catches him between the ribs with a nasty punch, knocking his wind into next week. Second guy rushes Nando only to catch one in the jaw.

He careens backwards, toppling into a group of onlookers and knocking them flat. More drinks spilled, more women groped.

That's when the real party starts.

A full-on melee breaks out as women shrill and their men make with the fisticuffs to defend their honor. It goes from zero to a million in a tenth of a second. I'm talking chairs broken over backs, tumblers smashed on heads, the whole enchilada.

This is the thing about operative work at this level—there are no fake punches. You have to sell it with the real deal. If those guys were willing to take this kind of drubbing, you can bet your sweet ass GSIA is cutting fat checks.

I even get in a few licks of my own, just to make sure the money is well spent.

Stealing a peek from the corner of my eye, I find Jacinto's table vacant.

Shit.

We may have miscalculated. If he's as paranoid as his file says, a rumble might just send him sprinting for the back door.

Someone grabs me by the hair so hard my scalp separates from my skull. It's Beer Stain, teeth bared for vengeance.

"Whore!" He spits in my face. I grab his hand, digging my nails in deep. He snarls through his teeth, but his grip loosens.

"Let me go!"

Suddenly, his eyes flash wide and his mouth falls open. His fingers untangle, and to my astonishment, he lifts off the ground.

Jacinto has him by the collar and the seat of his pants. The head of the Osorio Cartel hoists this grown man over his head and throws him like a rag doll over the bar.

I'm not gonna lie, I'm impressed.

Another fighter charges over, intent on clobbering Jacinto, me, or both. Without batting an eye, Jacinto heel strikes the dude in the shin, splintering the bone with a nasty crunch. Dude goes down squealing and clutching his ruined leg.

The sound of misery lights a fire in Jacinto and he lashes out at anybody nearby, meting out black eyes and broken bones like Easter candy. I've seen savagery in my time, but this level of brutality takes even my breath away.

When he's finally the lone man left standing in a circle of prostrate figures, Jacinto fixes his attention on Nando.

"So…" Jacinto's voice is alarmingly calm. "What do you have to say for yourself?"

Whether Nando is acting or not is impossible to tell. He stammers wide eyed as the cartel leader advances with calculated cool.

"I… Um… Listen."

A pistol snaps out of Jacinto's jacket and he chambers a round. Even so, he's easy as Sunday morning.

"I'm listening."

"It was a misunderstanding. That's all."

"Is it?" Jacinto gestures to the devastation surrounding him. "A misunderstanding caused all this?" Nando doesn't have an answer. "Well." Jacinto holds out his hand and one of his men puts the still lit cigar between his fingers. "Let me tell you what I understand." He levels the gun at Nando's forehead. "I understand how to settle things."

"It was my fault," I blurt. I can't let a contact go down less than an hour after landing. Jacinto looks over his shoulder, devouring me with his gaze.

"Your fault? Oh, my dear." He takes my hand and kisses it in a way that sends goosebumps shooting up my arm. "I can assure you, you are *faultless*."

Sweet fucking Lord.

Jacinto Osorio is mesmerizing in person. He's not tall, but radiates authority. The photos showed how broad he was, but could never communicate how *dense*. He's a compact package of pure muscle.

His dark hair sweeps to the side above a pair of almost pointed eyebrows. His eyes themselves are almost black. Vertiginous pools of lust, danger, and mystery.

The animal magnetism pouring off him lives in direct balance with a strange repulsiveness. Anyone can see the man has a soul so wicked the devil will run and hide when Jacinto gets to hell.

"Jefe," one of his men says. Jacinto acknowledges him without once breaking eye contact with me. "The car is out front."

"Good." He holds out his hand to take mine again. "You're coming with us."

He doesn't ask. He tells. Commands.

Awful as it is, his brazenness sends a shiver through me. Much as I hate myself for it, it's arousing.

Jacinto leads me over the wrecked dance floor, stepping over bodies and broken glass as if they were nothing. And I walk right beside him.

CHAPTER
FIVE

J acinto Osorio is a man of action.

By which I mean, as soon as the SUV door closes, he lunges for me like a jungle cat. His brawny body slams against mine, crushing my lips with bruising kisses. Feverish hands scouring over my body. If I was wearing a wire, I'd be toast.

It's startling, arresting, and undeniably hot. He pries his mouth from mine just long enough for me to gasp out a cry.

"Fuck."

This guy doesn't waste a second. His driver hasn't even pulled away from the curb and he's got his hands down the front of my dress. The fabric starts to pull, and I bite his earlobe and hiss.

"Don't rip it."

A convulsion judders over him as he struggles to control himself. Jacinto was born under a contrary star, so my plea only makes him want to strip me naked with a single swipe, shredding the dress with his powerful hands.

"Please." Another shudder, and his hand softens on my chest. It glides under the curve of my breast, and I know I've got him right where I want him.

As he massages me, I reach up and slip the straps down over my shoulders, then tease my top down. Just a little bit at a time.

Make him wait for it. Impatience thrums through the guy so intensely I almost pity him.

Almost.

When there's no more delaying it, I deliver up the goods, arching my back to give him an eyeful. But an eyeful isn't enough for a man like Jacinto.

He seizes my breasts like they're fistfuls of cash. Kneading to the point of mauling, he wrings my nipples between his finger and thumb. I reward him with all the right groans and whimpers, some of them perilously close to real.

Jacinto scoops me into his lap, feasting on my body with his eager, insistent mouth. I clap an arm over his shoulders, marveling at his solidity. He's everywhere. A one man tornado, licking, nibbling, caressing, growing ever harder beneath me.

That's my cue, and I position myself so I can rub against him. Reacting to his every move, I glide along his shaft, working him into a towering passion.

"Shit," he snarls into my chest. "You're perfect." His hand flies to my hip, gripping hard and pulling me into him. This is no subtle game, he's humping against my ass and kissing his way up my neck.

"Jesus," I gasp when he reaches the base of my ear. "You're amazing." He takes the lobe between his teeth and hisses hot breath over me.

"I know."

Cocky fucker.

It's like I've just given him an open invitation. Jacinto

nudges my legs apart, and sticks his hand up under my skirt, scraping his fingertips up the inside of my thigh.

I'm not gonna lie, the pressure is *scrumptious*.

Then he discovers I'm not wearing panties. They're not part of the uniform in this line of work.

Finding me naked, it's like he doubles in size. Those dark eyes harden with hot blooded determination, and his teeth flash between tight lips. Slicking a finger between my folds, he pushes into me as deep as he can reach.

The abruptness of it snaps my spine into a deep arch. This man has never even heard of a clitoris. It's penetration or nothing.

Still, he works in a slow, powerful roll that's undeniable. All the right pressure in all the right places. It's easy to moan for him when the sensations are this intense. Deception might be my business, but in moments like this, the body can't lie.

"You like that?" He grins.

"Yes. Yes, I do."

"Well." He pulls his fingers from me so fast I lose my breath. "Then you will love this." I'm off his lap, my ass landing on the seat with a thump. Jacinto shoves my skirt up my legs and over my ass, exposing me fully to his shimmering lust. He wrenches his pants down, taking his impressive cock in one hand and lowering himself over me.

"Wait." I try to scoot out from under him, but his sheer mass pinions me. "Wait," I repeat, louder this time.

"Trust me."

Why in the hell would I do that?

"I don't even know your name."

"Jacinto." His hips descend, the head of his swollen club drawing ever closer.

Look. If he fucks me now, it's no great loss. But if I can delay him? Keep him on the line? That's how you really spin someone up in your web.

"We can't. Not like this."

"I need you." His lips brush the shell of my ear. "Now."

"Please." I put a hand on his cheek, bringing him to face me. "Not for our first time." Jacinto locks in place.

Gotcha, motherfucker.

"What?"

"It's just…" I shrug and bite my lip. "Shouldn't our first time be special? We're better than the back seat of a car."

"That's for high school kids." He chuckles.

"Isn't it? Besides." I nod to the driver's seat. The guy might as well be munching popcorn he's watching the rear view mirror so hard. It's a miracle he hasn't run off the road with the show we've been putting on. But when he sees Jacinto look up, he's suddenly all business. I'm talking hands at two and ten on the wheel kind of shit.

After another low laugh, Jacinto looms heavily over me again, pressing me into the seat with his granite body. A row of vigorous kisses slather from my collarbone to the point of my jaw, then he hovers close to my ear.

"Perhaps you're right. But." He catches my eyes, staring into me with a bonfire in his pupils. "Soon."

"Thank God," I sigh as he pulls himself off me. "I can't wait long." Am I going to cover myself up? Like hell I am. My dress is bunched up around my waist, so I'm all tits and slit. The perfect picture to keep the blood out of his brain. Every drop of it is pooled somewhere else, and I have to say it's one hell of a sight.

Jacinto may not be tall, but he's by no means *short*.

He notices me looking and smirks proudly. Without pulling his pants up, he reaches into his jacket pocket and produces an expensive cigar. He displays his lighter before sparking up, just so I can see it's crusted with diamonds.

"So." The cab fills with smoke and he regards me for a long moment. "What is your name, my beauty?"

"Alana."

"Alana." He rolls it around on his tongue savoring my alias. "It means beautiful, yes?"

"It does. And precious. Peaceful." The last one makes him laugh. "Don't you think I deserve it?"

"You are beautiful." He nods. "And I can make you precious." He takes my foot in his hand, stripping off the broken shoe before raising it to his lips. "But your time with me will be anything but peaceful." He bites the bridge of my foot lightly, then harder.

You got that right, asshole. If only you knew.

Turning my foot loose, he removes the other busted pump and offers it the same treatment. The little game over, he leans back satisfied to indulge in another long puff.

"That's an expensive cigar."

"You have a good eye. Tell me, Alana." His hand runs up my thigh towards my exposed cleft. "Do you like expensive things?"

"Always."

"Me too. It made me determined to become rich."

"Is that right? And just how do you make your money, Jacinto?" The question hitches him up for a second, then an arrogant smile oozes across his face.

"I'm in the export business."

"Jefe," the driver says over his shoulder, and it's clear we're getting close. Jacinto gives me a nod, eyes twinkling.

"Sit up. You're going to want to see this." I do as I'm told, pulling my skirt down again in the process. When I go to cover my breasts, Jacinto puts a finger on my hand to stop me. I give him my most salacious grin and let my hands fall into my lap.

When I look out the window, my jaw hits my chest so hard it'll leave a bruise.

Just ahead is a massive set of gates. It's hard to say if they're actually gilded, or if it's just the long rays of the setting sun painting them gold. They're set in a wall ten feet high, the pillars on either side of the entrance adorned with sculptures and covered with mosaics. One side is a lion, the other a bull.

"Beautiful," I whisper.

"You appreciate fine work," Jacinto smiles. "Just wait."

The driver lifts his com unit and speaks into the receiver.

"El lobo está en la puerta."

The wolf is at the gate.

An apt code name for the man in the back seat with me. Ravenous, cunning, dangerous.

A hatch opens in one of the gates, and a guard peers through to confirm. Then the little door closes again and the gates start to swing open. As we roll through, I take note that the wall is over a meter thick at its base.

This place is a fortress.

Wait, holy shit!

"Is that a leopard?"

"Cheeta." Jacinto nods. I wrinkle up my brow, unable to stop myself.

"That's not a cheetah." *Did I really kick all this off by fucking correcting him?* Fortunately Jacinto laughs.

"No, you're right, my diamond — it's a leopard. Her *name* is Cheeta."

"Oh." I melt against him, rubbing my naked tits on his arm to smooth away the challenge I just tossed in his face. "Perfect. I love it!"

Other exotic animals scamper across the twilit lawn as we wind past topiary and water features. The guy clearly loves opulence.

We come around a tangle of open forest and the mansion itself comes into view. Lit from beneath against the purpling sky, it's a real showstopper.

A long colonnade of pillars and arches stretch across the front, and the second level windows are topped with Moorish detailing that's truly stunning. I expected a gaudy drug palace, but this is a paragon of sophistication and lavish wealth.

Jacinto may be a madman, but he's got impeccable taste in architects. A true renaissance man with his dick out.

We pull around the fountain in the circular drive, stopping directly in front of the wide steps. Looking to my host for approval, I finally pull the front of my dress up again and hide the girls. Jacinto follows suit, snugging his wiener away and zipping his fly.

Not a moment too soon because my door opens and a hand is offered to help me slide out. I take it, and as soon as my bare feet hit the ground, my breath flies high in my chest.

"Thank you," I murmur.

The man holding my hand is Diego Alamar himself.

Jacinto's right hand man.

His cousin.

And my downfall.

Because no matter how deadly the risks, no matter what it might mean for the mission, one thing is absolutely certain.

I'm going to fuck this man.

As often and as hard as I can.

Which means I'm in for some serious fucking trouble.

CHAPTER
SIX

DIEGO

Holy fucking shit.

Even disheveled from a ride with my cousin, this woman is the total package. Rich brown hair to her shoulders, fine bones, tanned skin, and a pair of eyes so large a man could get lost in them. And never want to find the way home.

Her chest is flushed, and I can almost see Jacinto's fingerprints all over her. The tight little dress clings to her curves, serving up a generous helping of cleavage. I'd sell my soul to the devil to yank it off and get a look at everything underneath. All the way down to her slender, sinewy legs.

Those supple lips part just a bit when our eyes meet, and I know in an instant that she feels it too. A fifty megaton bomb detonates between us, scorching me to the bones. One bone more than the rest.

She's so beautiful, when she was born the doctor slapped himself.

"Stop staring, Diego," Jacinto says as he comes around the back of the SUV.

"Can you blame me?"

"I can blame anybody I want." My cousin chuckles like it's a joke, but I've seen the proof of his bullshit first hand. "Here. Help yourself." Jacinto takes her hand from mine and lifts it to send her into a twirl. "Get a good look."

You don't have to tell me twice, motherfucker.

The ass, the slender spine, the toned shoulders. Jesus, I can already feel my hands on them as I drive into her.

"Would you like to know the best part?" He grins at me, then pulls her in and plants a toe curler on her. Leaving her lips with a smack, he cradles her head on his shoulder and looks me dead in the eye. "She's all mine."

The stink of challenge comes off him in waves. Like he'd love me to try and fuck her just to have an excuse to smack me down.

Let him lift a finger. Jacinto will get as good as he gives – maybe better.

He can smirk all he wants. The girl's eyes fix on my face, rich with complicity already.

"Don't look so serious, Diego." Jacinto releases her and pats my cheek. "I'm only teasing you." Drawing a cigar from his breast pocket, he holds it out as an olive branch. How can I refuse? The man smokes the finest cigars in the world.

"Gracias." I bite the end, and pat my pockets, but our new guest steps forward.

"Let me." A lighter appears out of nowhere, and she sparks it for me. I lean forward, penetrating her with my eyes as I suck the end of the cigar cherry red.

"Full service," I smile, smoke curling from my lips.

"Isn't she divine? My little Alana."

Alana, huh? Good choice.

Jacinto closes a hand around the back of her neck, squeezing and pulling her close so he can kiss her throat. She tips her head back to receive it, and the view alone is enough to make my dick hard. It's like I can taste her skin already, and it only makes me hungry for more.

"Looks like you've had quite the evening," I say.

"The best," he exclaims. "There was a fight. That's how I met this little diamond."

"I heard."

"You missed out, Diego. Breaking bones, crushing ribs. Blood and shattered teeth." He heaves in a chestful of night air and throws open his arms as he sighs it at the palm trees. "Paradise."

His knuckles are scraped and bruised, and I marvel that somehow there's not a speck of blood on his jacket. The man is a miracle of brutality.

"It hasn't exactly been quiet here either." That gets his attention, and my cousin's mood darkens with lightning speed.

"Oh?"

Of course I get to deliver the bad news. Everyone else hid like rats the second the transmission came he was returning.

"It's Osiris." Just hearing the name makes his shoulders tremble.

"Did something happen?"

"One of the leopards..." I don't even have to finish. Jacinto lurches forward, eyes filling. He clenches his fists in front of them to hide the tears, his teeth gnashing horribly.

"Which one," he croaks.

"Sanson."

Jacinto rocks back on his heels with an animal roar, body quaking with fury. Whipping around, he thunders off.

"Who's Osiris?" Alana asks.

"His chihuahua." My cousin rips across the lawn frothing at the mouth like a werewolf on acid. "Shit." I have to catch him. I take off, with Alana right behind me.

A trio of exotic cats cluster by one of the koi ponds, eyes

glowing as Jacinto closes on them. They've seen his rages before, so their tails barely twitch.

Until a pistol comes out.

"Motherfuckers!" Jacinto lets loose, emptying the clip. The cats never stand a chance. They vanish in a mist of blood and fur as agonized yowls fill the air. Within seconds, three glorious animals are reduced to one big pulpy mess shuddering on the grass.

"The fuck are you doing?" I shout, ripping the gun from his hand. It's red hot, and I drop it as he snatches me by the shoulders.

"Motherfuckers," he snarls again.

"Jacinto!" I grab him back, shaking him and forcing him to look me in the eye. "What the fuck was that?"

"They killed Osiris!"

"Those leopards were eleven thousand dollars apiece."

"They're worthless now!"

You got that right, I think as I look at the mangled heap.

"Jacinto." I grip him harder. "You can't do things like this."

"Get your hands off me!" He throws me off and squares up, ready to scrap right here.

"I'm only trying—"

"Nobody touches me," he shouts over the top of me. Lifting a finger, he jabs it at my chin. "Be careful, Diego. You'll wind up with a broken neck."

I don't give a fuck if he's blood or not, threats like that are a shortcut to an ass whooping.

"Mind what you say," I tell him, struggling to keep my temper under control.

"Make me."

Jesus, would I love to.

He didn't use to be like this. But now this brand of erratic bullshit is his signature. The God of Destruction, dressed in flesh and expensive suits. Given half the chance I'd beat the stuffing out of him and show him he's mortal after all. Push him to the brink of death so he knows what fear tastes like.

Instead I keep my hands down and take it on the chin.

"See?" A sardonic laugh sneers over his lips. "Coward."

That fucking does it!

My throat rattles out a ferocious snarl and I coil up to pounce and my cousin bristles for combat. Before I can, Alana glides in, coiling around Jacinto like the serpent in the garden.

"Jacinto," she purrs. "Are you really going to fight him?" Her lips dust his ear as she whispers, "After what you promised me?"

I swear she darts a look my way.

A woman like that could make a man forget his own name, let alone a fight in the making. As she runs her hands over his chest, Jacinto's anger melts into overt lust. Shit, I can see his cock swelling in his pants.

Who can blame him? Mine's doing the same thing.

"Eager, aren't we?" Before she can answer, he claps his mouth over hers, sucking her tongue with relish. He doesn't care that I'm standing here. If anything, he's putting on a show. Grabbing her tit, running his palm over her shapely ass. Displaying her perfection to goad me. It's a worse punishment than anything his fists could have doled out.

The son of a bitch is getting his revenge after all.

Jealousy courses like venom through my veins as he paws her. If I was ready to fight over killing some cats, I could murder him on the spot for enjoying her in front of me.

"You are very… persuasive," Jacinto says, licking her jawline all the way to her chin.

"Am I?" Batting her heavy lidded eyes at him is the perfect trap. And my cousin falls as hard as any man.

"You treacherous little witch." He takes her throat in his hand, squeezing just enough for her breath to gurgle. She puts her hand on his, and he laughs and cuts me a look. He loves mixing pleasure with pain, so long as he's the one dishing things out. "You're lucky I have another appointment, Diego."

"Right," I say, tight lips and tighter trousers. They walk past, and it's all I can do not to clobber him and run off into the bushes with her. Who am I kidding? We wouldn't make it to the bushes. I'd fuck her right here on the grass for anybody who wanted to watch. I might even save the security footage to remember it by.

They walk towards the house, his hands exploring her body the whole way. My blood boils, but I have to keep myself in check—for now.

When they get to the steps, Jacinto looks back and shouts, "Have someone clean up that mess, Diego."

"Of course." Cleaning up after him has become my full time job. But that shit is drawing to a close fast.

Alana looks back too, her gaze lingering just a little too long to be innocent. We make a deal right this instant, and it's ironclad.

I'm going to have her. Regardless of what it costs.

When I heard she was coming, I was told she was impressive. Even the pictures didn't do her justice. No camera in the world could hope to capture the amount of sheer sex that woman has crammed in her lithe little body.

But I'm going to cram even more into it.

CHAPTER
SEVEN

LYDIA

Jacinto doesn't just pick up where we left off in the car, he jumps ahead ten spaces. I'm naked with one swipe of his hand. He kicks the door shut at the same time, launching himself at me and tackling me to the ground.

If it wasn't for the plush animal hide rug, I'd bust my bare ass on the terracotta tiles. His mouth whips into a frenzy, a full-blown tempest of tongue assaulting my skin. The naked lust of it is electrifying. As if he wants to devour my body whole out of sheer sexual appetite. I spread myself on the floor and give over to it, surrendering to his ransacking hands.

"Fuck." He jerks upright, stripping his jacket off and hurling it aside. While he unbuttons his shirt, I yank at his belt, mirroring his carnal avarice.

My eagerness unleashes the monster inside him. Jacinto rips off his shirt, then smacks my hands away to undo his pants. His cock is out in less than a second, throbbing in his fist. A glistening bead drips from the crown, then glides along the underside of his shaft.

No turning back now.

There's no world in which a macho hunk of meat like him would ever go down on a woman. That's not how he gets off, so it doesn't exist.

But he's all for the shoe being on the other foot. I grab his hips and drag myself up, inhaling him into my mouth all the way to the root. That salty drop is lost in the sea of my saliva, and I work up as much as possible to grease his pole.

"Take it," he snarls. "Take it you fucking *whore!*"

Oh, so he's that kind of guy?

I know exactly how to handle him. Direct eye contact, and just a little bit of teeth.

Grabbing him by the base and squeezing, I suck him all the way into my throat and get to work. Tears flood my eyes as they bore up into his, and I make sure to gag when I draw him out again.

Jacinto's teeth are clenched in a grimace of feral rapture. His fingers tighten, claiming a stinging fistful of my hair as his hips buck forward. The only time he's satisfied is when he's *all the way in.*

Now, I'm skilled at what I do, but there's only so much of this kind of thing a girl can take. It's not exactly covered in the intelligence training regime.

I'm going to have to change the game.

Plucking his pulsing dick out of my mouth, I look up at him with as much rapacity as I can muster.

"I need you inside me."

A cruel smile tugs the corner of his mouth.

"Beg me."

I bite my lip and furrow my brow into a pleading mask of pure helplessness.

"Please, Jacinto." My hand never stops wringing his cock.

If I can get one out of him without having to spread out, so much the better. "Please. I'll die if you don't fuck me."

Turns out, that's the secret password.

With one sweep of his mighty arms, he lifts me off the floor. Again, I'm astonished by the brute's strength.

But this isn't some romantic step over the threshold in a bridal dress. No, he flings me onto the bed like a doll. I haven't even stopped bouncing amidst the luxurious bedding before he's on me again.

He licks his palm, slicks it across my lady bits, and rams into me. It's enough to force the air out of my lungs, and I claw at the sheets to try and get my bearings. Jacinto grabs my ankles, stuffs my legs over his shoulders and batters into me with demonic abandon.

With my legs locked in place, he pins my wrists together over my head without missing a stroke. There's no denying he's endowed, and the head of his cock hits the flickering point in my core as he stabs into me over and over again. It's barbarous, pitiless, and utterly *sublime*.

Demeaning as it can be, there's something profoundly satisfying about being held down and fucked.

Hell, the demeaning is part of the attraction.

Giving over to it, I lie back and let myself be taken. His hips hammer moans out of me, and I clench around him to feel every bit as he shoves in and drags out again. My body shudders under the overwhelming force of his lovemaking.

But I can't call it that.

There's not a scrap of love in the way Jacinto uses my body for his pleasure. The physical sensations are all there, and if I wanted to, I could come at any second. But the core of the clinch is empty. We're fucking like the vacancy sign is lit up, and just thinking it hollows me out.

I wriggle and moan like I'm supposed to, but that's all. Jacinto is an ardent, forceful lover, but I don't feel a thing. Which is exactly as it should be.

Then, out of nowhere, Diego's dark eyes flash across my mind. Jacinto thrusts in the same instant, and I rip my hands free and clutch his ass.

"Shit," I hiss, pulling him deep. All my synapses fire at once, and I screw my eyes shut as my imagination melts Jacinto into Diego. My spine becomes a flaming bullwhip, and I buck up against him with all my might.

His shoulders are slick with sweat, and my legs slip free. They lock around his hips, cinching him in place so I can grind my clit against his abdomen. His hands find my breasts, and a frisson in my core crackles to life.

"Pinch my nipples," I snarl. "Do it!" He does, and I turn into pure, chaotic light. With a kick of my legs, Jacinto is on his back and I hunker down to fuck this man to pieces. Keeping my eyes shut so he stays Diego, I ride like Lawrence of Goddamn Arabia. The sparkle in the pit of my stomach explodes into full on fireworks and I scream the adobe off the walls.

Each breath I take blisters out of me like dragon fire as my climax continues to climb.

"Fuck, my Alana," Jacinto groans, digging his fingers into my hips. "I'm going to come."

And that kills it. He's himself again, and the light in me goes out.

Oh, I keep hollering, but it's all for show. He spasms under me, member pulsing as he fills me to bursting. A tight thread of sound unspools between his teeth, and I keep up the furious career of my hips until he goes limp in the sheets.

Mission accomplished.

Jacinto is snoring in less than a minute. I lay next to him, spy brain taking over to scope out the room. Not admiring the vaulted beam ceiling or the antique rug. Not even the magnificent four poster we just defiled.

I'm looking for information. Anything I can use to my advantage.

Then I see it.

There on the lion skin rug where the party started, next to the rumpled tangle of his trousers, lies a shiny black jewel worth more than a whole blood diamond mine.

Jacinto's phone.

If I can get my mitts on that, we might be able to button this thing up without having to work up a sweat with him again. I might miss out on fucking Diego for real, but that's a small sacrifice to get my ass back on my speedboat.

Extricating myself from Jacinto, I scooch to the edge of the bed. Mastering my body, I force my pulse down to keep my head clear before I even think of standing up. No sense in rushing. Stealth is the best ally in the world.

My bag lies just beside the door where I dropped it. Inside is Nine's phone ripper. This whole thing could be over in less than an hour. Get the information back to headquarters, wait for Zero to give the thumbs up, and torch this heroin haven off the face of the earth.

Jacinto snorts like a car backfiring, and all those flaming fantasies go up in smoke. His cum groggy eyes flutter open, and he plants his palm on my thigh.

"My angel. That was…"

"The best sex I ever had," I coo, snuggling up to him.

Go back to sleep, dickhead.

Instead, he climbs out of bed with a yawn. Look there's no getting around the fact his broad back is impressive. It's criss-crossed with red scratch marks all the way down to his tight, marble hard ass.

To my dismay, he trots right over to his phone and picks it up. A quick glance at the screen, then the son of a bitch pads over to his *fucking safe*. Obscuring the combination with his body, he tucks the phone away and shuts everything again.

"Hey, lover," I murmur, doing my best brainless fuck doll. "Isn't that a little extreme?"

"In my line of work, a man can't be too careful." The son

of a bitch actually winks! Rubbing his eyes, he comes back to bed—hog bobbing from thigh to thigh with every step.

Cratering onto the mattress, Jacinto fumbles at my body with sleepy fingers. The guy is such a powerhouse, the fact that he's so worn out is a testament to how hard I just fucked him.

Gold star for me.

He latches on to one of my nipples, suckling for a second. It's strangely infantile, so I smooth his hair with my hand and hum tunelessly to lull him out again.

Works like a charm.

The man is snoring again in no time, and I decide to wait for him to drift all the way to dreamland before slipping out of bed.

A hot shower has a lot of work cut out for it. A couple of international flights, a sweaty club, and sweatier car ride, and a tumble with one of the most dangerous cartel kingpins in the world.

Not bad for a day's work.

Scrubbing the Jacinto spit off my body, I tick through my options.

If his phone is out of reach, I can at least case the joint. Get a feel for the layout and try to suss out where the money spots might be.

It's a job that requires stealth, but that's about it. Check for locked doors, and if you hit bingo, make a note of it for later. It's a rookie mistake to toss a location on the first visit. Save that for when you know the escape routes. Getting made on day one is a shortcut to a shallow grave.

And I get the feeling loverboy sawing logs in the bedroom would do the digging himself.

A quick glance at my phone tells me it's a shade shy of ten. Maybe a bit early for a midnight ramble, but fuck it. I'm taking this bull by the horns. I'm not sure how late shit goes down around here, but there's only one way to find out.

I don't exactly have the outfit for sneaky-sneaks, but I've got the next best thing—a great set of tits, and no shame. The only disguise I need is a towel and a pair of doe eyes.

Sneaking past Jacinto is no problem. The guy sleeps deeper than Captain Nemo. In two shakes of my naked butt, I'm dripping on the hallway tiles. It'll be like leaving a trail of breadcrumbs that'll be dry by morning.

And if I run into any guards, I'll act all startled and drop the towel. That oughta buy me all the good will I need to explain away my nighttime snoopery.

All I've seen of this place so far are the killing fields for exotic cats and Jacinto's bedroom. The trip from one to the other was a blur, so now I get to take my time. It's one long corridor after another, each one boasting nothing but locked doors. Well, locked doors and security cameras sprinkled around at regular intervals. It might be possible to get around this place without getting caught on tape, but it'd take some next-level cat-burglar shit.

And I left my catsuit in my other pants. This little moonlight gambit might just turn out to be a bust.

Just when I'm about to cut bait, a knob turns.

An opulent sitting room waits on the other side. A pair of genuine elephant tusks form an arch in front of the window, a heavy leather chair perched under them. The whole place is like a teenager's fantasy of a grown man's study. Bookcases line the walls, brimming with books I guarantee nobody here has cracked.

A mahogany desk holds down the rug next to a fireplace, and I traipse over to see what I can find out. Again, it's more like a museum display than an actual office.

The only giveaway is a hefty bronze ashtray on the corner. No question this is where Jacinto gets down when he wants to feel like a grownup.

Looking around, the whole room is littered with ashtrays. It's a no-shit Marlborough Man scavenger hunt in here. Smart money says it's the only way they can keep El Jefe from ashing all over the priceless rugs.

Naturally, the drawers are locked, but I'm guessing the façade of this room extends all the way to a set of empty drawers. The truth steals over me all at once.

It's a meeting room.

A den crafted expressly to impress visiting dignitaries. An overt show of wealth and power to cow any underlings who get out of line, and dazzle other drug moguls on the rise. Stepping back, it's an exquisite piece of theatre, but useless to me and the mission.

Still, it's good to know there's a hideout around here. Between the papier-mâché grandeur and the unlocked door, you can bet a ten pound bag of Pizarro's gold nobody ever sets foot in here unless it's meticulously planned.

Which could make it an excellent ditch point if I need to shelter in place and plan.

Taking a second to dab up any droplets my hair let fall on the desk, I make for the door. There's still a whole wing of this place I haven't gotten to yet.

I cringe as the door opens with a slight creak, so I skitter into the hall and close it as gently as I can.

"It always squeaks like that," a voice from behind me says. My adrenaline hits the sky, and I whirl around, clutching the towel to my cleavage and get ready to put on a show. But when I see who it is, I freeze.

It's Diego.

And his gaze is even hungrier than I fantasized.

CHAPTER EIGHT

Diego

"Well, well, well. Did someone get lost?"

I get the feeling nobody catches this girl off guard. There's genuine terror in her eyes nobody could fake.

From what I can see, *nothing* about her is fake. The damp towel slung around her isn't hiding much, which I suspect is the whole idea.

"I was looking for Jacinto's room."

"Oh, were you? How did you manage to get out of it in the first place? From the look in his eyes, I figured you two would be busy until breakfast."

"I'm sure that's what he hoped." The insinuation my cousin didn't measure up to his promises makes me chuckle. Though I'll admit I'm not surprised. There's also just enough invitation in her voice to make my dick harder than it already was.

It sprang to fucking life when I saw her ass creeping backwards out of our Situation Room. The subtle line of her spine working up to those perfect shoulders. But those sharp eyes gleaming above her plentiful spill of cleavage? I want to snap that towel away and ram her to the floor so hard we chip the tile.

"So," I say. "Are you telling me you didn't enjoy your evening with Jacinto?"

"I'm not saying that at all," she replies immediately. "I enjoyed it quite a lot." My throat gets hot, and I clench my fists. My eyes dart over her body, looking for traces of him. Telltale red skin from his embrace, bite marks, bruises. It's no secret how he uses his women, and my blood turns to lava thinking this one actually *enjoyed* it.

"Good for you," I grumble. It's enough to make me want to kick open the door and beat the shit out of him in his own bed. Stifle him in sheets still smelling of her body. It would be too good for him.

"Don't misunderstand." She bites her lip, and stops just shy of touching my arm. "I can imagine better."

My dick throbs so hard it damn near rips my pants. She's bating me, and we both fucking know it. It would be so easy to shove her into the Situation Room and bend her over Jacinto's desk. Sexual hunger fogs over me, consuming everything else. Which is exactly the distraction she's going for.

I force myself to rock back a step to try and break the spell.

Who the hell goes sneaking around a mansion in the middle of the night wearing nothing but a towel?

Someone up to no good, that's who.

I've got to take control of this situation.

"Do you mind telling me what you were doing in there?" My shift in tone makes her eyes flicker as she recalibrates. All of a sudden, she's a full-on babe in the woods.

"I got lost."

"Somehow I doubt that," I snort. "What are you doing so far from Jacinto's room, anyway?"

"Am I really that far?" She nibbles on her thumbnail,

never breaking eye contact with me. "I must have really gotten myself turned around."

I'd love to turn her around.

Stop that shit! Keep it together, Diego.

"Turned around, huh? Let me ask you again, what are you doing out of Jacinto's room in the first place?"

This time when she reaches out, her fingertips graze my arm.

"Can you keep a secret?" Her mouth curls into a grin so wicked the Witch of the West would take notes. "I worked up a bit of an appetite. I don't suppose you know where a gal could..." Those treacherous fingertips caress their way up my arm. "Satisfy her hunger?"

"Not satisfied after all, huh?"

"It was a nice appetizer." She shrugs. "But now I'm ready for the main course."

Jesus fucking Christ.

I've got to be careful. Every inch of my body—all the way to the tip of my aching dick—demands that I kiss this woman. Instinct is a motherfucker.

Don't fall for it, a tiny voice inside me screams. *She's using you.*

And I've been used before.

I'll be goddamned if I let another woman get the better of me. None of them are to be trusted, especially this one. If I know one thing in this rotten world, it's that I'm locking eyes with a viper. And I'd better not forget it.

"Alright." I harden my tone. "I'm going to get a straight answer out of you." Before I can even finish saying it, her towel slips. She squeaks and grabs it, but not before I catch a flash of pink. Not a whole nipple, but enough to set the wolf in my heart howling at the moon.

"Sorry," she gasps, flushed in embarrassment. Her eyes dart around, eager to look anywhere but my face.

Which is funny because mine know exactly where to look.

They're riveted to the deep crease of cleavage, and the supple swell of her tit.

"Goddamnit," I mutter, licking my lips at the sight. She's got me cornered, and she knows it. When I pry my gaze up to her face, her eyebrow is arched seductively.

"Do you like what you see?"

"You know I do."

She hugs herself closer, plumping the girls up even more.

"Would you like to see more?" Her voice is breathy. Secretive. Forbidden. Begging to be kissed out of her mouth and swallowed whole.

"Yes."

Without ever breaking eye contact, she takes the top of the towel in both hands. Moving with agonizing, deliberate slowness.

Just a peek. Get yourself a solid eyeful so you can get over this bitch and get back to the task at hand.

Just as her hands start to part, revealing a ribbon of nudity from her collarbone to her belly button, someone rounds the corner.

I jerk back, ready for the worst. If it's Jacinto, I'm as dead as yesterday's dinner.

Ortega.

"The fuck is going on?" he grunts, narrowing his eyes at us.

"I was looking for help," she gulps.

"Oh, yeah?" Ortega looks her up and down. "Help with what? Because if it's getting laid, you're barking up the wrong tree. And you." He turns his attention to me, face hard as granite. "You're really going to risk getting caught with Jacinto's girl out here in the hallway? For fuck's sake, if Jefe saw this, you wouldn't live to hit the floor."

"It's a misunderstanding," the girl pipes up. "I took a shower in a room Jacinto had set up for me, but when I tried to go back to his room, all I managed to do was get lost."

"Yeah, right." He laughs right in her face. "Jacinto set up another room for you? On your first night? Lady, everyone on the compound knows you shouldn't be out of his suite for a week at least." Ortega cracks off a lascivious cackle, cutting right to the red hot core of my temper.

"Be careful what kind of shit you toss around, Ortega. If Jacinto got the idea his girl was sneaking around naked in the middle of the night, it's not just my head that'll roll, and you know it."

He bares his teeth as he considers this, looking back and forth between me and the girl.

"We can fight this now, or he can let the dog keep sleeping," I say. "At the end of the day, you and I are in the same corner, and rattling this cage isn't gonna do either of us a lick of good."

"Yeah," he concedes.

Up to now, the girl's been silent, watching us chase this back and forth. I haven't been talking in code as much as I should, but I needed to squash this fast.

"What are you two talking about?" she asks. As if I'm gonna buy the innocent act she's dishing out.

"Never mind," I snap.

"You didn't hear anything." Ortega's face tells her that pushing the point comes with a steep price tag. The last thing we need is her sticking her nose in any father. A beat of silence vibrates over the three of us, then Ortega's spine slackens. "Come on." He offers her his arm. "Let me get you back to Jacinto's room."

"I'll take her," I say, putting a hand on his chest.

"Like hell! Just let the boss get a whiff of you anywhere near her in this condition and it'll be a three ring circus. But me?" He opens his arms to give me a good look. "Nobody could say I'm a threat."

Not when it comes to running off with a pretty young girl, anyway. Squat, stout, with a face like a hundred miles of bad road. If Jacinto sees him with the girl in a towel, the only thing he'd suspect Ortega of is spraying her with a water hose.

"Alright." I've got no choice but to back down.

This is the second time I've had to watch her walk off with another man. At least this time I know beyond a shadow of a doubt she's not going to fuck this one. He might steal a peek or two, but fuck it – he's earned it.

Ortega wanted my spot in the lineup. When my cousin took over the cartel, Ortega was right in line to step up and be his second. Decades of service busting heads and torching police cars should have sealed it right up for him.

In the end, Jacinto decided blood was thicker than sweat. I moved up, and Ortega kept his position as head of security. He's got every reason to resent the living fuck out of me, but we've got an alliance that runs deeper than bullshit hierarchies. He and I share the same goal.

Eliminate Jacinto Osorio.

When I'm at the top of the ladder, that puts Ortega squarely in the spot he covets.

Right now, the only spot I covet is his—with an armful of beautiful, virtually naked woman.

Lucky bastard.

This time she doesn't look back, but the back of her towel is hiked up just enough to reveal the bottom curve of her ass. Perfect rounds, bouncing back and forth as they walk away.

She knows exactly what she's doing.

And I don't mind a bit.

CHAPTER NINE

LYDIA

Jacinto must have woken up rejuvenated because he plows me again as soon as his eyes open. He certainly has his style. Not a lot of variety in the routine, but he's good at what he does. I'll admit to another little imaginary assist to put me over the top.

After my spicy little run-in with Diego last night, it's a lot easier to, shall we say, *achieve*? I achieve so many times Jacinto can't stop patting himself on the back.

"What do you think?" he asks as he fondles my breasts in the shower. "Spend the day in bed? Really treat ourselves?"

"You know what I'd *really* like?" I cradle his dick in my palm, and he's literally putty in my hands. "I'd love a tour."

"Oh?" He retreats a bit, so I rub up against him. We're both slippery with soap, so why not use it to my advantage?

"I only got a glimpse last night, and it's all so beautiful. So *elegant*." He starts to stiffen in my hand. "Don't you want to show off for me?" Sinking to my knees, I kiss the head of his cock and flick it with the point of my tongue. "Please?"

"For you, my diamond?" He puts his hand on the back of my head, showing me exactly what the admission price will be. "Anything."

I give him what he wants, and in half an hour we're dressed and walking down the front steps. Diego leans on the fender of a military style jeep, looking very sour behind his sunglasses. The front of his loose, linen shirt flaps in the breeze, giving a peek at the fruits of his workout routine.

He's easy on the eyes, no question. And better still – he's up to something. That little convo with the Ortega last night was a jackpot all by itself.

"Good morning," I say as brightly as I can, snapping my fingers. "Diego, right?"

"That's right." He hates my charade, which only tickles me more. "I understand you tricked my cousin into a *tour*?"

"Nobody tricks me," Jacinto proclaims, beaming in the morning sun. "Ever."

Diego looks like he just stepped off a beach resort, but Jacinto has gone full Castro. Olive drab everything, aviator sunglasses, that stupid little hat, and a pocket full of cigarillos.

"Please." He doffs the cap, encouraging me into the passenger seat. Diego rolls his eyes as I climb in, then Jacinto hoists himself into the back, standing and holding onto the roll bar. All he's missing is the machine gun to complete the storybook picture.

He's like a kid playing dictator, and I'm absolutely here for it. His type are so easy to topple. Play up to their ego and they never see it coming.

The ones who think they're invincible are always fish in a barrel.

"Dieguito?"

The diminutive? That pisses Diego right the hell off. He grips the wheel like he's going to rip it loose and beat Jacinto to death with it.

"Si?"

"Vamanos!" He pounds on the roll bar and Diego grits his teeth.

Me? I'm fucking *loving* it.

We roll out, taking a gravel path around the back of the mansion. It's all tiered stonework, pools, and succulent gardens for about a quarter mile, then the terrain opens up.

It's all I can do to keep my jaw from dropping. The compound rolls on so far I can't even see the back fence. What I *can* see is a massive field of crimson flowers. Like, acres of the goddamn things.

"Oh, my God," I gasp in delight. "They're so beautiful!"

"Aren't they?" Jacinto fills his chest.

"It's like heaven. What are they?"

"Poppies."

"Oh," I cry. "Like in the *Wizard of Oz*?"

Diego shakes his head, but Jacinto throws back his head, laughing to split himself. He drops into a crouch and snakes an arm around me.

"Aren't you adorable?"

"So they're the same?"

"Yes, my diamond." He grips my chin and tilts my head so he can kiss me. And I kiss him right back. If he's gonna be ardent, I'll be a goddamn house fire. True to form, his hand slides inside my top, seeking out my nipple.

I open my eyes and Diego is ready to explode.

Perfect.

"So," I say when Jacinto's lips turn me loose. "What do you need all these poppies for? So you can put people to sleep?" It's my turn to laugh, and Jacinto's eyes gleam sneakily.

"Something like that." He exchanges a look with a visibly unhappy Diego, then stands up again. I smile at Diego, but he won't even look at me. Making him jealous is going to be a party in a box. If there's already a rift between them, I'm going to turn it into a fucking *ravine*. These men will rip each other to shreds, and all I have to do is screw the right one at the right time.

"Oh, come on." I crane my neck up at Jacinto, every inch the petulant child. "Really. Why are you growing all these flowers? Are you a florist?"

"You should know better than anyone I don't play with *flowers*." He scoffs at a profession so feminine.

"What then?"

That devious shine lights up his eyes again.

"Do you really want to know?"

"I wouldn't," Diego says, his voice flat. Jacinto flares.

"What?"

They switch into Spanish—as if I don't speak it. Amateurs.

"I wouldn't tell her if I were you."

"Because you're a coward," Jacinto claps back. "What is there to be afraid of? She's just a silly girl. Besides, who is she going to tell?"

Diego shrugs. "It's a bad idea."

That does it. Jacinto gets all puffed up, clenching his teeth and glaring. The surest way to get him to do something is to tell him not to. I'll remember that for later.

"Keep your opinions to yourself," he shouts. I sit up in my seat and look back and forth between them.

"Is everything okay? What are you fighting about?" Poor little me. The stupid American who only speaks English. Jacinto turns his gaze back to me, softening instantly.

"We're not fighting, sweetheart. But we Mexicans are passionate people." He thumps his chest with his fist. "But you want to know, I'll tell you." One last glance Diego's way, then he leans over me.

"Have you heard of heroin?"

I'm all naive astonishment.

"You mean, like, *drugs*?" My pearl clutching wins another boisterous laugh from El Jefe. He wags finger at me.

"You are very smart. All of this," he sweeps his arm at the opioid meadow, "has one destination. You smell flowers, I smell money."

We come up to a series of long tin barns and Diego jams it in park. Hopping down, Jacinto scuttles around to offer his hand to help me out. Say what you will about the guy, he's putting in a world class effort. And this cow has already given up the milk!

Inside the closest tin barn are dozens of shirtless men processing the flowers. This isn't some rinky-dink little operation, it's a full-on industry. Escorting me past work station after work station, Jacinto rattles on about numbers and productivity. I soak up as much as I can, thanking my lucky stars for Nine's recording device. It drinks in everything so I can focus on playing up to my host.

"I can't believe it," I coo, hugging his arm between my boobs. "All this is yours?"

"Every bit."

Diego trails behind, sullen. Even his sunglasses can't hide the heat in his glare.

Back in the jeep, the fields of red give way to acres of green. A half mile later, another series of barns dry and process countless strains of marijuana. Hydroponics buildings foster seedlings and more delicate varieties. The sheer scope is fucking astounding.

Leaving that behind, we roll still further into this dusty, narcotic saturated wonderland.

A shed with a single door stands along the side of the road, and Jacinto calls for a halt.

"I know what you're doing," Diego whispers while his boss clambers to offer his hand.

"What? What am I doing?"

Jacinto appears and all Diego can do is scowl at my back as I alight. His rage has been climbing all morning, and I've fed the flames at every opportunity. Draping myself on Jacinto is easy, and he's glowing like a million watt bulb.

Even so, I steal glances Diego's way whenever I can get away with it. Best of all when neither of them are looking. We're all glistening as the day heats up, and Diego's shirt is starting to cling to him. I don't know what his regime is, but the guy has sculpted his body for pure sin. And I'm ready for a trip straight to hell—as long as he's the devil waiting at the gate.

Jacinto throws open the door on the shack, revealing a spiral staircase leading down. Because, of course.

"After you."

If the motherfucker had the brains to spring a trap, this would be it. And I've got one of those explosive pellets on me in case things go sideways.

Then the odor of loam and manure hits me in the jaw and I figure I'm in the clear. The metal staircase clanks with each step, and when we reach a dim, humid room nobody looks our way. Deep bins filled with rich soil run side by side, row after row. Each one is studded with enough psilocybin to bring Jerry Garcia back from the dead.

I have to hand it to my buddy Jacinto, he doesn't think small. He's basically running a one family empire, cornering every drug market imaginable. Most cartels specialize, but this man is truly a Jacinto of all trades.

"Magic mushrooms," I murmur. "Wild."

"The best is yet to come." He puts a hand on the small of my back, ushering me towards the far end of the room. Naturally, by the time we reach the door, he's full-on grabbing my ass. And why not? After all, it's the key that opened all this up for me.

"Are you ready for something special?"

"Jacinto," Diego's cautioning voice cuts in. "Are you sure?"

The sneer on Jacinto's face says exactly how sure he is. He turns the knob, and bright light makes my eyes water. I have to hold up an arm to shield them as we cross the threshold.

Everything up to this point has been boilerplate Mexican drug manufacturing. Cheap and cheerless, dripping with sweat and despair. The only real difference has been the scale.

But this? This is something else again.

It's bigger than I ever could have imagined, and I guaranteed Zero doesn't have a clue how extensive this is. She wouldn't send me on this mission for nothing, but I'm starting to wonder if it's really a one-agent operation.

"Woah."

My eyes adjust, and I look around at a laboratory any teaching hospital would sell their accreditation for. We're talking Frankenstein for the 21st century. This isn't about processing some cut rate snoot to sneak over the border in a rusted El Camino. It's a manufacturing hub for some next level shit. And I have a pretty good idea what.

"What is all this?" I ask anyway.

"You haven't guessed?" Diego hangs behind me, apathetic to all the high tech goings on. "Fentanyl production. Where the money is." His face is an impervious mask, unreadable for the first time since I laid eyes on him.

I turn to Jacinto, but he's already trotting away. When he realizes I'm not right behind him, he waves for us to follow, a giddy smile lighting his face.

He's merrily punching a code into a keypad by the time we reach him, and I kick myself for not keeping in step with him. Three seconds earlier and I'd have that code in my brain.

"Before I show you the best part—how do you like things so far?"

"Oh, Jacinto, it's..." I look back over the lab with unfeigned astonishment. "Beyond belief."

"Believe it." He calls my eyes back to his. "You're sharing

the bed of a very powerful man." With one pull of his arm, the door swings open and my eyes shoot out of their sockets. "With a lot of money."

Brother, you ain't just whistling Dixie.

Money.

And not just a little bit.

We're talking a warehouse full of pallets piled high in shrink-wrapped cash. The Home Depot of drug money. There's so much dough here, it's where God comes when he needs to take out a loan. I couldn't give a rat's ass about getting rich, and even I'm blown away.

"I don't understand," I say, looking into his egotistical face. "How does one man make all this happen?"

"Determination," he crows. Then he leans close and clamps his hand on the back of my neck. "And friends. In very high places."

Diego heaves an exasperated sigh. His boss just dimed out the last thing an outsider should know, let alone a straight-up spy.

"Unreal."

"Oh, I assure you." Jacinto slings his arm around my waist and squeezes me to him. "Everything is very real." Taking my hand, he plants it on the front of his pants so I can feel how swollen all this self-congratulatory shit makes him. "*Very* real."

I tremble with nubile excitement as waves of resentment pour off of Diego.

"Jacinto." I whisper his name in the husky voice of someone overcome with desire, bewildered by money and power. It may not be my best performance, but the kiss is real. Well, real enough to make Diego storm out of the treasure vault.

As Jacinto's tongue slithers around to count my teeth, I tick back over all the information I'm going to send back to

Zero. She was right. Nobody could move this kind of volume without someone in the US turning a blind eye.

Judging by the scope of this place, I'd wager on a lot of someones.

CHAPTER
TEN

DIEGO

"I don't fucking like it." I grip the neck of a bottle of tequila, trying to decide whether to open it or throw it in the fucking pool. "He's blinded by the end of his dick."

"Keep your voice down," my dad cautions. After all, my cousin is less than thirty steps away.

"Fuck him, he's asleep." Shit, I can hear him snoring. Passed out on a deck chair, getting burnt crispier than a chicharron, his own bottle of tequila ready to boil in the afternoon heat. Direct sunlight can be a motherfucker, and his lounge chair is slap in the middle of it.

"I don't like it either," Ortega grumbles. He sucks his teeth, the señorita tattooed on his chest peeking out of his open shirt. "We don't even know this girl."

You don't, maybe, I want to say, but keep my fucking mouth shut.

"That's just it." I rock forward, looking back and forth between the two old heads. "He snatched her up at some bullshit club just last night, and this morning he shows her *everything*?"

"When you say everything…?" Ortega trails off, eyeing me seriously.

"All the way to the money locker."

"Goddamn." He rubs his forehead, then cuts a look at my father.

"Even you have to admit, that shit's not good, Eduardo."

Dad inhales sharply through his nose, staring at the patio tile.

"Yeah." He hates this.

There's a good reason my father didn't succeed his brother-in-law to take over the cartel. First, his name is Alamar, and the Osorio name was well imprinted on the region. And two, he doesn't have the stomach for it. He's a numbers guy, so when it comes to pumping dope into people and slitting noses when it goes wrong, let's just say he's not a fit.

"I have to hand it to her," Ortega says with a filthy smirk. "Her pussy must be tighter than a dolphin's blowhole to get that kind of access after just one night."

Hearing him talk like that about her makes my insides itch. As far as I'm concerned, I'm the only man on the planet who should even be able to *think* about her pussy, let alone say the word out loud.

But he's right. She worked her magic. Fast.

"He shouldn't have done it," my father admits. "But what difference does it make? So what if some piece of ass from the club gets a look? It's not like we're hiding. The whole region knows what we do."

"Region?" Ortega laughs. "The whole fucking country!"

"Maybe. But, they don't know the layout, do they?" That shuts them both right the hell up. "We scramble airspace around here for a reason. Security has orders to shoot down drones on sight, right?" I look at Ortega hard. That's his department after all. He should know better than anybody that an outsider getting an eyeful is a liability. Even if she was just some dumb slut from a bar.

That girl is many things, but a bimbo barfly ain't one of them.

"Jesus Christ." My father's mouth hangs open in awe, and Ortega is dumbstruck. They both look past me, and I already know what I'm going to see before I turn around.

Trick is, there's knowing something, and then there's actually seeing it. When I crane over my shoulder, I almost have a goddamn stroke. In every sense of that word.

The woman glides out of the shade of the colonnade at the far side of the pool almost in slow motion. Her lightly tanned skin is more blinding than an atomic flash once the sun hits her. I squint, but don't dare close my eyes. I'm not missing a second of this.

Brown hair down to her shoulders, and nothing left to the imagination. Shit, her sunglasses cover more than her bathing suit does. You can damn near see where the white bits turn pink. It's enough to bring tears to a man's eyes.

She knows we're watching. She has to. Time itself has stopped to ogle this perfect, nearly naked witch laying out to sunbathe.

Her chair is a good ten feet from my cousin's and she goes belly first, thank God. We all get a good look at the flowers as she eases into place, ass up just long enough to leave us all crossing our fucking legs. I have to grab the arms of my chair to keep from flying over there and pounding her into the ground.

"Fuck." I turn around, slouching in my chair. Who would have thought seeing 99.99% of a beautiful woman would put me in such a foul mood? "Are you done?" I snap, leaving my dad and Ortega shamefaced. "What really matters isn't what that tramp tricked Jacinto into—it's what it says about his mind. Shit is getting more unstable by the day."

"Yeah." Ortega shakes his head. "It's not good."

"No," my father agrees. "So?"

"We need a meeting. Call Don Manuel. I'll reach out to our man in Texas."

"Careful." Dad holds out a hand, looking over my shoulder again at my cousin beached by the pool.

"Fuck careful," I whisper, heat rising in my chest. "It's time to go hard."

"Not yet."

"*Soon*. We all know it. We need to stop talking and start fucking *doing*. And if I can make things work, we might just wind up with an ace in the hole." I hadn't intended to play my hand yet, and clamp my mouth shut. But my father knows when I'm holding back, and narrows his eyes at me.

"What's that supposed to mean?"

"Nothing. Forget it."

"Diego?" His teeth clack together, bared to take a hunk out of me. "What did you just say?"

"I'll tell you when I'm ready."

That has the old tiger ready to pounce, and Ortega rocks forward in his seat, putting himself between us.

"Alright, cool it. Fighting amongst ourselves is just going to fuck things up. Let's get that meeting together and decide as a group. Because, your boy's right, Eduardo." He looks at my father. "It's time."

Dad's not happy. But he's outnumbered. He pulls his lips tight, then fires back a shot of tequila and stalks off without a word.

"Stubborn son of a bitch," I growl as I watch him go. Ortega laughs.

"Like father, like son. Tell you what." He smacks my knee. "I'll go talk him down, then I'll call Manuel Barrera."

"Sounds good."

He hustles off after my dad. Two elder statesmen, content to sit in the shadows. If it weren't for my ambition, they'd stay under Jacinto's thumb until he burns the whole goddamn cartel to the ground.

Well, I'm not waiting around for him to shit on the cake. I'm making moves.

With that in mind, maybe it's time to make one very specific move. Because if I let that woman have another day to work her magic, all our plans might not amount to jack.

I can tell you one thing, Jacinto's going to be cranky when he wakes up. The sun has *roasted* that motherfucker. Most of us don't sunburn down here, but he's damn sure going to feel it.

Getting a closer look, his tequila bottle is well over half empty. Impressive considering he did it all himself. On an empty stomach, too—he claimed he wasn't hungry after we got back from his little song and dance tour. Just dragged her back to his room for a victory lap and shambled out already three sheets gone.

Maybe he couldn't get it up and decided to drown his sorrows. I'm told cocaine does that to folks.

I wouldn't know. I never touch the stuff, and I've never had a problem getting my dick hard. Just the opposite— sometimes it's too hard.

Like right now.

The closer I get to the American laid out on her chair, the more fiercely I want her. Her body is just begging to be touched, and my fingers are ready to volunteer. She knows I'm watching. I can tell.

"Hey, what's your name again?" I ask when I arrive next to her. She lifts her head, pulls her sunglasses down her nose, and looks at me. Those eyes cut straight to my core, and the hint of a smile lights the fuse.

"You remember."

"I do."

It's almost enough to make me laugh if her come-hither stare didn't make my dick throb so bad. This woman knows the effect she has on men, and I knuckle down to keep from giving her the upper hand. "Can I make you a drink, *Alana?*"

She holds my gaze for a long moment, then almost winks.

"Sure." Sitting up, every bit of her glides and bounces in just the right way. Bodies like hers should be illegal. At the very least, she should have to license it as a concealed weapon.

For all I know, maybe she has.

I lead her to the bar under the colonnade and step behind it. She climbs onto a stool, folding her arms on the bar top, then resting her breasts on her forearms. Lift and separate? More like divide and conquer.

"Want anything special?"

"Can I tell you a secret?" She wrinkles up her nose and leans forward, hiking her boobs up even higher.

Fuck, she's good.

"A secret?" I follow her move and lean close. "Don't tell me a girl like you actually has *secrets*?"

"Wouldn't you like to know?"

"I would, actually." That catches her a bit, or at least seems to. "But, let's start simply. What was it you were going to say?"

"That I don't like tequila."

It's the last thing I expected to hear, and I rock back on my heels and laugh.

"I hate to tell you this, but you came to the wrong country."

"Oh, I think I came to the right country." Her voice is sultry, and I find her eyes again. "For a variety of reasons."

"Are any of those reasons stretched out beside the pool?"

She looks back at Jacinto, and while she's distracted, I get myself an eyeful. Not that I haven't been, but holy shit, this woman.

"Perhaps." Even that crumb of acknowledgement lets the

pit bull loose in my guts. "But he's not what I'm interested in right now."

"What are you interested in?"

She bites her lip, considering me with a half-smile.

"Rum."

"I know just the thing." I grab a glass, sling some sugar into the bottom with some fresh mint.

"Ah. I love a mojito." She lifts her ass off the stool and sticks her nose over the glass, inhaling deeply as I crush the two together.

"I aim to please."

"Oh, I'm sure you don't have to aim." She stays close, lifting her gaze to mine. "A man like you could please with his eyes closed."

"Flattery will get you everywhere."

"Aw." She sinks back into her seat, her lip stuck out in a pout. "I was hoping I already had an all-access pass."

"Try me."

"A challenge?" Her eyebrow arches and she tilts her face away. "Alright. Can I ask you a question?" She thinks she's so good at this game.

"Ask away."

"I'm curious… who were those men you were talking to?"

"That's what you're curious about?" I scoff and juice a lime into her glass. "You already know Ortega. Or didn't you get cozy when he walked you back to your room last night?"

"Very cozy." The way she says it makes my blood hot, and when my eyes flash to her, she snickers.

"You're too easy."

"Wrong. I'm not easy. In fact, you might like to know that I'm very, very hard."

Her lips part and I have to look away to keep from reaching over the bar to taste them.

"And the other man?" she asks. "With the long silver hair?"

"Eduardo Alamar." Rum in the glass. "My father."

"I can see where the good looks come from."

"Is that right?" I scoop some ice into the glass. "You think I'm good looking?"

"It doesn't matter what I think. It's a fact. You *are* good looking. Better than good. But I'm nosy by nature…" *You got that right.* "You all looked so serious. What were you talking about?"

"You can't guess?"

"No."

"Come on." I flatten my hands on the bar and look at her dead on. "Don't pretend you don't know."

"What?" She laughs a bit, then sips her drink. "Why would I know anything?"

"Because you know a lot more than you let on. Don't you?"

"Don't get all serious on me, Diego," she giggles. "I'm just trying to rile you up."

"Are you?"

"Maybe?" She shrugs, toying with the straw between her teeth. The flirtation is so overt I have to wrestle myself back into control.

"I think we can stop playing this game. I know who you are, and I know what you're doing here."

"So do I. I'm the gal who's fucking your boss. That's what I'm doing here."

Having her say that to my face makes my mouth go dry. It's the last tactic in her belt, and I know she wouldn't use it if I didn't have her backed into a corner.

"Please don't condescend to me, Miss Slick. Or should I say, Agent Slick?"

CHAPTER
ELEVEN

Lydia

I almost drop my fucking glass.

But hard training has taught me not to give away a goddamn thing. Pulse normal. Not a single bead of sweat.

"Agent Slick?" I shake my head with a wry smile. "Diego, what the hell are you talking about?" With a roll of my eyes, I take a sip of his mojito. I have to hand it to the crafty son of a bitch—not only does he get crackerjack intelligence, he knows how to mix a fucking drink.

"You're good," he says. "But I'm better."

I'll believe that when I feel it.

Still, it's too close for comfort. I need a smokescreen, and waking up his booze soaked cousin should do the trick nicely.

"Look, this was cute, but it's starting to get boring. I'm not into role playing, so if you'll excuse me." I set down the glass. "I'm going for a swim." He's got me by the wrist before I can get a foot on the tile.

"Nando Rivera." The name stops me dead. If Diego actually knows my contact from the club, he might not be as full of shit as I thought. "I think he started a fight over you?"

"I know, poor thing. Jacinto really worked him over. Poor Nando…"

"Hector," he corrects me.

Shit.

"Excuse me?"

"Your *old friend* Nando Rivera? Yeah, his real name is Hector Ruiz. Which you would know if you'd ever laid eyes on him before last night."

"Okay, now you're talking crazy."

"Cut the shit, Lydia." He clamps down harder on my wrist. "Hector Ruiz has been in my pocket for years. Petty thief, junky, stool pigeon, and all around mercenary shitheel. When I realized how useful he could be, I dragged him back here, put him on the payroll, and kept him juiced enough to stay loyal. Then it was just a matter of dangling him where some GSIA operatives would find him."

Airtight.

I need to relay that information to Zero. ASAP.

As if he's reading my mind, Diego lets out a sinister chuckle.

"Don't worry, he's already dead. They all are."

"Him and the other two?" I shouldn't have let it slip, but the cat's already out of the bag on this much. Diego cocks his head, the corner of his treacherous mouth curling.

"There were more than that, but yes."

"I see. May I have a cigarette?"

"Sorry, it's all cigarillos." He grins and holds one out.

"That'll do." I put one between my lips and he lights it like he's to the manor born. "So." I exhale the smoke in his face and pick up my glass. "If you put so much work into this Hector, why kill him?"

Diego just shrugs.

"He served his purpose."

"Really? And what purpose was that?"

His grin widens and he points a finger in my face.

"*You*, Lydia. We needed you here. I needed you."

"Needed? Or *need*?" I take that finger and put it between my teeth, biting down just a bit. As if that's not enough, I flick my tongue on the tip before letting go. He chuckles, then licks the tip of his finger where my tongue touched it.

"You're good. I have to admit, you really know what you're doing."

"But you see through me?"

"Please." He plants his palms on the bar and puts his nose mere inches from mine. "I know what you're doing. I know why you're here."

I roll back in my chair and cross my legs, smiling like the cat that ate a whole flock of canaries. If he's going to speechify, who am I to stand in his way?

"Go on."

"GSIA sent you here to distract my cousin Jacinto. Turn his head. You're here to lure him into your web and make him spill everything you need to ruin the organization. And the dumb fucker is too blind to see it."

"Oh, I'd say he's more than blind." We both look to Jacinto twitching in his sleep under the brutal Mexican sun. If I had any pity left in my blood, I'd throw a towel over him. Or kick him into the pool. Whichever felt right in the moment.

"You're not wrong." Was that vulnerability in Diego's voice? My eyes dart back to him to find unexpected concern in his face. "My cousin..." He frowns and shakes his head. "He's changed. Coming unhinged. You saw last night, the way he slaughtered those cats."

"That's not normal for him?"

"It didn't use to be. But now?" Diego takes my drink and downs half of it. "He's dipping into the supply."

"Even I know the rules." We say it together—

"Never get high on your own supply."

"Exactly." Diego nods, chewing his lower lip at how blind his cousin is. "That's his favorite movie. Only he looks at it like a blueprint instead of a warning." Inhaling sharply through his teeth, he looks like he could spit. His level of fed-up with Jacinto is so sky high, it's a miracle the boss man hasn't clocked it yet. Because Diego's poker face is for shit. "When my cousin first took over, it was all business, but when he started to see how powerful he was, it took over him."

"So, the violence at the club last night is a new thing?"

"No, he's always been cruel. Sadistic, even. It's one thing to beat the shit out of someone who steals from you, or kill a rat, but Jacinto takes it too far. Killing isn't enough, he needs to torture too. Warm blood on his hands gets him off."

"Among other things."

"Don't talk like that," he shouts with startling vehemence, slamming his hand on the bar. We both look to Jacinto for fear of getting caught. He just snores lazily, and I turn my attention back to Diego. "You can't say those things. Not to me."

"Oh?" I lean forward to put my elbows on the bar, snugging my boobs between them. "Why not?"

"You know why. And don't pretend you don't feel it too."

He's got me there.

"Look." Diego straightens up and steadies himself. "If my cousin keeps on like this, it could jeopardize everything. The manufacturing, the supply chain, the cash flow, our connections—" He snaps his mouth shut and clenches his fists, furious to let that last part slip. Which is my cue to start digging.

"Connections," I ask innocently as I pick up my glass. "And who might those be?"

He sucks his teeth, then smiles and wags a finger at me.

"Nice try. I said more than I should, but I know when to stop."

"What if I begged you not to stop?" The heat in my voice

flickers from his face all the way down to his cock, and I see it swell through the front of his pants.

"Don't distract me."

"Don't you want me to?" Rocking forward, I do everything I can to get the girls directly in his line of vision. The guy takes an eyeful, but it only seems to rev him up—and not in the way I'm after.

"Look." He grips the edge of the bar, teeth clenched. "Your mission is going to fail. I'll do everything I can to ensure that."

"Fair enough. I'll call for an extraction team."

"Not so fast. Your mission is going to fail, but I can't let you go."

"Because?"

"Because I need you to help me with mine. That's the real reason you're here."

The real reason? Diego clearly fancies himself a mover and shaker of the first order, and the whole scheme cracks wide open for me. Why he's stood by and let Jacinto go full Pacino without butting in? He's got his eyes on a higher prize. Shifting sideways in my seat, I let him lay the breadcrumbs for me.

"I'm listening."

"Jacinto is going to fall," Diego says, dropping his voice and leaning close. "Either he can do it on his own..."

"Or you can give him a little push?"

Diego nods.

"And rise in his place."

"Well, *well.*" I take a long drag from the cigarillo. "Ambitious, aren't we?"

"I have to be."

"You do. But it has nothing to do with me."

"That's where you're wrong, Agent Slick."

"Lydia, please." Reaching out, I trace my finger across the back of his hand. "I think we're past formalities."

"You may be right. Now." He pulls his hand away. "Erratic as he's become, there are still many loyal to Jacinto, both here in the compound and spread across our network. That makes it impossible to stage an outright coup. Everything would fall into chaos. We need something subtler. And since you have found your way into my cousin's bed, you're just the person to enact our plan."

"Really?" I squeeze my tits together and stare in his eyes, daring him to look at the goods. "You think I'm *subtle*? Oh, Dieguito, I'm flattered."

He wheels on me like a viper.

"Don't call me that!" Flecks of spit pepper the bar, even speckling the back of my hand. When he sees it, the beast runs to hide and he rubs them off with his thumb. "Don't."

Volatile.

I love it.

I have to cross my legs to squash the heat his little outburst flared up. Point that kind of passion in the right direction and who knows what could happen? Actually, I have a pretty good idea exactly what would happen.

Will happen.

Much as I'd love to leap over this bar and ride him from here to Sunday, I've got other things to focus on.

"Diego, I admire how neatly you have everything planned. But what makes you think I'll help you?"

His tender touch flips harsh and he clutches my hand hard, twisting my wrist.

"You don't have a choice," he hisses. "All I have to do is *suggest* who you really are to Jacinto. Barely even mention it, and his brain would take care of the rest." A mirthless laugh wheezes out of him, and his eyes shine like blood diamonds. "You wouldn't last to sundown."

"Pity," I say, yanking my hand free. "I do my best work after sundown."

Much as I hate to say it, my Mexican Mephistopheles has a

point. Toppling Jacinto is already part of my prime directive. Integral, even. I could put Diego on the throne and it wouldn't make a cunt hair's difference to my mission. Shit, I'd probably enjoy myself along the way.

Whether it's Jacinto or Diego at the helm, as long as I get the information I want, everything works in my favor. Growing fields burn regardless of whose name is on the letterhead.

"Fuck it," I say with just enough sigh for him to think I'm conceding. "I'm in." Triumph swells on his face.

"Excellent!"

"Did I do well, Diego?" Diminutive pet is one of my most seductive looks. "Have I done what you want?"

Lust clouds over him so fast I half expect a foghorn.

"Yes."

Time to spring my trap.

"Tell me, Diego… is that *all* you want?"

The fact his dick doesn't smash through the bar and into my mouth is a brass tacks miracle.

"Lydia, I want so, *so* much more."

I look back to his sleeping cousin to give the whole assignation an extra soupçon of peril.

"When?"

"Tonight." The word comes off him low and hot, like a furnace is burning in his linen pants.

"Tonight it is, then. Now." I ease off my stool, stretching my body to show all my best angles. "I think I'll finally take that swim."

I don't have to look back to know his eyes are on me. I can feel him glutting himself on my skin, rubbing himself over his pants just looking at me.

Plunging into the water only makes me miss home. Chlorine is so much less romantic than Adriatic salt, but a girl has to make do.

Water caresses me in ways no man ever has because it

doesn't want anything from me. It just holds me and lets me be. Which is delicious, but has a habit of leaving me wanting.

And I've got a strong suspicion I won't be left hungry tonight. If Diego's cock makes good on his eyes' promises, I might actually regret double crossing him.

Much as I hate to admit it, night had better gallop a-fuck-ing-pace so I can find out.

CHAPTER TWELVE

DIEGO

"**I**'m just saying I would have appreciated a heads up," I snarl. My father puts on his martyr face.

"You and me both."

Jacinto loves springing shit, but this is something else. The pavilion around the pool is fucking slammed with people in their Sunday best. Political figures from Matamoros, members of Mexican *and* US Coast Guard we've paid off, and a pack of hyenas to laugh at every stupid word out of my cousin's mouth.

I guess showing Lydia around this morning put a bee in his fucking bonnet, and this last minute cocktail party is the honey. Who the fuck am I kidding? We all know what the honey is, and it's dripping off Jacinto's arm in a dress made for mortal sin.

"He's playing with fire," I mutter, unable to take my eyes off the literal fox in the henhouse. "You know that, right?"

My father just shrugs.

"All my nephew does is start fires. We could take away the matches, but he'd just find a flamethrower."

This is a damnsight more than matches. If my father knew what I knew, we'd snuff Jacinto's candle tonight.

Agent Slick is getting an all access pass, and I'm ready to spit blood. She's shaken hands with more smuggling heavyweights than members of the actual fucking cartel. And I guarantee she's got every name committed to memory. Her reputation for that kind of shit is unparalleled—along with her other attributes.

Jacinto has no clue what kind of serpent has coiled herself around him. She glitters in that dress, but I know the shine is all scales.

I may have cornered her earlier, but Lydia's slippery. Deal or not, she's learning more than I want her to know. Jacinto may not give a shit, but he's not going to live to reap the consequences.

I need to squash this shit, pronto.

"Your cousin knows what he's doing." My father's words snap down my spine like the crack of a gun.

Keep it casual.

"Oh, yeah?"

He nods to a clutch of women in bikinis strutting around the far side of the pool.

"Those are the most expensive hookers in Matamoros." I don't ask how he knows. "I guarantee Jacinto plans to pass them out like party favors. Every hombre with deep pockets is getting a top tier ride tonight."

My eyes lock on Lydia. Nobody's getting a better tumble than me.

As if she can read my lust in the wind, she glances my way. Even at this distance her gaze has the power to make me rigid.

There's just the faintest glint of triumph, then she turns around to shake hands with the goddamn former governor.

I've got to get over there.

"I'll be right back, Dad."

"Where are you going?" he asks as I head down the stairs for the courtyard.

"To get a drink." God knows I fucking need one watching this. Coming around the far side of the pool, I do my best to keep it free and easy. One of the sex workers tries some of her magic on me, but this shop is closed for business. At least as far as she's concerned.

I make my way through a baker's dozen women so close to naked they'd have to put something on to get thrown out of a bar. Hard nips or not, they might as well be invisible. According to my dick, Lydia Slick is the only woman within fifty square miles.

The back of her dress scoops all the way down to the dimples above her ass, each vertebrae a magnet tugging at my zipper.

I've got to keep my fucking head.

Hot as she is, when Jacinto takes the Big Nap and I'm in control of this cartel, she's going to become a king-sized problem. The kind that needs decisive action before things get out of hand.

Much as I hate to, I'm probably going to have to kill her. Every breath past her plump fucking lips is a liability. Jacinto can't smell it, but I've got a keener nose for poison than he does.

Peeling her attention away from the row of medals on the ex-governor's chest, her eyes shoot a pair of heat seeking missiles over her shoulder aimed directly at my chest.

Maybe I won't kill her.

There has to be a cage around this place with a lock she couldn't pick. Having her as a sex slave wouldn't be so bad— at least for a while. Problem is, someone's bound to come looking for her eventually, and there's only so many people I can throw in the crocodile pond before she's not worth it anymore.

I get close enough to graze a finger across the small of her back, then give Jacinto a smack on the shoulder.

"I'm getting some champagne. Do you want one?"

He looks up at me with a toothy grin and holds up a bottle of twenty year old scotch.

"I've moved on to bigger things, Dieguito. But help yourself."

I was fucking going to.

He and his lapdogs chuckle amongst themselves as I swing over to the bar. A white coated bartender looks me over solicitously.

"What would you like, señor?"

I'm not in the mood for phony class at the moment.

"Find somewhere else to fucking be," I snarl. His greasy smile vanishes in a puff of pot smoke and he takes a powder. Stalking behind the bar, I crouch down and shove into the fridge for something cold and strong.

"Did you find any champagne?"

Lydia followed me, just like I knew she would.

"Looks like it's all gone, Alana. Is there anything else you'd like?"

"Plenty." She runs her tongue over her lower lip, begging me to bite it. "But for now I'll take one of your mojitos."

"You're getting tequila." I jam two tumblers on the bar, slash some ice into them, and pour a gout of reposado into each glass. Sliding hers over, I lift mine and we clink. "What the fuck are you doing?"

Her lids barely flicker.

"Having a drink. Why?"

"You know what I'm fucking asking you." My voice comes out hot, and I glance around to make sure nobody's clocked us yet. Lydia raises an eyebrow.

"I'm not doing anything. If your cousin wants to show me

off, who am I to refuse? If that means shaking hands with some *very* important people, that's just part of the job."

"Whose job? Because it's not the job you and I agreed on earlier."

"Which one?" she purrs, leaning closer. "I seem to remember us discussing a couple of *jobs*."

"Cut the shit," I hiss through clenched teeth. "GSIA. Are you in touch with them?"

The coy shit falls from her face like a veil and suddenly I'm facing an ice hearted spy.

"Of course."

"We had an agreement—" She cuts me off with her hand.

"I have to maintain contact. What do you think would happen if I cut off communications? An extraction team arrives and it's operation scorched earth. Is that what you want?" She stares at me as I rise to my full height. "Ruling over the ashes isn't what you're after, is it?"

"What are you telling them?"

"Enough." She takes a long drink. "More than you'd like, but less than I should. Minor league names. But I could go bigger…" She leans over the bar, dropping her voice to a sarcastic whisper. "And there's nothing you could do to stop me."

The fuck there isn't.

My hand clamps around her upper arm so hard she lets out a squawk. I yank her into a corner a little too roughly, but I don't give a shit. If she's going to provoke me, she doesn't get gentle Diego.

Hauling her around the side of the bar, I smack her bare back against the stucco wall.

"Now you listen to me, you little bitch. You don't even know the game we're playing right now. All you need to know is that I'm the one making the rules."

"Big man," she coos, batting her eyelashes at me.

"Fucking right." I back up just enough to show off my

chest. "Take a long look at what you're up against. You and I both know there's nowhere to hide a gun in that dress."

"I don't need a gun to take you down." She chuckles, looking me over from top to bottom. My temper flares.

"What did you just say?"

She pushes off the wall, putting the tip of her finger on the front of my shirt.

"I said, I don't need a gun to put you on the floor."

"Is that right?"

"Yes." She cocks her head over her shoulder with a flirtatious smirk. "That *is* right. Now the real question is, what are you going to do about it?"

I shove her back against the wall, pinning her there with my body. Gripping her chin, I twist her head back. A tiny groan sneaks past her lips before I cover them with mine, claiming her as my own with a violent, animal kiss. This storm has been growing in my gut from the second she climbed out of Jacinto's SUV, and it finally makes landfall.

Then she kisses me back. Her hands snake under my jacket so she can ball my shirt up in her fists. Arching against me, she licks the inside of my mouth like a honeycomb, exploring each pocket with the point of her eager tongue.

Digging my fingers into her jaw, I wrench myself off her and stare straight into the core of her molten soul.

"Make whatever excuse you can. Upstairs bathroom. Now."

I rip away from her without looking back. She's going to follow. She has to.

Say what you want about spies, there's no faking the electricity I just felt out of her. Jacinto is her mission, but I'm something else.

I'm the risk.

And she's mine.

The stairs are deserted, and I steal up them like a wraith.

A damned soul loosed out of hell clawing its way towards the only slice of heaven it's ever going to get.

Thank Christ, the bathroom is empty. If some unlucky fucker had been in there, I'd have dragged them off the can and thrown them over the balcony. There are more urgent bodily functions about to unleash in this room.

I pace like a tiger, pulse pounding in my cock so hard it's ready to split. Then a series of faint knocks dust over the door. I jerk it open and snatch Lydia in with me, devouring her before her feet hit the tile.

My hands have been so hungry for her, they blast across her body with demonic fury. I need to touch all of her at once.

The skin on her back is smoother than silk, and I'm ready to spoil every bit with my touch. Her heart thunders through that flimsy dress as I soak her neck with sloppy kisses. When my teeth graze the underside of her jaw, she grabs my hair hard.

"Fuck," she whimpers. "Diego, fuck."

"We will." Crushing my mouth over hers again, I bite down on her lower lip and pinch as I tug out of the kiss. A raspy breath chases me from her throat, and I know she's completely mine.

The clasp on the neck of her dress is too complicated for lust numb fingers, so I scoop it over her head and let it fall. Rosy points stand at attention, pleading to be sucked. And I'm a generous man.

I push her breasts together so I can get readily from one tingling bead to the other in record time. They pebble against my tongue, and each swirl and nip fetches a new moan from Lydia. There's no faking what this is doing to her. She's helpless against the tide of her own rising desire.

"Shit." I spin her around and she grips the edge of the sink for dear life. That ivory skin is blotched red, her lips puffy with longing. I clamp my hand at the top of her throat, taking her jaw between my thumb and forefinger.

"Look at yourself," I order her. "Look at how fucking beautiful you are. She trembles, and I grind against her ass, pinning her to the counter. "Do you see that? Do you see what I've done to you?"

"Yes," she murmurs. I let go of her neck and grab her shoulder, pushing her forward until her face is pressed against the glass. Her breath fogs it while I open the front of my pants and pull out my cock. She sees it from the corner of her eye, and a shudder races along her spine.

With one swift move her skirt is up over her ass. Just as I'd prayed, it's no panties for her. It's all trembling thighs and glistening pink. Every tender bit of her quivers, and I run the underside of my cock along her dripping slit. It aches in the best possible way.

She feels it too. Her whole body heaves up and she pushes back into me.

"Not so fast." I shove her back into the mirror, jamming her in place.

"Fuck," she gasps, and I slick my cock through her juices again. The friction makes her knees tremble. Easing back, I part her folds with the head of my swollen cock, teasing against her entrance.

"Is this what you want? Hm?" Barely nudging into her, Lydia's body jolts and she claws back for my hips.

"*Yes.*"

"Is it?"

"Jesus!" She pants, her ribs swelling and contracting with each ravenous breath. "Diego, please. I can't wait anymore. *Please.*"

A wicked power surges inside me hearing her like this.

"Please!"

Hearing her beg me is enough. For now, anyway.

"We can't." I pull my throbbing cock away from her cunt, and she collapses breathless across the sink. I'm ready to burst from wanting her, but this keeps her under my control. "Someone's going to come looking for you."

"Ugh!" She groans, then reaches back for me with her hips, spreading herself in invitation. "They can wait."

"No, they can't." I tuck myself away and zip up my pants to put a period on the discussion. "Besides." I take her by the arms and drag her up, smashing her against my chest. "We don't have the time. Not for what I want to do."

Wandering over her torso with my hands one final time, I graze each nipple, then kiss the back of her neck.

"Now." I push her roughly to the sink. "Put yourself together. We have to get back out there."

Lydia spins around and catches me across the face with a blinding slap. I still have stars in my eyes when she pounces on me with a vicious kiss. Biting my lip just shy of drawing blood, she backs away and lifts her dress back over her head.

It's like she casts a spell. As the dress glides back into place, her skin is pristine again. All the flushed redness of our near clinch evaporates.

"You're right," she says, voice icily regal. "Mustn't leave my host waiting." Facing the mirror, her lipstick is perfect again with two swipes of her finger. A shake of her head and not a single hair is out of place.

The woman is a fucking witch.

"Give me at least a three minute head start," she says, fixing her gaze on me in the mirror. "We can't be seen coming back together."

With that she shoulders me out of the way of the door and slinks through it.

My own reflection is less forgiving than hers. Hair askew, shirt rumpled, face reddened by need, and more than a bit of a handprint. The painful bulge in the front of my pants will have to go down before I dare head back to the party. That in itself would give me away. I'd have to steal one of the whores to throw Jacinto off the scent.

What I need is a cold shower, but it's just a powder room. Splashing a little water on my face will have to do. When I catch my eyes in the mirror, they're dark and deadly.

"Be careful," I tell my dripping reflection. "Never forget what she is."

For all her passion, she put herself together again in the blink of an eye. Is it what we needed her to do to keep us out of trouble?

Absolutely.

It's also exactly why I can't trust her.

Fuck her? No question. But trust her? Never.

I dampen some toilet paper in the sink and wipe her face print off the mirror. It's a shame to erase the emblem of our lust, but that's the kind of life I'm living right now. Leave no traces.

Satisfied I'm essentially myself again, I open the door and freeze.

"The fuck is going on?" Ortega's creased face scowls up at me like a cigar store Indian.

"Taking a piss is what's going on. Is that a security risk?" I try to maneuver past him, but he plants a heavy palm square in the middle of my chest.

"Don't bullshit me, Diego. I asked you what's going on, and I expect a straight fucking answer." There are times when it's easy to forget that an old lion still has fangs. Ortega may be a grunt, but when he puts on his war face, it's best to stand down.

"Look, nothing, okay?"

"I've got fucking cameras on every square inch of this place," he growls. "Now do you want to tell me the truth this time?"

"Fine." I put my hands up and look him in the eye. "Maybe it's not *nothing*, but it's nothing I can't handle."

He exhales hard and smooths down his mustache.

"You better pray to God you're right, Diego. Because if

Jacinto even imagines you're making him a cuckold, they'll be pulling pieces of you out of the Gulf for the next thirty years."

He's right. Which is a sobering fucking thought. Enough to kill the last of my erection, anyway.

"Heard."

It's not the answer he wants, but it's the one he's willing to swallow. Ortega bares his teeth and glowers at me one last time before turning and stomping down the hall. Good thing he's in my corner. One breath from him and it'd be lights out for me.

Not that I'm giving up Lydia. I just have to be more careful about where I finally have her. Because that's happening, whatever the cost.

Treacherous as Lydia is, a night between the sheets with her just might be worth dying for.

CHAPTER
THIRTEEN

<u>LYDIA</u>

Jacinto isn't one to leave a party until the last ring kisser has peeled off into the night. It's after four in the morning when he finally flops into bed, snoring before the first bounce. Just like after we got back from our *very* informative tour, he's too far gone to paw at me again.

I should be thankful for small mercies.

In truth, I wasn't sure how things were going to square. Between the booze pouring down his gullet and the heap of booger sugar he snorted, it was anybody's guess which was going to win. Coke is notorious for manufacturing limp dicks, so I was probably in the clear either way. It's just a relief not to have to lie here pumping his flaccid turnip while he rambles about how respected and feared he is.

He's half right. The people fear the living shit out of him—and with good fucking reason. But respect? Not so much.

When they weren't cringing away from barely veiled threats of violence, they were laughing up their sleeves. From the dignitaries to the dishwashers, Jacinto is like a bushel of hotdogs with a stick of dynamite hiding in the scrum. Tasty to the unscrupulous, but one of those fuckers is waiting to blow.

I couldn't see Diego when I manhandled this strapping idiot up to his room, but I could feel his eyes on me. Shit, there are eyes and ears all over this place.

A girl has to mind her p's and q's.

Because I'll admit I was tempted to sling Jacinto over my shoulders like a side of beef and carry him up here, but that wouldn't play. Not with the demure sex kitten persona I've carved out.

The cameras around every corner also mean I'm going to have to watch my step. It's all well and good to get footage of me guiding Jacinto to bed like a wounded moose, but sneaking out again for a spicy rendezvous with his cousin? I'm liable to wake with my throat cut.

Good thing I'm a girl who thinks ahead.

After the appetizer I got during the party, there's no way I'm missing the main course. Of course Diego decided to get all cute about making me wait, but tonight I'm not letting him go until I've cashed that rain check as hard as I can.

Security is gonna think this brown-haired bimbo has shitty luck with shoes. Well, let them. The stupider they think I am, the better this whole shebang is going to work.

And believe me, this she-bang had damn well better.

One of my black pumps is still loitering down by the pool, so it's time for me to pull a drunk act and go fetch it.

Jacinto should be a full-on lumberjack the way he's sawing logs, but I give him a nudge on the shoulder with my toe just to be sure. The whole bed jostles, but he's so deep in dreamland they'll have to name a neighborhood after him.

When trying not to get caught, don't sneak.

Make sure they see you.

I get out into the hall and immediately bump into a side table. Giggling as I careen off it, I stumble forward a few steps, then take off my lone shoe and dangle it from my finger.

They can't miss me. And I've established exactly what I'm doing out here. Keeping a hand on the wall, I weave my way to the stairs and bumble down. Some goon in a black tee shirt is waiting for me when I hit the ground level.

"Everything alright, miss?"

"Hm?" I close one eye and squint at him with the other. "Oh, it's fine. I just need to find my other shoe. I think it's by the pool."

"We'll find it for you and bring it up to the room. Jacinto will be waiting for you."

"Jackie's sleeping. Can you believe it?" Putting a hand on his chest, I lean close enough for him to smell the tequila on my breath. "Passed right out without giving me my medicine." I bite my lip and roll my eyes, rubbing my thighs together so he gets the picture. "And now I'm all alone..."

Flirty enough to spook the guy, but not so much I'll be hearing about it later. Sure as shit, he backs off. The last thing anybody wants is to get caught tangled up with me. Well, they all want it, but nobody's itching to brave the consequences.

Nobody except Diego, that is.

"Do you think you know where it is?" the galoot asks, sweating and shooting furtive glances at the camera.

"I think so. But maybe having a little help wouldn't hurt after all." Stutter stepping for him, I try to get a hold of his hand with a coquettish wink. Dude leaves a henchman shaped cloud of smoke in his wake.

That oughta clear my path.

After the rigamarole of the party, the night is shockingly still. Bits of clothing and discarded glasses litter the poolside. Even the help is too wasted to clean up. Fucked up as their intrepid leader is, they ought to have until mid-afternoon to clear everything away before having to worry if he'll see it.

From the dark under the colonnade comes the clink of a glass. Of course Diego's at the bar. It's in danger of becoming our spot.

"Hey," I say softly. His reply comes from behind the glowing cherry of a cigarillo.

"Hey." His voice is a caged panther ready to pounce. And I'm more than ready to be pounced upon. "Can I mix you a drink?"

"I'm not thirsty," I reply as I approach him through the shadows.

"Bullshit. You're the thirstiest bitch in all of Mexico."

"Guilty." I've reached the bar beside him and lean an elbow on the cool tiles. "Maybe I'm just not thirsty for a drink."

He's on me in a flash, pouring kisses down my throat like scalding wine. I drink every last drop. Diego crushes me to his sculpted chest with such force I think my ribs will crack. I mold myself to him, reveling in the way his firm body responds to my touch.

"Fucking shit, Lydia," he groans, pinching my lower lip between his teeth. "I wish we had all night."

"There's time," I whisper. "Jacinto will be asleep for hours."

"I have a meeting. At dawn." The seriousness of his tone cuts through the lascivious fog shrouding my brain. He's not saying and I'm not asking, but we both know what the meeting is about.

"Well then." I slide my hand down and grip his cock through his pants. "We'll have to make the most of the time we do have, won't we?"

I don't have to tell him twice. Diego takes me by the wrist and steals deeper into the shadows. If he's worried about the cameras, he damn sure doesn't show it. I bet he knows where all of them are pointed and who's beating off to the view.

Wrenching open the door to a small closet, he pushes me

through. Cleaning supplies aren't the sexiest smell on the planet, but fuck it. I'd lie on top of a thousand damp mops if it meant this guy would hump them to splinters.

I'm still in my party dress. Well, I say still. He snatches me naked before I can catch my breath, smothering his face in my breasts. Sucking my nipple into the damp cave of his mouth, Diego rolls it with his tongue until I could scream.

Well. I kind of do scream.

He clamps his hand over my mouth hard, which only makes my thighs wetter. Because, brother, they are *wet*. I was slick before I got to the pool, but now I'm goddamn *dripping*.

"You can't do that." His breath burns across my chest. "We can't make a sound."

"I won't."

"Oh." A low chuckle pulls my eyes down to his, glinting in the darkness. "Don't misunderstand. I'm going to make it hard for you."

"I thought it was already hard for me."

A rumble from his core washes over me, and he lunges up to strip off his shirt. Even in the half-light his chest is dazzling. I don't know his workout routine but it's *working*. I scrub my hands over him, each dense plane giving rise to another.

Speaking of rising...

His trousers drop and his weapon jabs into the open.

I guess big dicks run in the family.

Jacinto's cock is just like the man himself—not the tallest, but thick and powerful.

But Diego has him beat in every department. The instant I saw this man, something in his confident swagger told me he was packing heat, but nothing could have prepared me for the bonfire behind his zipper.

I grip him at the base and draw him close to me, placing him between my thighs to glide my clit across his shaft. He got to tease me earlier, now it's my turn.

"Shit," he hisses, planting his hands on either side of me. I keep after him, teasing my glittering nub along his length while stroking the sensitive underside with my fingers. "Lydia." His voice is low and thick. "You have no idea what you're doing to me."

"I know exactly what I'm doing to you."

A furious daring combusts behind his eyes and I know I'm in for it. Grabbing me under the legs, he lifts me off my feet and slams me to the wall. Finding my opening without his hands, he presses ferociously and invades my body.

He's hot and solid, stretching me as more of him just keeps coming. My spine arches into the wall and I blink at the ceiling unable to comprehend how I could take more of him. Then more of him arrives.

"Fuck," I grunt when he finally hits bottom. Diego crams a hand across my mouth, punctuating each word with a sharp thrust.

"I. Fucking. Told. You. To. Keep. Quiet."

He was right about one thing—he's not making it easy for me. The pace is set, and he bucks into me tirelessly. Clamping my thighs around his waist, all I can do is hang on for dear life.

Dear, sweet, delirious life.

The room clouds with our breath, the cool evening giving over to sweaty, humid paradise. My body shines so much I'd slip to the floor if Diego wasn't so intent to pin me in place. Shoving so deep it pinches in my core, his pelvic bone grinds my clit to diamond dust. Each sparkling facet keen with ecstasy.

I moan into his fingers, biting down when the surges pulsing through me are too severe to keep back.

Why is sex so much more intense when you *have* to keep quiet? All the noise you want to make blisters under your skin until your brain shatters.

You know what it is?

It's the fucking *danger*.

Danger is the cornerstone of my life, and sex is at its most potent when it's the most perilous.

And this is downright lethal.

"God," I growl between his fingers. "I'm so fucking close."

Most men would take that as an invitation to switch things up. Harder, faster, or whatever. Diego stays the fucking course like a thoroughbred and is rewarded as such. My inner walls grip him tight as a blaze of light explodes from my core. My nails flay his back as I search for anything to keep from spinning off into the universe.

I can't breathe. I can't see. My ears ring.

And the motherfucker keeps on pounding. Each plunge drives me further into boiling mayhem. I shatter into a galaxy of throbbing stars shooting across the darkness.

I may not be screaming, but my throat is ready to split.

An agonized breath rushes into my lungs, and I realize tears are streaming down my cheeks. This is living. Really living.

"Jesus." Diego's tight voice drags me back down to earth. "Jesus, Lydia." He's thrusting faster, his spine coiling and his breath high in his chest.

"Are you gonna come?"

"Yes."

"You can't." I unlock my ankles, but he keeps driving into me.

"I don't have a choice."

"Diego, no. You can't come inside me."

Burying himself in me as deep as he can, then ripping away from me in rage. He abandons me so fast I'm stunned by my emptiness. A thrumming weakness radiates from my deepest reaches, and I fling myself at him.

Plastering my skin against his, I grab his cock and wringing it with steady, firm strokes. His whole body responds, reaching back to grab me tight. A shudder crashes over him, and he throbs in my hand.

A rattling groan steals past his teeth as spurt after glorious spurt erupts from his cock. I've pointed him directly at a grease stain on the concrete, and plaster it with the first shot. Even tingling all over from a brain splitting orgasm, my aim is on point.

Diego's chest heaves, and my eyes dazzle at the sheer volume of what he kept pent up in store for me. It's enough to make my knees weak all over again. Rope after rope lashes out, and I hit every target I draw a bead on.

"Fuck," he gasps as his body goes slack. I keep stroking, pulling aftershocks out of him until he bats my hand away. "Hang on. I need… I need…"

"To catch your breath," I finish for him. A panting laugh falls out of him, and I join in. "Me too."

The room stops spinning, and we fumble around in the dark for our clothes. I've only got a dress to find, but he's got trousers, underwear, a shirt, and God knows what all else. If he leaves anything behind with the generous helping of cum on the floor, someone's bound to come asking questions.

"That was," he says softly, sliding his shirt over his shoulders.

"Forbidden." Even in the dark I can hear him smile.

"Which makes it all the sweeter." His lips find mine, and I run my hands up his back. When he pulls away, I straighten his collar.

"Can't have you looking like you just got laid." I straighten his collar, devouring him with a knowing smirk. "You've got business to attend to."

"I do."

Giving his collar one last graze with my fingertips, I manage to tuck away one of the listening devices Nine sent along with me. It's been in the folds of my dress all evening, lapping up names. But part of me swears it was just waiting for this opportunity. Maybe he'll change his shirt before knocking noggins with whoever he's in cahoots with, but it's a gamble I'm willing to take.

There's a secret meeting in the works, and I'll be damned if I miss a word. So, it looks like the evening is business and pleasure. I just got my world rocked, but this girl still has her mission to attend to.

Diego may not know the full extent of it, but I guarantee he'd agree—I'm the best at what I do.

CHAPTER
FOURTEEN

DIEGO

I can still smell Lydia on my skin even after dressing. It's like she's permeated my body and stolen into my brain.

Hopefully, I'm the only one who's picking it up. If Ortega sniffs sex on me, he's going to know exactly what I've been up to—and with who.

Which is just one more piece of grit in my gizzard.

Staying up all night has my nerves shot all to hell. Bagging Lydia should have taken the edge off a bit, but instead it sharpened me right the hell up. I'm already jonesing to run it up in her again, but there are serious things that need attending to.

Our clinch didn't leave me time for a shower before this meeting, and I'm not eager for the others to catch me reeking of sex. Ortega already has his nose in the air, and if he tips off the others, it'll be a whole thing. For now I just grit my teeth and hope he's got the good sense to keep his fucking mouth shut.

"Why the hell are we doing this at dawn again?" The others look at me warily before my father clears his throat.

"So Representative Myer knows the scope of things before going to the state house."

"He needs to be able to brief his colleagues on where we are, Diego." Don Manuel Barrera always has such a level head for a man who built an empire on cocaine. The guy swears he's never touched the stuff, and I believe him. If only Jacinto took a page from his book, we wouldn't be having meetings like this.

The phone in the center of the table starts to ring, and I exchange looks with my brothers in conspiracy. My father, Don Barrera, and Ortega. It's a small, tight knit group, but it has to be. The wider the circle, the greater the chance of a rat.

"We ready?" Ortega asks, and we each nod in turn. The line goes live, and Ortega puts it on speaker.

"Good morning, Representative Myer," I say, voice smooth as fresh cream.

"Diego, how the hell are you?" It blows my mind the fucker can be so upbeat at this hour. Maybe he's dipping into Barrera's shipments. "Is everybody there with you?"

"We are," my father answers. "This is Eduardo Alamar, and we've also got Lope Ortega and Don Manuel Barrera on the call."

"Good to hear it," Myer crows. "Gentlemen, thank you for your time."

"Our pleasure." The others shoot me a look given how I just complained. "It's good to be able to touch base about things to keep you apprised of any developments." Ortega raises his eyebrows and mouths 'apprised' as the others chuckle. Fuck 'em. Talk for the job you want, not the job you have.

"Well, I have to ask," Myer says, all Texas charm, "*are* there any developments? Or are the three of you still huddled around a table in a pool house or something?" It's one of the marijuana barns, but he's got us pegged.

"Things are progressing," I reply. He drawls out a condescending laugh.

"I gotta say, you Mexicans sure have a funny idea of progress. We've been spinning on about a regime change for what feels like a year and so far your boy Jackie is still on the throne."

"It's a delicate matter, Representative." My dad folds his hands and leans close to the phone. "It has to be handled carefully if we want things to run smoothly. We would hate for there to be a disruption in the supply chain."

"Yeah." Larry Myer gets that one. If a drug shipment is delayed, everybody takes a bath on it. "You're saying it's too close to a shipment?"

"We are," I confirm. "The next run is slated for Saturday. After that we have fifteen days before the next drop."

"Two weeks is a hell of a window. You boys think you could get a bit more specific with your timeline? Folks up here are getting antsy, and frankly, I don't blame them. We've been hanging on a line over this since you pitched the idea, and I don't mind telling you—hot friends are getting cold. Some folks are getting the idea that things aren't quite so bad under Jacinto." The way he always hits the hard 'J' puts my teeth on edge.

"They're bad enough," I reply.

"If you say so. But the deliveries have been coming on time, and that's all my colleagues and I give a hoot in hell about."

"Well, they should give a hoot in hell about a lot more than that," I grumble. "Because Jacinto Osorio is a bigger liability every day. He's spinning out of control, and others are starting to see it. He's not careful with his connections, and that puts people like *you* and your friends in jeopardy."

I'm sharper than I ought to be, but so fucking what? It's

not like this Republican dickhead has the first idea what it's like down here.

"Don't raise your voice at me, Alamar," Larry barks, coming in hot. "I won't have it." I'm ready to let the fucker know just what he will and have, but Don Barrera holds up a hand.

"Representative Myer," he says, the picture of elegance.

"Yeah?" The Texan is ready for a scrap.

"Manuel Barrera here. My associate may have let his passion run away with him, but not without reason. He's right about Jacinto's—shall we say—lack of discretion? Just tonight he held a party for any number of dignitaries in our region and was loose with information. Trust us when we say his removal is essential."

"And in short order," Myer agrees. "Look, you boys know I'm in your corner about this whole thing. I'm just saying others in the chain wonder why it's taking so goddamn long, and if what you tell me is true, I can't blame them. Every day it doesn't happen is another day your little coup loses support."

"What if we upped the percentage on your end?" The others look at me, shocked. Judging by the silence on the phone, I've caught Larry off guard too.

"How much are we talking?"

My co-conspirators stare open mouthed, so I make the call.

"A point." Snap decision. "And a half."

"Well..." Suddenly all the fire and brimstone the Texan was slinging vanishes. "I think that might unruffle quite a few feathers up my way. Let me spread the word."

Fucking politicians. All you have to do to win them over is wave a dollar bill under their snouts.

"Give them all my best."

"I'll give them better than that—I'll tell them their share just got bumped. Have a good morning, fellas. Keep me posted when Topple Time comes. Because even with this little windfall... tick tock, gentlemen."

"You'll be the first to hear," I say. The guys look ready to eat glass, but they're all smiles in their farewells.

"Thank you for your time, Representative Myer," my father coos, but as soon as the call ends the veins in his forehead bulge. "Are you out of your fucking mind, Dieguito?"

"What the hell, man," Ortega croaks. "A point and a fucking half?"

"I did what I had to do. I bought us the time we need."

"That may be..." Don Barrera plants a hand on the table and rises to his feet. "But with whose fucking money?" His jaw is tight, teeth bared. He's not a man to be crossed, and I've overstepped.

"Look—"

"No, *you* look!" He pounds his hand on the table so hard even Ortega flinches. "It's one thing for the three of you to play these little games. You're already part of the Osorio organization. But what about me? The Barreras only join when Jacinto is out of the picture, and you take money off my plate before I've even publicly allied?"

"It's a shitty move," Ortega says, standing to join Barrera.

"It was the only move," I shout back. "I don't know if you were listening, but American support is falling. If we lose the Americans, we might as well burn the whole fucking place down. Which is exactly what's going to happen if Jacinto stays in charge."

"But the money," Barrera growls, but I thunder over him.

"The money is why I made the fucking call! The Texas pipeline is the only reason any of us are making the kind of returns we are. Before this it was crossing the border in busted pickups like every other two bit dealer from here to Tijuana. You know it's true. If coughing up another point and a half keeps that door open, and buys us time to handle this coup correctly, then so fucking be it."

"That's not how this works," Barrera shoots back. "We discuss these things."

"Discussing loses time."

"My brothers." My father holds up his hand, then scoots back from the table and slowly rises. "It's a dead snake that eats its own tail. I've watched the Osorios rise for many years. More even than Ortega." As if to prove it, he smooths his hands over his white hair. "I joined when my sister married Jacinto's father, but I was aware of the cartel well before that."

"Long time," Ortega grunts in agreement. My father looks at me.

"Your uncle Esteban was savvy. Level headed. He knew what to do, and who to keep close to tell him the truth. He knew how to deal decisively with enemies. And when he died, Jacinto had all the makings of a leader like his father. A natural successor. Dynamic. Charismatic."

It's almost like he's throwing the words in my face, and I seethe in my seat.

"He was really something in the days right after Esteban died." Don Barrera nods, smiling at the memory. "Jacinto carried inevitability on his shoulders even before his father was killed."

"He did," my father says. "And look at what he has become. This is a man who believes his own myth. When a man thinks he is a god, he inevitably becomes a devil."

A silence settles around the table as we all consider this.

"Thank you," I say. "We all needed to hear that. It's a reminder of what brought us together in the first place."

"True..." My father steps over to align himself with the other side of the table. "But I meant it as a warning."

I'm in the hot seat again, and I fucking hate it.

"Why? Warning who?"

"You."

That brings me to my feet.

"But it's what I had to do! You know it was."

"That may be, but my son," compassion floods his eyes, "going rogue like that? Changing fundamental financial arrangements with international business partners? It might have been the right move, but it's the move Jacinto would make." The comparison slices bone deep.

"*Jacinto?*"

"Damn right," Ortega says.

"Don't lose sight of the rest of us." My father's gaze is cool and direct. "The four of us are in this together. We're working to put you in the seat of power, but none of us are underlings. If we're working this hard just to install another tyrant, then the plan is off."

"Agreed." Don Barrera hasn't taken his eyes off me. None of them have.

"Agreed." Ortega's tone is an invitation to mend my ways.

I get to my feet and straighten my shirt.

"Agreed. Forgive me for overstepping. In the future, I'll do my best to be the kind of leader men like you deserve."

"That's all we ask." A tiny smile creeps into the corner of my father's mouth. "Do that, and you will make an old man proud."

I'll do my best, papa. For all of us.

CHAPTER
FIFTEEN

Well isn't that just the fucking sweetest? I wonder if they're hugging it out over there? Maybe gearing up for one big circle jerk?

Still, Eduardo Alamar's portrait of Jacinto confirms everything from the dossier. It's terrifying to consider, but Diego is actually a much better option for a cartel leader. If he can keep his ego in check, he'd do a good enough job that I almost regret having to torch this place when I take off.

Almost.

Despite the royal dicking down I got under the cover of night, I'm itching to get the hell out of here. Sex like that clouds the brain, and I need to be razor keen if I'm going to get out of this alive.

If those poor fuckers knew I've been listening in, it would be lights out before breakfast. Thankfully Nine's device works like a crackerjack. Every scrap of info is duly recorded, ready to be encrypted and fired off to GSIA headquarters. Once Zero gets a listen, she'll send the jet toot sweet.

I mean, come the fuck on. A goddamn Texas state representative?

Anybody could look at Larry Myer's face on tv and know he's crooked as a duck's dick, but this? One thing's for sure – if one politician is getting his beak wet, the rest are right in line behind him.

Considering government officials are part of this mule train, small wonder Zero sent me down here. This shit could run all the way to the top.

Just get good ol' Larry squealing and the bastards will gladly give themselves up for a chance to turn state's evidence on the next loser up the ladder. When I get back, I'm gonna need to treat Nine to lobsters and champagne. That dotty old sweetheart just handed me a golden ticket.

I'd send the file right now, but I need to backtrack and edit the section where I take it in the sweet bits from Jacinto's right hand man. That's decidedly off mission and could get me into a world of hard times. I'm not jumping in that briar patch, thank you very much.

All the same, I need to relay this to base muy pronto.

Whipping out my phone, I dash out a message to Zero.

> Recorded conversation between Eduardo Alamar, Diego Alamar, Lope Ortega, Don Manuel Barrera, and Texas Representative Larry Myer. Audio file to follow.

No sooner do I hit send than I've got company.

"What are you doing here?" It's another one of the countless thick necked brutes the place is crawling with. Armed to the teeth with everything but brains.

That said, it wouldn't take Neil deGrasse Tyson to figure out I'm up to no good.

What a snapshot I must be, crouched outside a doorway at the far end of an empty corridor, headphones on, my supply pack at my feet, and a guilty look on my face. Not to mention it's a cunt hair after six in the morning.

I'm not some drowsy pillow queen looking for a plate of poached eggs. I look exactly like what I am—a spy. With an earful of treason against the guy signing the checks.

"Um." Gotta bluff this one out for a second. "I was looking for the bathroom?"

He's not buying it. The lunk takes a step closer, pointing to the receiver connected to my headphones.

"What's that?"

"White noise machine."

This guy has no sense of humor.

He grabs me by the arm and yanks me off the floor, and I just manage to snag my pack before he hustles me along.

"Come on."

Time for the helpless damsel act. I go full rag doll under his grip and whimper.

"Where are you taking me?"

"To Jacinto. El Jefe will make you talk."

After seeing what he did to a cluster of exotic cats? No thank you.

The guy's not interested in answers. Just swift, bloody justice is the only thing ringing his bell. Well, I wasn't born to get shot in some heroin mansion. If I'm gonna die in Mexico, it damn well better be with an ice cold cerveza in my hand and a shirtless man under each arm.

The guy drags me behind him, and I scan for the best escape option I can find. No use breaking and running until I've got a sure thing. That said, Jacinto's room gets closer with every stomp.

Just around a corner is a flight of stairs leading to a portico on the side of the villa. Open air is always the best call when evading capture.

"Wait," I cry, tugging back. "I'm gonna pee my pants!"

He looks back and I catch him right on the bridge of his

nose with a top tier knuckle duster. That familiar crunch echoes, and his head snaps back. Miraculously, his grip doesn't slacken, so I pinch a pressure point to free myself.

Sweep the leg, and I'm at the bottom of the steps before he hits the carpet.

Clattering through the doors, I pull up short in front of the most beautiful sight I've ever seen. Right next to the topiary is a brace of motorcycles with sidecars, gleaming under the rising sun.

I straddle one in a flash, and there's even a set of keys in the ignition.

"Somebody up there likes me," I mutter, and crank that puppy to life. It vibrates between my thighs like it knows whose keister is on the seat. "Let's ride."

The security guy hits the doorway, and I crank the throttle. Gravel peppers the fuck out of him, and I fishtail around to rocket off. Any head start I can get is aces.

Sure as shit, I haven't even hit a bend in the road before a bike kicks up behind me. The rear view mirror confirms Jacinto's thug is open for business. He's not gaining like crazy, but he knows the territory better than I do.

I'm going to need to get creative.

First order of business is to put some distance between me and the villa. The place is covered with windows and visibility isn't my friend. Motorcycles aren't exactly subtle, and if Jacinto wakes up and takes a gander outside, I'd have to come up with one hell of a story to cover my little joyride.

That means point my crotch rocket square down the middle of the path and gun it for the edge of the property. Once I'm past the recognition zone, I'll sort out the bruiser on my tail.

It's early enough nobody's in the fields yet, so I set my sites on candyland. Poppies are shit for cover, but pot plants can take on a life of their own. Especially if you spill water on them the way Jacinto's men do. It's a veritable goddamn forest, and I plan to go full-on Lewis and Clark in that bitch.

When I hit the outer edge, I don't ease back on the gas a bit. The bike rips straight in, pot branches whipping me until I smell like a Berkley dorm room. The sidecar cuts a wide path, so if I'm going to lose the prick in black, I'm gonna have to ditch the bike.

Skidding to a fragrant stop, I dig into my pack for a roll of tape. Wrapping up the throttle nice and tight, I wrench it back and lash it in place. The bike karate kicks into the air, and I turn her loose to thunder off into the back forty. That'll give my adversary a bogus trail to keep an eye on.

Easy as it would be to take off and let him chase the wild goose, I can't bag out. The mook's put eyes on me, which means I need a more permanent solution.

Slithering through the brush, I crouch down and get ready to pounce. His engine gets louder, and I can hear the instant he thuds off the main path to follow the trail I carved into the reefer rainforest.

My muscles tighten to fiddle strings as he roars closer.

Don't think.

If I think about what I'm about to do, I'll just wind up fucking the whole thing up. The brain's a tricky bastard like that. It's instincts or nothing on this one.

He's twenty feet to my right and closing fast. My crouch deepens, and the second he's in view, I launch out of the brush and tackle him off the bike. He's built like a sack of doorknobs, and smacking into him damn near knocks the wind out of me.

Whatever. Breathing's for pussies anyway.

Guy lets out a squawk as I unseat him and we topple to the dirt.

I know, buddy. Sometimes I surprise me too.

At least he breaks my fall. He flattens beneath me, eyes wide in shock. They give me the best target in the world, and

I hit him between the eyes with enough force to rattle his teeth. His head ricochets off the ground, and it's night-night time.

My hand stings like hell, but that's part of the job. Busting heads ain't for the faint of fucking heart.

Standing over him, I go into my kit for some zip ties. Time to cinch this mother up and get back to the chateau before anybody notices I'm gone.

Then I hear it.

Another engine in the distance. The way it rumbles, I can tell it's not another motorcycle.

That's a fucking jeep. Which can only mean one thing.

Jacinto's on the hunt.

I need to move. But this isn't some cut-and-run-and-hope-for-the-best situation. This is gonna take some strategy.

Alright. What do I have at my disposal, and how can I use it to my advantage?

I've got a motorcycle, and a hibernating henchman.

I can work with that.

"Motherfucker," I grunt as I deadlift my companion over my shoulders. He's one hell of a prize hog, but I bear him up and lug him to where his abandoned bike idles in a bed of tattered ganja. Into the sidecar he goes, and I mount up. Scooting back to the main road isn't an option, so I pick a direction and hope for the best. I'll see where we are when things thin out.

The growing field should offer me cover from Jacinto's prying eyes for the moment. Take the wins where you can find them.

Zooming through this stuff would be enough to give Willie Nelson a contact high, but those are the breaks. My arms and face smart like hell from the constant assault of branches and leaves. Just when I think I can't take it anymore, fresh air breaks through and we bound back into the open.

Dirt banks up to the gravel road and the bike grabs some

serious air. Enough to jostle my buddy awake when we thump down again. He shakes his head, blinking with that adorable 'where the hell am I' expression goons always have after getting their clock cleaned. Before he can get his bearings, I jab out and hit the snooze button for him.

The open road is no place to stay, so I scan the horizon for cover that's not so vicious. Off my right hand is some lush greenery that ought to fit the bill just fine.

We're not talking hedge mazes and koi ponds. This is no-shit vegetation.

As much real estate as the growing fields take up, there's still a healthy bit of jungle closer to the compound. I imagine partly for coverage, and also because nobody wants to look out the window at pot leaves and smack posies every day.

Whatever the reason, I'm grateful for the cover.

Hunkering low over the gas tank, I aim straight for the promised land. Servals scatter, spitting to beat the band as I blow past them into the scrub.

One thing about a marijuana field—the terrain is pretty even. You're not dodging rocks and tree roots all over the place. The jungle is something else again. That means slowing down at a time when speed should be my best buddy. Evidently my luck has turned because I damn near pitch over a steep ridge. The bike wails as I pull up short, grinding to a halt just at the edge of a fifteen foot drop.

Jacinto has to be gaining ground, so it's time to pivot.

I could ditch the bike, but that would still leave my prisoner with a mouth full of stories. Add me on foot into the bargain, and it's a losing proposition all the way down the line.

That means the unconscious stooge in the side car is about to have a really shitty morning. Turning back to my trusty pack, I start working out my story. My fingertips hit my zippo and a tube of lighter fluid and it's go time.

Knocking the gas cap loose, I strip off one of my sleeves

and stick it into the tank. Easing the bike back, I rev her up for one last ride.

The security guy's eyelids flicker open just as I start dousing the makeshift fuse and sparking my lighter. Flames have a way of waking folks up. Suddenly, he's seven different kinds of concerned.

Well, too bad, champ.

Setting the front tire directly at oblivion, I let her rip. The bike hurtles towards the precipice, my pal scrambling like fuck to get out of the sidecar. He gets a knuckle sandwich as my parting gift, and I dive off the bike just as she sails over the edge.

Rocks and sticks aren't the most forgiving landing pad, but right now a little bit of blood is gonna be my friend.

Nice as it would be to watch the explosion and bask in the smoky fireball, there's other shit on my plate.

"Help," I scream in my best helpless maiden voice. "Someone help me, please!"

Ripping open my blouse, I scrub a fistful of dirt across my sternum, then grab my exposed arm as hard as I can. Mama needs a bruise if she's gonna sell this trash.

As if that ain't enough, I pull back and give myself one hell of a fat lip.

Oh, the things we do to stay alive.

Zero's gonna have to buy me a caviar brunch after this one. Who the hell am I kidding? I'll let Sir John do the honors. He's better morning company anyway.

"Help!"

"My diamond?" Jacinto's voice splits above everything else, and I can tell I've already got him on the hook.

Out with those trusty zip ties to bind my wrists. Grabbing the loose end with my teeth, I pull until the plastic bites into my skin. Shit has to look convincing after all. Now all I have to do is lie back and wait for Jacinto to swing to the rescue.

Arranging myself against a boulder, I scream my head off

as gouts of black smoke swell up through the leaves. Damnit, I hate to miss an explosion. It sounded like a good one.

"Alana!" A shirtless Jacinto crashes through the underbrush and teeters on the point of hysteria when he finally lays eyes on me. "Ah, mi tesoro," he cries, flinging himself down beside me. Stupid prick bought it hook, line, and sinker. I can already tell.

Diego is a different story.

He sidles up behind Jacinto looking less than convinced. Good thing he's not the one that needs fooling. He may be trouble later, but I'll burn that bridge when I get to it.

CHAPTER
SIXTEEN

Diego

This has super-spy stink all over it. My cousin Jacinto is many things, but observant ain't one of them.

You'd have to be blind in both eyes to think that Lydia was some sort of—*holy shit, are her wrists bound?*

My dick gets hard in record time. The whole poor-help-less-little-me thing has got to be an act, but I wouldn't mind having her at my mercy.

"What happened, mi diamanté?" Jacinto's in full sympathetic hero mode. "How did you get like this?"

"It was one of your men. I don't know his name, but he grabbed me. He tried to… to…" She buries her face in his chest, choking out sobs. He cradles her until she can speak again, and it's all I can do not to give the girl an Oscar. This is academy-level shit.

"When I tried to fight back, he did this to me." She holds up her wrists to him. The tie pinches her supple skin, and I clench my jaw looking at it. If she did that to herself, she's got a high tolerance for pain.

Noted.

"Animal," Jacinto bellows.

"I tried to run, but he chased me on a motorcycle and abducted me. If you hadn't come after us, he would have done *terrible* things to me."

He'd have to wait in fucking line.

I've got a laundry list of terrible things running through my mind, and I have a sneaking suspicion Lydia would love every last one of them.

Jacinto rocks back on his haunches and howls at the moon. It's enough to knock me back on my heels, and Lydia looks suitably petrified. I wonder if she knew what brand of monster she was letting out of his cage.

Surging to his feet, Jacinto rushes to look down into the ravine. I'm right behind him, curious just how far this whole charade is going to go.

Sure enough, the twisted remains of one of our motorcycles sits at the bottom of a pillar of smoke and fire. Just beyond it is one of Ortega's top men with his head busted like a watermelon on a crag. It must have been one hell of a fall.

"Puta madre," Jacinto screams, yanking his gun from its holster and letting loose. The dude's already dead, but that doesn't stop my cousin from pumping a full clip's worth of hot lead into him. I'm surprised he doesn't throw the gun. It's the behavior of a brass tacks maniac, and Lydia and I exchange a look as this sinks in.

She pulled the pin on this grenade, and now she's facing the shrapnel.

But when Jacinto jerks out his hunting knife and sweeps back to her, my heart leaps into my throat. Lydia scrambles backwards as he advances on her, and I'm between them before I can catch myself.

"The fuck are you doing?"

Maybe he sees through her bullshit story after all.

Jacinto flashes me one of his patented smoldering scowls,

pushing past me to tenderly help Lydia to her feet. Easing his knife between her arms, he cuts the zip tie and frees her. She crumbles against his chest, breathless with relief. I'm willing to bet that part is genuine as hell.

"My darling," he moans. "I'm so sorry this has happened to you."

Girl can't get a word out before his mouth is on hers. My fists clench at the sight of his tongue slipping into her mouth. Then she scrubs her hands over his bare torso and I'm ready to kill. She arches into him, her kisses growing more desperate, and I could slap her. I know for a fact she's playing this up to get a rise out of me.

Well, part of me has risen, so bra-fucking-vo.

When he finally pries his mouth off her, Jacinto scoops her into his arms and heads for the jeep. The image would be comical if it didn't chap my ass so much. She's even got an arm over his shoulder, tracing a finger along my cousin's spine. Even though she doesn't look my way, I know it's all for me.

I'm ready to blow a gasket by the time I get behind the wheel of the jeep. Jacinto is ready to burst as well, but for completely different reasons.

Settling Lydia on his lap in the passenger seat, he turns to me with pride and wrath battling in his face.

"Tell me… why are you in such a shitty mood, Diego?"

"I'm furious that anybody would do that to her." Not the phony kidnapping—Jacinto's kiss.

"If you can be so angry over it, imagine how *I* feel." He hugs her close to him and I grip the wheel like I'm gonna twist it into a pretzel. "Nobody takes what's mine. *Nobody.* Radio back. I want everyone in the courtyard when we arrive. Everyone."

"Yes, sir."

Jamming the jeep in gear, I pull her around and we head back to the compound. Every bump in the road jostles her in his lap, and Lydia starts to fucking *giggle*. Nibbling on his ear, the works. As always, my cousin gives as good as he gets and in seconds I'm fuming next to an all-out make out session.

"Ortega," I bark into the radio, hoping to spoil the mood.

"Ortega here."

"Jefe wants everyone in the courtyard. No one left out. We'll be there in five."

"Copy."

The couple next to me haven't broken their stride. I swear, if she starts fucking him I'm shoving them both out of the vehicle.

We come around the front to find people shambling out to meet us. More than half of them sleepy-eyed from being dragged out of bed. What good is a party at a drug lord's villa if you can't sleep in the next day?

Seeing them brings the demon out in Jacinto again and he all but pitches Lydia out of his lap. Climbing into the back to stand and glower at everyone, he draws his pistol and goes to fire it at the sky.

Dumb fucker forgot he wasted those bullets on a dead man.

"Fucking shit," he mutters, then punches me in the shoulder and waves for my gun. "Dieguito."

I fork it over with gritted teeth and Jacinto racks off a dozen rounds into the air. If people weren't awake before, they sure as hell are now. Rows of petrified faces stare back at us, and I wonder if Lydia's doing a headcount.

"Are you listening," Jacinto roars. "Because I want everyone to mark my words, and know I mean it. Ortega?"

"Yes, sir?" Ortega steps forward, and blanches when Jacinto levels his gun at the woman tattooed across his chest.

"Lope, one of *your* men—*your* security detail—tried to force himself on my Alana here. On my diamond." He strokes Lydia's hair as disbelief runs through the crowd. Judging by his shifty eyes, Ortega buys this even less than I do.

"One of my—?"

"I've already said," Jacinto screams, cutting him off. "Tell me. Did you know about it?"

Ortega's jaw drops, and so does mine. Even Lydia seems startled at the fallout of her little escapade.

"No, sir."

"Are you sure?" Jacinto hops down and walks to his head of security with deliberate slowness. "I want you to think very carefully." When he reaches Ortega, my cousin reaches out and takes the man's face in his hand. "Look at me, Lope. Look me in the eyes."

Nobody moves.

Shit, nobody dares take a breath. A long moment passes, then Jacinto turns him loose. "I believe you. Now." He stalks in a wide circle, pacing around everyone. "I want you all to know that *no one* touches her."

Jacinto points to Lydia with the barrel of his gun, and she squirms in the seat. Even I lean away in case his finger gets itchy.

"And I don't just mean sexually. No one lays a finger on her for any reason. Or any of my women!" With a sweeping gesture he takes in the clutch of girls under the portico above the door. They cower together in their night dresses, unused to being in the sunlight.

I watch as it dawns on Lydia for the first time. Perhaps she's special now, but all flowers fade in Jacinto's garden. She's not the sole object of his affection—she's become a part of his harem.

All the future holds for her is the same shattered look on all of the rest of his concubine's faces. Beaten to submission with his cock and bent to his will with his fists. Lydia's finally come face to face with the possibility she may never get out of here.

Not without my help.

"I want to be clear about the consequences." Jacinto points

to the smoke rising from the trees in the distance. "The man who *dared* touch my diamond was dead when I found him, but he will still pay. I want some of you to bring his body back here, and we will string him up as an example. I want his ears cut off and sent to his mother."

What the actual fuck?

"Jesus Christ," Lydia mumbles, stealing a quick look my way.

This is unhinged even for my cousin.

He carves his way back over to the jeep, tossing me my gun. Holding out his hand like some sort of fairytale prince, he helps Lydia out of the jeep. It's a whiplash move after the batshit speech he just gave.

As soon as her feet are on the flagstones, Jacinto dips Lydia into a kiss. This time she's stunned enough she doesn't put on a show. She just takes it, and the jealous tiger in my chest doesn't snarl for revenge. This isn't a romantic kiss, it's a statement of power. A public exercise to demonstrate his claim.

Jacinto turns her loose and Lydia stumbles back, nearly falling to the ground. My first impulse is to jump out and steady her, but I swallow that shit in a hurry. This isn't the time to test the water.

"Ortega!" Jacinto snaps his fingers and makes for the front door. "My office. I want to know why one of your men would *dare* to reach for what's mine."

Ortega and I exchange an uneasy look, but he falls in step behind the boss.

"And some of you clean up this fucking courtyard," Jacinto shouts, kicking an empty ice bucket from last night's shindig down the steps. "I won't have this place looking like a fucking pigsty."

Only when people start to disperse do I climb out of the jeep and pace around to Lydia. Much as I'd like to touch her, I'm not risking my neck.

"We need to talk."

Making a long arc around the side of the villa, I lead her to a series of cabanas beyond the pool. There's a shady spot behind one of them where we'll be out of sight of the windows. Jacinto's scolding room is on the other side of the mansion, but better safe than sorry.

True to her profession, Lydia follows at a safe distance. It would take a keen set of eyes to work out that she's trailing me.

"What really happened?" I demand when she lands.

"You don't believe me?"

"I don't believe a single word out of your lying mouth." I take her chin roughly and she winces. It's enough to soften my temper. There are a lot of things a woman like her can fake, but the bruises are real.

"Are you badly hurt?" The honesty of my question makes her shoulders drop. I could almost swear her defenses drop with them—almost.

"All in a day's work."

"The day's just started and you're already pretty worked over." I run my thumb along her jaw, then dust it over her busted lip.

"Did it hurt when Jacinto kissed you?"

A coquettish glimmer sparks in her eyes.

"I think those kisses hurt you more than they hurt me." Lydia takes the very tip of my thumb between her teeth. "Or am I wrong?"

"Did it hurt?" I ask again, voice thickening. She shakes her head, keeping my thumb in place.

"But if you'd like, you can try to hurt me."

The dam breaks and I taste her lips, eager to erase my cousin from them. Lydia pushes up to meet me, kissing so hard the faint, coppery taste of blood dances on my tongue.

I pull away from her, and her swollen lip has split just a bit. It does nothing to dampen her come hither smile.

"That's a very dangerous thing you just did," she purrs. "Kissing me out in the open like that? After what your cousin just said?"

I crush her to the wall with my body, loving the way her softness gives way to me.

"It's worth the risk."

So I do it again.

CHAPTER
SEVENTEEN

"We need to go somewhere," Diego says when he's able to abandon my mouth. "Now."

"Not another broom closet, I hope?"

A ferocious look smashes across his face.

"No. Not for what I want to do to you."

Holy shit.

Everything below my waist combusts. He grabs me by the wrist, and I hiss between my teeth from the pain. Diego's head snaps around, and he looks at the red marks the zip tie left behind. He traces a thumb along one, then grips me harder and drags me along behind him.

Storming right out into the open is some brazen shit, so I make a show of looking terrified. I'm anything but. Oh, I'm trembling alright, but with anticipation.

We bolt the compound, and he pulls me through a door and down a staircase. The cellar is dimly lit and stuffy. There are no windows for prying eyes to catch us. No cameras tucked in corners to record our assignation.

Diego hauls me to the far end of the cavernous cellar and flings me to the wall, then mashes me against it with his body. Grabbing a fistful of my hair, he tugs my head back to gorge himself on my lips. The split burns, but not half so hot as my crotch. Straddling his leg, I grind against him hard.

He yanks my hair again and bites down on my earlobe, whispering, "Did you like having your hands tied like that?" He pinches harder. "Did you?"

"Yes."

I did. Especially once his eyes were on me.

Suddenly, he backs away and I stumble forward at his abrupt absence. He grabs a chair and shoves it across the concrete floor to me.

"Do you have any more zip ties?"

I dig into my kit, keeping my gaze locked on his. He doesn't need to know what else I have stowed in here. My fingers deftly avoid anything incriminating and come up with some ties and my roll of tape. He raises an eyebrow at it.

"Electrical tape, huh?"

"Just in case you're feeling inventive."

Diego relieves me of them and grabs me by the back of the neck, steering me towards the chair. It's an old wooden office chair with solid arms and a straight back. I face it, and he nudges the back of my knee with his own.

"Kneel on it."

"Yes, sir."

Normally I bristle at taking commands from an arrogant man, but this moment is anything but normal. We're through the looking glass, and I'm ready for some madness.

Lifting my knees, I settle on the seat while Diego zips my wrists to the back of the chair. It pinches, but I need more.

"Harder." The hunger in my voice catches him, and he looks at me sharply. I smile and stretch my neck for him to whisper, *"Harder."*

He yanks me to the razor's edge of pain, and a tiny cry

slips out of my throat. Thank God, he knows better than to ask if it's too tight.

Coming around behind me, he strips my pants down so hard I almost pass out. Then he shoves my right leg against the arm of the chair and starts to bind it in place with tape. It's just rough enough that when he gets to the other leg, I'm already slick. I exhale sharply as he whips my panties after, my own breath echoing back to me across the dim room.

"Fuck," he grunts, slicking his fingers over me and stuffing them in his mouth. His greediness for my taste makes me even wetter. Searing humidity spreads from my core until I'm vibrating with need. "Goddamnit, Lydia." He rubs his fingers across my throbbing lips, then glides one up the seam. The prickle of it has me grasping the air and tugging against my restraints. The bite of my ties is exquisite agony. The struggle only intensifies as he delves his finger into me.

My throat burns with the need to cry out, but there'd be no explaining our way out of this one. Instead, I grit my teeth and push back into his hand.

The motherfucker pulls out.

I toss a furious glance over my shoulder to see him opening his fly and taking out his cock. Fucking hell, it's just as impressive as the first time. I reach back for him with my body, and he shies away.

"Careful," he warns, delivering a vicious slap on my ass. "Don't get the idea you're in charge."

"Fuck." The chair groans beneath me as my whole body rebels.

I'm always in fucking charge.

Then his cock glides in where his finger was and my mind goes blank to anything but pleasure. The hot, hard strength of him pushes everything else out. He swells into me, parting my body with one livid thrust.

Those firm hips clap against my cheeks with enough force to rock the chair off its legs. Diego's fingers anchor in my hair, tugging my head back to the point the ribbons of my throat ache.

Pummeling into me again and again, my ass stings pink from the assault. I've never been dominated like this.

Used.

Obliterated and shamed, purely for the purpose of gratifying someone else's thirst.

It's *divine*.

Surrendering control of everything, I let him pound ecstasy out of me in fat, glowing drops. Tears pool in my eyes and saliva slops down my chin.

Then a ball of fire thunders up in my gut, each stab of his cock stoking the flames higher. I kick my feet, helpless in the face of the climax rising to consume me.

"Shit," I mouth, unable to find my voice. "Shit." Over and over again in a rising crescendo until everything topples down around me. I writhe and pull and kick and pry at my bindings, my spine twisting like a snake.

Diego keeps fucking. A spasm rocks through me with such force the chair is ready to come apart.

"God," I cry. "I can't take any—" He covers my mouth.

"There's someone walking upstairs," he snarls.

Maybe, but I could never have heard them over the blinding sparks showering behind my eyelids. Fireworks cascade as orgasms dogpile on top of each other. My hands and feet are numb. Shit, all of me is except for the parts scorched with carnal rapture.

Just when I think I'm going to rattle to pieces, Diego strokes his hand down my belly and starts rubbing my clit. Slow circles to accompany rapid fire thrusts.

"Harder," I moan against the fingers covering my mouth. "Harder!"

The pressure on my clit intensifies, a golden glint rising like steam. His hips buck into me with a new fury.

"Harder."

I'm gonna die.

"Harder."

He's fucking the absolute life out of me. The orgasm hasn't stopped, just compounded to the point where it transforms into something else. A hole opens up beneath me and the universe snaps in half. I bite down on Diego's hand to keep from shrieking the building down.

A drumbeat pulse inside me tells Diego's about to explode. That telltale throb that says the inevitable is upon us.

"You can't," I gasp, wresting my mouth away from his hand.

"Fuck," he roars.

"Diego, you can't!"

With an animal growl, he snatches out of me so fast I almost slam shut. He comes around the chair, gripping his swollen cock in his fist. As soon as he arrives, a spurt of rich white cum surges out. It caches my neck, and I arch my back to offer him my chest. My shirt is ripped open from my ruse, and Diego plasters me from chin to navel. Every inch of exposed skin hot, sticky, and slick.

Then he grabs the front of the chair with his free hand and slumps forward, stealing kisses from me like my mouth is Fort Knox. I can feel our shared pulse in his tongue as his breath slackens.

When he pulls back, I collapse in place. Everything hurts and shines at once. I hear the snap of his knife, but don't even look up. One wrist is freed, then the other. Then his blade snicks up the wooden arms of the chair, and the tape peels free. The rip of it against my quaking thighs is *heaven*.

Unbound, I twist in the seat and liquefy into the chair, raking in deep, shaky breaths.

"God," I sigh. "That was..." There aren't words. I look in his face and can see that he's exactly where I am—satisfied and starving all at once.

Then I glance down at my tattered shirt and flushed chest, both soaked with the evidence of his lust.

"It, uh…" I fix him with a flirty smile. "It'd be pretty awkward if I got caught like this." Something in his face changes. As if the danger of it all settles on him for the first time.

"We should leave separately."

I can't hold back a laugh.

"You think?"

With a brisk nod, he looks me over one more time, then turns and walks away. He doesn't look back.

Of course he shouldn't.

And I shouldn't expect him to.

This isn't some grand love affair. This is a clandestine liaison under perilous circumstances. Diego Alamar isn't even my target. If anything, he's a distraction from the matters at hand.

An entertaining distraction, but that's not the point.

Sitting upright, I put Lydia away and summon Agent Slick from deep within. Pulling out my phone, I find a message from Zero waiting for me.

Because, of course there is.

Call.

I do, and she picks up on the first ring.

"When can we expect that audio file?"

"Hello to you too."

She dismisses my quip. "The file?"

"Soon. The morning got away from me a bit."

"Trouble?"

"Not entirely. I had to take out a member of the security detail and frame it as an attempted kidnapping. Osorio is even more invested in my cover now."

"Good. The Larry Myer intel is valuable. Following the

trail we've gotten several other pings with potential accomplices. Well done."

Was that an actual compliment?

"Is it enough to send me home?" It's not like me to be optimistic, but I'm wrung out of anything but first impulses.

"Negative."

Shit.

I can always count on Zero to bring me back to Earth.

"Okay," I stifle a sigh. "What are my next moves?"

"We need access to either Jacinto's hard drive or his phone records."

"Well, Nine equipped me with a cell ripper, but it could still be a tall order. I haven't seen Jacinto anywhere near a computer since I got here."

"And his phone?"

"He was paranoid about that before this morning's dust up. I can only imagine that's skyrocketed now."

"Paranoid how?"

"He locks his phone in a safe while he sleeps."

There's a long beat as Zero considers this.

"I see," she says at last. "Who else is in his circle? Are there others high enough up the ladder that it would be worth ripping their phones?"

"No question."

"Do you think you can manipulate any of them to get close enough to rip that data?"

I look down at the sticky mess Diego made of me, and take a deep breath.

"Absolutely."

CHAPTER EIGHTEEN

I really need a shower to get the smell of Lydia off. Maybe I'm imagining it, but the aroma of her body has soaked into my clothes. No matter how many times I wash my hands, there are still traces of her on my fingertips.

Not that I'm complaining. It's just hard to keep my head straight.

That woman is clouding my mind. And I've got the sneaking suspicion she's doing it on purpose. It's what she was sent down here for.

Maybe her agency knows more than she's saying. Jacinto might not be the target at all. If they know Jacinto is already crumbling, it's possible she was sent to target me as the heir to the throne.

Shit, I'm starting to think like my cousin.

This brand of paranoia isn't like me. It wouldn't be hard for the outside world to learn Jacinto is coming apart at the seams. He's not exactly hiding it, and soirees like he threw last night put it on full display.

But the only way anybody could know about my plan to rise would be if someone in our group was a rat. Which is impossible. We've kept the circle small, and each member is iron clad.

My father would die before giving me up. Don Barrera has too much to gain from the alliance we've forged, and Ortega? He's a foot soldier. The man doesn't have the brains for treachery. Like any junkyard dog, he's loyal to his master and bites any other hand he can reach.

No, Lydia's not here for me. At least not like that.

At the same time, I know better than to trust her. Her reputation in the world of espionage is sterling, and I've seen what a consummate liar she is up close. The way she twisted Jacinto around her finger was masterful. If I didn't know what and who she was, I would have bought into her kidnapping story just as deeply as he has.

Wait.

I stop in my tracks, blinking up into the blinding midday sun.

What the fuck did she need that cover story for?

I've been so caught up in everything else it never dawned on me to ask the real question – what was she doing with the security guard in the first place? I didn't get a good look at his body, so I don't even know who it was yet. I just know he was one of ours.

What could Lydia have been doing to run afoul of him in the first place? It was serious enough to get him killed, so she must have been in real danger. A spy of her caliber never kills in a situation she can talk or fuck her way out of. The next time I get close to her, I won't let her distract me with those bedroom eyes. I'll get some answers if I have to break every finger she has.

"Diego?" Ortega's voice grits to me across the patio.

"You're alive," I joke. "I was wondering if Jacinto ate you for breakfast." Ortega's not laughing. He comes to stand right in front of me, his thick lidded eyes searching my face. Something's up. "How did it go in there?" I ask more earnestly. "Was it bad?"

He watches me for a long moment, the muscles in his jaw popping as he grinds his teeth.

"Jacinto wants to see you." Flat. No inflection, no hint of what's waiting for me.

Fuck.

Brave it out with a smile.

"Thanks for finding me. Which room?"

"Situation Room." The guy is a brick wall. I keep right on grinning, slugging him on the shoulder as I head for the house. Just before stepping through the door, I call back over my shoulder.

"Who was it? On the bike?"

"Chucho Rozin." Ortega doesn't even turn around. Just stands with his back to me, and I can hear my funeral bells start ringing.

Of course I was playing a dangerous game tangling with Lydia, but mostly I was worried about what she might do. I've fucked enough of Jacinto's women to know how not to get caught, but maybe somebody heard us. Try as I might to keep my head, that woman is a fucking maze it's easy to get lost in.

Of course Jacinto is in the Situation Room. The only reason we set up that joke is so he has a place to intimidate people. I've spent countless hours laughing up my sleeve as greasy pricks snivel under Jacinto's maniacal posturing.

Well, now that I'm the one in the hot seat, I'm laughing out the other side of my mouth.

It doesn't help that it's the first place I saw Lydia's skin. The woman spread it out like a blanket, and I was dumb enough to take a nap on it.

Two quick knocks on the door, and it springs open. Jacinto looks up at me with black, searching eyes. His mouth twists into a treacherous smile and he claps his hands on my arms.

"Dieguito! You came to see me."

As if I had an option.

"Ortega told me you were looking for me."

"I always have an eye out for you, my cousin." He ushers me in, and I look around warily. "Here, I was just about to have a cigar. Join me."

We clip a pair, and Jacinto holds out his lighter for me. I roll the end in the flame, making a show of relishing my first puffs. Anything to give the appearance of ease.

"Perfect," I sigh, blowing smoke at the ceiling. Jacinto lights his own, then takes a moment to dabble his fingers in the little shard of orange.

"Fire." It glistens in his eyes. "I love it. The kiss of it. The sting. The danger. Tell me," he looks up to me. "Do you like playing with fire?" He gets in moods like this from time to time, so it's impossible to tell whether or not I should be ready to fight. Best to keep cool and see where this leads.

"Everyone does sometimes."

He snaps the lighter shut.

"Some people play too much." Jacinto paces away from me, and I keep my attention riveted to his back. If it's time to trade punches, I'll be goddamned if I'm catching the first one unawares. "Tell me, Diego—how well did you know Chucho?"

"The same as any of the security detail. No one could say we were close."

Jacinto wheels on me.

"You hired him!"

Oh, so that's it. Guilt by association.

Jacinto didn't have the pleasure of killing the man who interfered with his woman, so everyone associated with him gets a turn on the whipping stool. Now that I know the game, I'm willing to take my stripes.

"I didn't know then that he was capable of something like this."

"Every man is capable," he roars. "Especially with a woman like Alana. She brings out the beast in a man. The most loyal could turn traitor just to be near her."

I know I shouldn't but I have to poke the bear. He just makes it so goddamn easy.

"Are you saying you can't blame him?"

"Of course I blame him!" Jacinto punches his desk hard enough to rattle all the drawers. "The fact that someone thinks they could take her from me is like poison in my blood. I can feel it burning in my veins so hot I want to scream. Where's the loyalty? I can't believe I put my life in the hands of a man like that."

Chucho put himself between Jacinto and danger countless times. But I choose not to bring that up.

"Worst of all—he thought I wouldn't find out? Tearing around on a motorcycle, practically rubbing my nose in it. You know what this means, don't you, Dieguito?" Jacinto plants his hands on the table, hunkering low and baring his teeth like a wolf. "My power is slipping."

His face is terrifying, but I force myself to laugh.

"You're not serious?"

"I am!" He pounds the desk again. "The fact that Chucho —that *any* man on this compound—could think such a thing is proof. I demand total loyalty, and that kind of faith comes only from *fear*!"

"No one doubts your strength, cousin."

I'm walking a razor wire tightrope, and sweating like a priest in a preschool. Jacinto straightens, studying me for a long moment. Then he strides for the door.

"Follow me."

We walk down the stairs, across the foyer, and out into the open. With a single bound, Jacinto vaults into the back of the jeep and puts on his sunglasses.

"Drive."

It makes my stomach seethe when he goes all dictator like this, but I do as I'm told. I've got too much to hide to get defiant now.

"Where to?" I ask, cranking the ignition.

"The labs."

It's a dusty drive to the far end of the growing fields, but Jacinto stands the whole way. A tinpot tyrant puffing on his cigar. Posturing for nobody but the cheap labor watering his crops.

"Look at this." He throws his arms wide, basking in acre after acre of marijuana and poppies. "I've built a *kingdom*, Diego. Larger than anything this side of Mexico City. I command a wider selection of drugs than anybody. Billions of dollars—tens of billions! More money than anyone could spend in a dozen lifetimes. Money like this buys more than *things*, Diego. It buys power! Respect. If that starts to go…"

He goes quiet. Fucking *finally*.

Just as the shack entrance to the underground labs comes in sight, Jacinto kicks the back of my seat.

"Stop!"

I jam on the brakes and Jacinto hops to the ground before the engine is off. Dust swirls up around him, and he breathes it in like perfume.

"Do you know how many senators I have in my pocket, Diego?"

Oh, goddamnit. Not this fucking game.

"Sixteen."

"Name them."

I stifle a sigh as I count out on my fingers. "Travis. Ivers. Reed. Satchell." I've had to do this so many times I stop listening to myself. But my cousin conducts me like it's a goddamn symphony.

"How many representatives?"

"Twenty." I start to list them, but Diego jabs his finger in my face.

"Twenty *six*!" A look of hellish pride oozes across his face, and I gape at him in disbelief.

"Who?" is all I can think to ask.

"Ah, ah." Jacinto shakes his finger. "A man must have some secrets. When people know everything, they don't need you anymore." There's something eerily pointed in the way he says it, but he snaps his fingers before I can think too hard about it. "But tell me the ones you know. You might surprise me."

It makes me sick to my stomach when he gets puckish like this, but I reel off the names. It's not like they're a secret. Hell, the peasants picking stems could do as much. Then he makes me run down the list of CEOs.

"Jacinto," I laugh when I'm done. "Did you really drag me all the way out here to sweat me through a pop quiz?"

"I wanted to prove a point. Because all of this—the things you've listed, the things you've seen driving us out here—it's all *mine*. And if I thought someone was trying to take that from me..." He lashes out, catching one of the field workers by the scruff of the neck. The unlucky bastard gives a yelp as Jacinto jerks him off his feet and shoves him to his knees. In an instant, Jacinto's pistol is out, jammed against the man's head.

"Woah," I shout, but he just glares at me.

"I would burn it all down, Diego. Every bit. To the fucking ground."

"Jacinto—"

"All of it," he shouts over me. "I built it, and I'd destroy it before I let another man have it."

"Jacinto..." It's like approaching a copperhead. I just shake my head and spread my arms easily. "You say these things... my cousin?" Fixing him with a knowing smirk, I lean in. "All this over a *woman*?"

The whole world stops breathing. Jacinto stares into my soul with spine tingling stillness.

Then he laughs. Throws his head back and cackles at the sky. The gun goes away, and he yanks the hostage to his feet, slapping his back until the poor fucker has no choice but to join in laughing. Soon all the onlookers are in on the act, and I join in to boot.

"You know something, Diego? I forget how funny you are." Slinging a careless arm over my shoulder, Jacinto draws me in close. "Let me tell you something, my friend. If you knew what it was like to have sex with Alana, you would kill any man who tried to come between you."

"Oh, come on." I make a wry face and try to wave him off.

"I'm serious, cousin. That woman?" His tongue swipes across his lips with sickening abandon, and I batten down the hatches for the coming storm. "Her skin is the creamiest, most delicious thing I've ever tasted. You've never seen tits like hers. Nipples so hard you want to cry. And a pussy…" He trails off into a series of sickening licks and groans, jostling me as he humps the air. "Heaven."

"I can imagine."

"You *can't* imagine!" He punches me in the arm. "It's impossible! I never dreamed sex could be like this. The way she writhes and wriggles and moans. Her body is made for pleasure."

I know it.

Better than anyone.

Better even than he does.

Because I guarantee whatever slice of affection she's given him doesn't come close to the ocean of passion we've shared. Hearing him talk about her like this fires up the furnace of my jealousy to the red zone. The more he spews about cramming his dick into her, the harder I grit my teeth.

Then I realize he's right.

Because just thinking about him being with her has me ready to kill him where he stands.

CHAPTER
NINETEEN

LYDIA

I check my receiver for the hundredth time to make sure it's still recording. And taking furious notes just in case the audio file is a bust.

Thank Christ Diego hasn't changed his clothes since his secret meeting. Between the motorcycle extravaganza and some hardcore fucking, he's been a busy boy. And that microphone has ridden his collar every step of the way.

Jacinto's little grandstanding tirade is mother's milk to an intelligence agent. Stupid son of a bitch just gift wrapped the whole caboodle. Hearing him talk about me like that isn't easy on the stomach, but it'd bother me more if I gave a single fuck about him.

That said, after the way he just spilled the frijoles for me, he probably deserves a great big smack on the lips—and not the knuckle flavored variety.

"Zero's gonna cream her pantsuit," I mutter as I jot the last name down. This just might be my ticket out of town. I'll be back on my speedboat by the end of the week. Maybe a night in Sir John's flat to bring me back to earth, then it's off to the Adriatic for some rakija and some Ston oysters.

I can taste them already.

The audio file still needs to be cut down before I can zip it over, but at least I can kick the names her way. My handwriting is for shit, but they've got codebreakers at GSIA, so I bet they can figure it out.

Snapping a picture of my notepad, I send it to Zero.

Jacinto spilled names. More details to come.

As soon as it's delivered, I rip out the leaf with my chicken scratch list. Can't have that hanging around Jacinto's room.

It's dangerous doing actual spy work in here, but it's the only place I can be caught alone. After my brush with security last night, I'm on high alert. Jacinto, on the other hand, is at def-con five. One look at me with my gear in hand and it'd be lights out.

Fortunately, I know he's out in hell's half acre, so I've got a minute.

If I had a room of my own it'd be different, but for now, I'll just have to make do. I'd campaign for my own little boudoir if I thought I was going to be here long enough to use it.

Now, there's nothing like the smell of burnt paper to let a mark know you're up to no good. Ashes in the trashcan have a way of getting agents killed.

But I've got Nine on my side, and that nutty old cuss is a genius in his stocking feet. Crumpling up the evidence, I plug the sink and run the tap. Smoke is a dead giveaway, but paper that dissolves in water is a girl's best friend.

Feels like regular paper, writes like regular paper, and melts like cotton candy as soon as it hits the drink. Ten seconds after my intel hits headquarters, there's no blood on my hands for the hounds to sniff.

Apart from my equipment on the bed, that is.

Which reminds me...

I tap my ear piece to check in on the boys. The jeep is rumbling again, which means they're on the move. Probably back this way. I turn up the volume and Diego's silent stewing crackles like static over the line. I may not give a damn in hell about the locker-room diarrhea Jacinto just spewed out of his mouth, but I bet Diego is boiling in it.

It's one thing to inspire blinding jealousy in a man like Jacinto. He's the lowest apple on the tree, ripe for the picking. Diego is something else.

Imagining him quaking with envious rage is enough to make my knickers damp. Especially after the kinky drilling he gave me an hour and a half ago. Maybe it'll inspire him to throw me against the headboard again to try and claim me back.

Well, come and fucking get it, Dieguito.

If they're on their way back, I need to get myself in order. Giving my reflection a once over, I see how my scrapes are shaping up.

My lips have gotten a lot of attention, so the pop in the mouth I gave myself looks just fine. Thanks to the freshening up Diego saw to, the pink lines on my wrists are still clear and deep. The bruise on my upper arm is coming in nicely, so that's the icing on the cake.

The ripped, cummy shirt is disposed of, but I've put on another sleeveless number to show off all my scratches and nicks to best advantage. An operative's first objective—sell the story.

I debate getting into a bikini to go wait down by the pool. That would really show off the number my chase through the pot fields did on me. It'd also give me a chance to taunt Diego with my body.

But it might seem a little too casual after my faux abduction. Do tender hearted lambs go sun themselves after a near violation? Best to stay here and cower appropriately.

It also keeps me close to my technology in case Zero gives me the thumbs up to bust out of this joint. The bathing suits I brought barely cover the pink bits, so there's nowhere to hide a phone.

Footsteps echo in the hall and my breath catches. I've memorized the gait of each major player in this farce, and I'd bet a peso to a pinch of shit that's Jacinto.

They made good time.

Too good.

I dive on the bed and scuttle my gear behind the headboard just as the door opens. Clutching the sheets, I gasp and lurch back against the pillows, staring petrified at the man on the threshold.

"Oh," I sigh, a delicate hand on my chest to still my racing heart. "It's you."

Jacinto fuggin melts.

"Si, mi diamante."

"Sorry." I scrunch up my nose in shame. "I don't speak Spanish." It's a big fat lie, but it does the trick. An indulgent smile warms his face so he almost seems tender.

"I'm sorry, my diamond. I'll try to remember." He closes the door and comes to sit on the edge of the bed. "How are you feeling? You must have been so afraid."

It's go time.

"Don't worry about me, darling." I roll forward and put my hands on the duvet, smashing my tits together with my upper arms. "How are *you*?" The ploy works and Jacinto gets an eyeful of my cleavage, then sours when he sees the bruise purpling my skin.

"Oh, Alana. I'm so, *so* sorry this has happened. Don't worry." Those black eyes ignite with violence. "He's been made an example."

Yeah, no shit.

Unless I'm mistaken, the henchman's mom is going to get one fucker of a present in the mail.

"Thank you for protecting me. I feel so safe when I'm with you."

"You are. I promise you." His attention flicks back down to my arm, then he reaches for me timidly. "May I see?"

Did he actually just *ask* me? The guy is just full of surprises.

I offer my arm and he takes it gingerly with his fingertips, dabbing over the bruise and pressing lightly at the edges. There's an odd sweetness to how earnestly he seems to care. If only he knew the creases on my wrists are courtesy of his trusty second banana. Who am I kidding? Diego's banana is second to none in this place.

He presses a bit more firmly in the center of the bruise, and I hiss through my teeth like a coward. Jacinto starts back, then caresses my arm.

"Did I hurt you?"

"Just a little."

"Well." That glimmer dances in his gaze again. "Let me kiss it better." Lifting my arm to his lips, he brushes it with the softest whisper of a kiss.

Then another.

Then the tip of his tongue outlines the dark area before slicking across the broad plane of my arm. Sensitive attention flies out the window in favor of fervent hunger. Slobbering his way up my arm, Jacinto tries to take my whole wrist in his mouth, lapping at the sensitive furrows my bindings left behind.

"God," he murmurs, tugging me closer to him.

And we're off to the races.

His other hand wanders my body as he chews his way back up my arm in search of my neck. Breath heavy and fast, moaning lightly as he cradles my tit.

So much for gentle. Well, two can play at that game.

I throw my head back, crying out under the weight of his kisses. My fingers tangle in his hair, guiding him down the plunging neckline. He fumbles at it, grunting with impatience when his fingers can't figure out how buttons work.

I'm running low on tops, so I take matters into my own hands.

"Wait." I peel his mouth off me, my face flushed with giddy desire. "I need your mouth on my body." We both get what we want. He gets to think I'm mad with yearning for him, and I get to peel my shirt off in one piece.

Jacinto latches on like a lamprey, sucking my skin so hard he leaves red marks everywhere. I arch into him, offering him more and more of myself. Dumb bastard is happy as a pig in shit.

"Yes," I squeal, forcibly burying his face in my breasts. "God, Jacinto, *yes*!" A crumb of encouragement is a loaf of permission for this guy. Jacinto gobbles greedily at my chest, burbling with libidinous longing. The more I scream, the wilder he gets.

This party ends one of two ways, and if I'm being honest I'm a little fucked out. It's been a party in my panties in the two days I've been here, and I wouldn't mind sitting out a round.

Raking my nails up his thigh, I find the granite lump in the front of his trousers and get to work. Stroking him with *just* the right amount of pressure, I do everything I can to paint the inside of his zipper with spunk.

It has to feel good because his breathing skyrockets. My chest is slick with saliva, and he's nowhere near done drooling.

A small shudder runs over him, and I know I'm winning.

"Easy," he whispers, trying to pull my hand away. "You've got me so close." That's all I need to hear and I double down, rubbing his crotch like I'm trying to start a fire on his pants. "Fuck." He shoves me back and stands, grappling with his belt.

"Let me," I plead, sliding onto my knees. "Please, Jacinto, let me."

Permission granted. His hands forsake his belt to tangle in my hair, and I rub against him as much as I can while undoing his fly. All the requisite noises slip out of me, making his muscles tight and his breath short.

Fly comes down. Pants to ankles. It's just me and a pair of boxer briefs peppered with love drops.

"Oh, my God," I wheeze, running my hand up the underside of his erection. I slip my fingers under his waistband, ease his underwear down and… bingo.

As soon as air touches his knob, it bursts with a healthy squirt. I grab with both hands, aiming so he gets as much on himself as possible. Jacinto doubles over me, clawing at my back while I milk him dry.

I know the second his orgasm passes because he goes dead weight. We topple over to the floor and he lies back with his chest heaving.

He sighs like he just ran a marathon. My dude just entered varsity league in premature ejaculation, and he's not even a little embarrassed. If anything, he glories in it. Looking over to me with a sly smirk, the fucker winks.

"See what you do to me?"

Unreal.

Getting to his feet, Jacinto strips buck naked and whistles his way into the bathroom. For a second, I fantasize that he's going to bring me a damp towel. Then the shower starts and I know I'm on my own. I wash ejaculate off my hands and arms while he goes full Pavarotti through the clouds of steam.

Who says chivalry is dead?

One thing in his favor—Jacinto loves him some creature comforts. A hot shower buys me a minimum of twenty minutes, and I have no intention of wasting the time.

Scratching behind the headboard, I manage to drag out my phone and receiver. My earpiece is dead, which tells me Diego finally stripped off that shirt. The agency's loss is my imagination's gain as I picture his impeccably toned chest. Maybe he's treating himself to a shower too. Water cascading over him until he's shiny and smooth.

Snap out of it. You've got work to do.

I flick through to the audio editor and scan back over the files to weed out extraneous conversation. It can be painstaking work because something that sounds like an inconsequential detail could carry the motherlode. That means leaving conversations intact and snipping out the silences.

And the not-so-silences.

Scrolling back for the meeting of conspirators, I go just a bit too far. Hushed grunts flood my ear, along with the unmistakable slap of flesh on flesh. Nothing feigned here. No cloying pleas. This is desperate, famished fucking.

The equipment damn near catches on fire.

It's Diego and I in that cramped closet, letting our respective devils out of their cages. The sound of us ravishing each other sends a rush of heat straight down to the sweet spot.

"Goddamnit."

I ought to be working. I *need* to get this edited so I can send it over. But the incendiary audio won't set me free. Diego's panting rises, ratcheting closer and closer to the brink. Then I hear it.

"Jesus, Lydia." The raspy snort of a man about to lose himself to me. My nether regions burst to life.

I have to do this.

It will clear my head and I can get to work. Which might be a lie, but it's the one we're going with for now.

Scrolling back just a hair, I play it again.

"Jesus, Lydia."

And again.

"Jesus, Lydia."

I put it on a loop so that my name on his husky voice pours into my ear like molten sin. My fingers sneak into my panties and I tease myself to pieces.

"Jesus, Lydia."

"Jesus, Diego," I mouth as lightning ripples under my skin. It's cruel the effect that duplicitous criminal has on me. At the same time I wonder if maybe—just maybe—he's somewhere in this mansion thinking of me.

CHAPTER
TWENTY

<u>*DIEGO*</u>

Getting off base is just the medicine I need. Even a little bit of physical distance from Agent Slick helps me see her for what she is. A world class manipulator. A liability with great tits. Thanks to them, I haven't been keeping my eyes on the prize.

It's hard to miss the prize when the team is loading kilo after kilo of top flight juice onto our fleet of speedboats. That gulf breeze hits me in the face, blowing away anything but the smell of salt water and money. Jacinto may be crazy as a shithouse rat, but I've got to hand it to him – the man has built a cartel superpower unlike anything else on the planet.

And once I take control, it'll run like the Swiss clock it should. Because right now we're a half tick off.

"What's the holdup?" Ciges asks. He's captain of our fleet, and the fastest goddamn boat driver on the gulf.

"I'm working on it." Bringing my binoculars back up, I take another hard look at the patrol boats in the distance. With the sun going down, I can't make out if they're US Coast

Guard or the Búsqueda y Rescate Marítimo. Not that it should make any damn difference. Every police pontoon within five hundred nautical miles is on the Osorio payroll.

That should mean there's nothing on the water but blind eyes. Problem is, these sons of bitches aren't turning their backs. If anything they look open for business.

"Ciges, do we have any boats that aren't loaded yet?"

"A couple."

"Fire one up. I need to go talk to these boys." If they're just farting around, that's one thing. But if some naval official has a wild hair up his ass, I'm sure as hell not going to face him with a hold full of prison powder.

We slice through the wine dark water, straight towards the closest patrol boat. The closer we get, the more my heart balls up like a fist.

They're ready for action, alright.

The US Coast Guard boat is porcupine sharp with assault rifles just waiting for us. We pull up and Ciges bops the horn to hail them. The commanding officer steps into the clear, and it's Coastie Regina MacManus. Five foot four inches of rock hard curves. I should know.

"Regina!" I salute her with the biggest smile I can muster. She's not smiling back.

"Señor Alamar." Guess she's got her no-nonsense panties on today.

"I don't know if you checked your calendar today, but Jacinto Osorio has a candy delivery on the books for tonight."

"I've been made aware of a possible shipment, and have orders to intercept any vessels attempting to ferry illegal cargo into US waters."

The fuck is she talking about?

"Run that by me one more time?" I'm smiling, but my teeth have turned into fangs. Regina leans closer, softening just a bit.

"I know the plans Jacinto has in place, Diego. But we don't have the all-clear from the American side."

"Meaning?"

Regina sighs and shakes her head. "Meaning until I'm told otherwise, you're looking at a closed shop." She must see the explosion of anger in my face because sympathy blinks into her eyes. "If it were up to me, Diego..." She almost reaches for me, then checks herself.

Somebody's watching.

"I understand," I say, putting up my hands. "Just following orders."

"I'm sorry."

"It's okay." At least I fucking well hope so. Regina can look as remorseful as she wants, she's not the one who has to tell Jacinto his shit's still sitting in the harbor. "Get me back to land, Ciges. I've got some phone calls to make."

"Yes, sir."

By the time my boots touch sand, I'm ready to shit down someone's throat. And I know who candidate numero uno is.

"C'mon dickhead," I mutter as I pace the shoreline. The phone's been ringing for over a goddamn minute. All eyes are on me, and they burn like fucking hell. Nothing like having fifty smugglers standing around with their dicks out while I try to sort out why we can't ship.

"What the hell are you doing calling me right now, Diego?" Representative Larry Myer hisses as soon as he picks up.

"We've got a problem."

"I'm in the middle of dinner with my *family*."

"I've seen the pictures," I snarl back. "I guess my dinner invitation got lost in the mail—should I just come on up? Remember, *I know your address*." That gets his attention. I can hear him chewing back some choice words while he calculates his next move.

"What do you want?"

"You know what I want. I've got damn near two dozen powerboats loaded to the teeth, and the Coast Guard says I'm looking at a no-fly zone. Care to tell me why that is?"

"Shit," he grunts. "That order came down already, huh?"

"What order?" He doesn't want to answer. "What order, Larry?"

"Look, I don't know the whys of it all, but things are on hold."

I all but throw my phone into the fucking gulf. Looking at the mule boats and idle smugglers, my blood pressure shoots for the moon.

"That's not good for us," I growl.

"I don't know what to tell you, partner. If you want details, you're gonna have to talk to Deke Mulholland up in Austin."

"Gimme his number."

"Look, Diego—"

"I said gimme his fucking number, Larry!" My voice echoes up the beach so far I'm sure his family doesn't have to overhear the call to know he's getting his ass chewed.

"I'll text it to you."

"You better." I hang up, fuming. As soon as the contact info comes through, I dial it up. This Deke better be willing to play ball or I'm gonna reach through the phone and rip out his goddamn throat.

A woman answers.

"Hello?" God, she even sounds rich. It's like she's got diamonds in her throat. Tamping down the barracuda in my guts, I put on my polite voice.

"Yes, I was wondering if I could speak to Mr. Deke Mulholland?"

"May I ask who's calling?"

"Tell him a friend of Jack Poppy." Jacinto's code name rattles her. "I was given this number by Representative

Myer." There's a long beat, and when she speaks again, she's hoarse as hell.

"Hold on a moment."

Deke picks up the line, smooth as glass.

"You're one of Jack Poppy's boys?"

"I'm Diego Alamar. That name mean anything to you?"

"Yes, it does."

"Then maybe you'd like to tell me why I'm standing on a beach outside of Matamoros with a shipment ready to move, and the whole coast guard telling me to stay put?"

"Because I said so."

So this is the fucking guy.

"I'm gonna need a better reason than that. Because," I drop my voice and turn my back on the workers, "if this is about the *coup*, I thought an extra percentage point smoothed the path."

"That ain't it, Alamar."

"Enlighten me."

"Shit." He sighs. "Look, let's just say there are ripples in the water. Nobody's sure where they're coming from, but irregularities in the system have pinged up. It could be anything from a bug in the software, to a lone hacker, all the way up to an outright malware attack. We're looking into it, but until we confirm it's nothing, the pipeline is closed."

"You're telling me this is over a computer glitch?"

"Maybe it is and maybe it isn't." God, guys like this chap my ass. "I'm just saying glitches shouldn't run through the entire chain. We have to be sure."

"I want you to listen to me, Mulholland—and listen well. If this shipment doesn't go through *tonight*, there's going to be hell to pay. And not just down here in Mexico. If Jacinto Osorio gets the idea his amigos up in Estados Unidos are running cold, he might cancel shipments indefinitely. And if *he* doesn't, you're talking to a man who will."

Deke laughs, and I clutch the phone so hard I almost crack the screen.

"You're gonna just stop shipments?"

"Try me."

"What are you gonna do with the product? Burn it? Stockpile it for a rainy day? Maybe old Jacinto will just juice himself to the gills and have one hell of a party." He doesn't know how close that last one is to right. "Don't worry about it, son. This should be cleared up soon, and we can all get back to printing money."

Easy to say from an overstuffed chair, but I've got seawater in my socks.

"What the hell am I supposed to do until then?"

"Well, Diego, that sounds like a problem of *yours*."

And the son of a bitch hangs up.

"Fuck," I roar, gnashing my teeth and stomping back up the beach. Ciges is right behind me.

"What did he say? Diego, talk to me."

"Port's closed."

"*What?*" He's mad as hell, but I don't have room in my chest for anybody's anger but mine. I spin on him, ready to bludgeon anyone stupid enough to get close.

"Don't fucking start with me right now, Ciges! Because I'm *this* fucking close to killing someone, and I don't give a fuck who. Got it?"

"What are you yelling at me for?" he bites back. "I just want to know what's happening!"

"I'll tell you what's happening, Ciges. *Nothing.* Not tonight anyway. Get these assholes to seal up shop. Anything that's already aboard can stay there, the rest of it goes back to the warehouse."

"You want us to just leave product out here on the fucking boats?"

"Yes," I scream. "What, you think anybody around here is dumb enough to touch it? The biggest junkie in Mexico would rather throw himself down a flight of stairs than cheat Jacinto in a *dream*. That shit is safe right where it is."

"Diego." Ciges looks me dead in the eye, letting the weight of his age carry through. "You're letting your temper cloud your judgement. We've got a problem, but that's no reason to be foolish. You know better than that."

Fuck.

Ciges is my father's age, and all the men of that generation have a cool that's hard to argue against. I squeeze my eyes shut and exhale hard through my teeth.

"Alright. Unload, but keep everything close. The second things open up again, I want the shipment out. No wasted time."

"Yes, sir." He salutes, and I turn to make for my jeep. "Where are you going?"

"Where do you think?" I call back over my shoulder. "Someone has to tell Jacinto."

"Better you than me, Diego. Better you than me." Ciges knows as well as anybody Jacinto's habit of shooting the messenger. Much as I'd like to pawn the job off on someone else, this one is squarely on my plate.

Not only that, the way I handle this should be a signal to everybody the kind of leader I'm going to be when the time comes. Time to square my shoulders, take my lumps, and do everything in my power to be the voice of reason.

Even so, dread pools between my ribs as I fire up the jeep and head back for the compound. Jacinto blows his stack at a minor inconvenience, so this is going to be a bloodbath. I just hope it's a metaphorical one. I haven't worked this hard to wind up rolled in a carpet because Jacinto got pissy.

As if the shutdown wasn't bad enough, I have an idea what might have caused the ripples Deke mentioned, and a software glitch ain't the culprit.

I'm willing to bet hard cash I know who is.

CHAPTER
TWENTY-ONE

LYDIA

I have to say one thing for my fake kidnapping story—it's got Jacinto so worked up over security, he's forgotten all about fucking me. Lope Ortega is getting the worst of it, which means I've had time to edit files up and get them to headquarters.

Now it's just biding my time until I get the word to pull the ripcord and blow this popsicle stand. I've opted to confine myself to Jacinto's room for the day. The less time I spend out wandering the grounds, the less likely it is that someone looks at me sideways. Sometimes the best cover is just being out of sight.

It doesn't hurt that Jacinto's got the single most comfortable bed on the planet. I'm going to have to check the tags before I start setting fires so I can get one for my place back in Croatia. Shipping in and out of that country can be a bitch, but maybe I can pull some strings.

For now I just lay back in my undies and a crop top and let the hot Mexican breeze pour in through the French doors.

Do they still call them French doors if they're in Mexico? I'll have to look that up.

My phone buzzes before I can bring up Google.

It's Zero!

Just the text I've been waiting for. I swipe through, straightening my spine as if I expect her to walk into the room.

Excellent work, Agent Slick. The list of names you captured from Osorio and Alamar is fulsome. Preparations are underway to enact sweeping action. More details to come, but know that your work deserves top commendations. Well done.

For Zero, that's effusive. It damn near brings a tear to my eye. But it doesn't touch on what I really want to know.

Have we reached the extraction point? I can move to the scorched earth portion of this operation any time.

Negative.

My heart drops.

In the recording Osorio mentions nameless contacts higher up the chain, and we suspect there may be more he's keeping secret as well.

How long will that take to flush out?

I hold my breath and wait for her reply.

Unclear at this time.

Definitely not what I was fucking hoping for.

We will keep you apprised. In the meantime,
be sure to double check your transmissions
to ensure all attached files are relevant.

What the hell is she talking about?

Okay.

It's about a million miles from okay, but what the hell am I
supposed to do?

Much appreciated. We will reach out when
more information comes to light. Keep after
Osorio and see if you can extract anything
farther. Signing off.

"God fucking damnit," I groan, dropping my phone in the
covers and shoving my fingertips in my eyes. The only thing
I've truly been able to extract from Jacinto so far is semen. The
rest of it has been dumb luck and Nine's inventions.

My phone buzzes again, and while my brain knows it's
impossible things have moved this quickly, my heart scampers away like a rabbit. But it's not Zero.

It's Sir John.

I don't suppose I could steal you for a quick
chat?

A phone call? Come on, Sir John. We both know an agent in
the field isn't exactly in the position for a good old fashioned
Sunday jaw. Especially given that I'm in the literal lion's den.

And yet...

Fuck it.

Sure.

Getting caught just might be worth it to hear a friendly voice. Even if it's just for a minute or two. It rings, and the prickle in my chest makes me hesitate before picking up.

"Alana here."

"Hullo, Alana." He always roughs up his accent when he's teasing me. It warms me to the pit of my stomach. "So. Good to hear you've been having fun on your little trip."

"Fun?" I scoff out a laugh. "I've had better times."

"Well, that's flattering to hear."

"What is that supposed to mean?"

"Wait." A sly chuckle creeps into his voice. "You really don't know? In the future, you should check your files more carefully before you send them along."

"Zero said the same thing. What the hell is everybody talking about?"

"Amidst all that very pertinent information was a rather salacious recording of you, shall we say... executing your duty?"

"Oh, shit!" My hand shoots to my mouth as a bleat of laughter flies out. I cringe, wishing I could go back in time and scrub the file as hard as I'd scrubbed my clit listening to it. "Please tell me you're joking."

"I presumed you just wanted to prove that you were working hard for the good of the mission."

"Who all heard?"

"We spared Nine."

"Thank God for that! He's like my grandpa. I'd hate him to hear me rutting for God and country."

"Well, as I said—at least you're having fun."

"Let's just say the job has its ups and downs." That earns a laugh of true appreciation.

"Oh, I remember the ins and outs of this kind of operation. They can be tricky, but I rose to the occasion a time or two when I was in the field."

"I've heard the legends."

"Legends," he cries in mock offense. "You speak as if I'm an *antique*."

"Burnished, but never rusty."

"Bitch." He sighs and we settle into a cosy quiet. I was right—this was worth the risk. "Lydia my darling, much as I hate to broach more serious territory..." he drawls and I groan.

"You're going to anyway."

"I'm going to anyway," he says along with me. "It may not be any of my business to say so, but from the evidence you submitted, I gleaned this is perhaps more than merely a honeypotting job?"

My hackles rise on instinct. "Meaning?"

"Lydia. The orgasm I heard was real."

"Bullshit."

"Lydia." Sir John draws out my name expectantly. "I of all people should know."

He's got me there.

I sigh and settle back among the pillows.

"Are you saying you always faked under the covers when you were under cover?"

"I'm just saying..." His tone softens. "Protect your heart."

Jesus, I'd give anything to be able to take his hand right now.

"I will. I am. My heart is never at risk."

There's a long beat before his weary answer.

"I know."

Better than anyone, Sir John.

"Listen," I say softly. "I should go. It's dangerous having a conversation behind enemy lines."

"Of course." There's more than a dash of melancholy in his voice. "Thanks for picking up."

"Only for you, Sir John. Only for you."

I hope he knows how much I mean it. The line cuts and I let my phone fall in my lap.

Is it possible to be homesick for a person?

Not for want of getting laid. God knows I've had enough sex to last me 'til Christmas. But... to share a glass of fine whiskey and look out of his window over the London skyline would be a balm to the soul.

This is dangerous to think about.

Sir John said to protect my heart, and he knows deeply that I've welded cast iron plates around it. And yet anyone who welds knows cast iron has brittle joins. Cracks form no matter how many times you hammer things closed again.

Which means people can sneak through.

And after Jeremy...

It's silly. Nothing in life can ever touch that first love. And when that ends as severely and definitively as Jeremy's life did, it leaves a wound that seeps for the rest of your life.

Knowing that love can die—really and truly *die*—has left me unafraid of death.

Which is why the GSIA came looking for me in the first place. I'm the perfect recruit. Broken in all the right places, and whole in the ones that matter most to intelligence work.

Love makes you weak, and Lydia Slick refuses to be weak. Even with someone like Sir John.

Explosive as the sex with Diego is, the man doesn't stand a chance.

Speak of the devil, Diego comes strolling in without so much as a knock. I scramble to hide my phone under the covers, but he just waves me off with a snide laugh.

"Please, you don't need to play that bullshit with me. I know who you are, remember?" He's a little too loud for my liking. Careless with my identity in a way that brings out the panther in me.

"What makes you think you can come in here without knocking? Jacinto—"

"Jacinto's in the lab sampling the latest batch. So it looks like we've got time for a *chat*." The word is powerfully different in his voice than Sir John's. Diego struts to the bed, looming over me with blood in his eyes.

"What's gotten into you?" I ask.

"What's gotten into *you*?" he sneers, taking me by the face hard. "We had an agreement, *Lydia*." Diego hisses my name as if it burns his tongue. "You work on my side of the fence, and I don't blow your cover. In case you haven't noticed, Jacinto's on the warpath."

"What does that have to do with me?" I try to pull free of his grip, but he clamps down. Easy as it would be to break his hand, I don't need that kind of attention.

"It makes things dangerous for *everybody*. And it's going to get a hell of a lot worse when I deliver the news about his shipment."

"I don't know what you're talking about."

"Don't you?" It's a bullwhip question, and I realize there are plates spinning I don't know about. Diego sees the shift in my eyes, snorting a nasty laugh in my face.

"Exports are frozen indefinitely. Evidently there have been disruptions in the chain. Someone's been sneaking through the encryption and poking around. Any idea who that might be?" Diego glares at me, then brings his nose inches from mine. "I know you've been sending information back to GSIA." He shoves me away from him, and I work the stiffness out of my jaw.

"I told you as much," I say, but he roars over me.

"More than you said!" Anger's got the best of him, so I elect to give him room to vent. Maybe even play the victim card a little.

"Is that really what you think?"

"It's the only explanation."

"There are dozens of explanations for something like this. Criminal organizations' biggest Achilles heel is paranoia. And Diego?" I roll onto my knees to face him better. "Even if I *was* relaying that kind of intel, it wouldn't make any difference."

"Why not?"

"Because they want the whole fish, not just the scales. They won't make a move until they know every last link in… *the chain*, did you call it?" He shifts uncomfortably. "If I'm still here, they haven't touched a thing. Because if they did, I'd be gone. You know I would."

Diego squints at me, chewing that over. He's gonna bite. I can feel it.

"Do you promise?"

Gotcha, fucker.

"Yes."

Like a fool, he believes me. To be fair, it's a half truth.

The lies:

1) I've sent back every scrap of information I get my grubby little paws on.

2) If there's a disturbance in the force, it's 100% because GSIA has been snooping. I'll have to tell Zero they're leaving fingerprints.

The truth:

1) They're not doing anything major until it's locked up tight. That means getting whatever names Jacinto is keeping from his men.

2) As soon as the storm breaks, I'm out of here like last year.

"You'd really leave?" he asks. "Without saying goodbye?" That famished look flits over his features, and I get all tingly in spite of myself.

"Oh…" I shine my eyes right back at him. "I might be convinced to make an exception."

"You'd better." He advances on the bed again, and I rise up to meet him. It's a panty soaker of a kiss. There's that danger again. The door is open, I'm less than half dressed, and we're on Jacinto's fucking *bed*. Good luck getting out of this one if the cavalry came.

When he snakes a hand up under my crop top to dabble with my nipple, it's time to pump the brakes.

"Diego," I whisper against his lips. "We can't. You can't have sex with me in Jacinto's bed."

"Are you sure about that?" He rocks forward and grinds his cock against my side. It shouldn't move me like it does, but *goddamn*. The man has one of the truly great penises of history.

"I'm sure," I say, putting some air between us. "So far what we've been doing is dangerous, but this? Lethal."

"Hm." He looks at me for a long time, tracing his hand up the line of my neck. He cradles the exact same jaw he was ready to crush less than two minutes ago, grazing his fingertip over my lower lip. Then he slides his thumb into my mouth and a sizzle races through me. He looks past my pupils and straight to the bottom of my worst nature.

"Later."

The digit slides from my mouth and he walks out, studiously leaving the door open. This man is treacherous as a mountain road. No sooner have I thought it than the word *treachery* lights up in my brain.

The one thing I haven't relayed to Zero crackles to life, and I grab up my phone.

Potential mutiny.

Conspiracy to topple Jacinto Osorio and replace him with Diego Alamar.

The response is immediate.

Squash it. We need Osorio right where he is until it's time to bring the hammer down.

Heard.

I take a deep breath and put my phone aside. This is really deep water. Fortunately, I'm an exceptional swimmer.

CHAPTER
TWENTY-TWO

DIEGO

L ydia is up to something. I fucking know it.

The second I'm away from her, the blood rushes back to my brain. I see things as they are. Of course she's lying to me—*that's what spies do*. But she bats those eyes at me and mashes her tits together and suddenly I'm eating out of the palm of her panties.

I walked in on her fiddling with her phone for Christ's sake! It's not like she's texting her mom. No matter how much she swears she's dealing fairly, I know she's relaying intel to her superiors. She can feed me all the bullshit she wants. There can only be one cause behind the ripples in the pond, and it's a pebble named Lydia Slick.

Maybe Nando Rivera lied about why she came down here in the first place. What if she's not here for Jacinto at all? What if *I'm* the goddamn honeypot? I never thought I'd fall for a trick like that, but here we are.

I tried to put the idea beside before, but I have to admit it makes perfect sense. Just when plans for a coup start coming to a head, the universe drops a bombshell like Lydia Slick on the end of my dick to scramble my brains.

Nando started that fight in the club because he knew Jacinto would sweep in to claim her, and that would put her in direct proximity to me.

That has to be it.

Snitches are notorious liars, and I'm almost sorry Nando is too deep in his shallow grave for me to torture a confession out of him.

Which is exactly what Jacinto would do.

Jesus, I'm even starting to think like him. Conspiracy theories and paranoia. I have to keep a cool head and remember the warning my father gave me. If we pull off a revolt just so I can turn into some suspicious lunatic, I'll have a target on my back bigger than his.

Once you kill a king, everyone knows the king can be killed.

"What are you doing?" Ortega asks when he finds me by the bar.

"Stalling."

His mouth falls open.

"You haven't told Jacinto yet?"

"Do you want to do the honors? I'd be happy to pass the torch."

"Listen to me." Ortega pries the glass out of my hand and slings the liquor on the ground. "If I start to get the idea you're chickenshit, I'm bailing. I thought after what your father said you'd straighten your shit out."

"A frozen shipment has nothing to do with our plan."

"It has *everything* to do with our plan," he snarls, leaning in close. "What the fuck good is seizing control if you can't do anything with the bunk but sit on it? Look." Ortega lays a hand on my chest. "Get up there and break the news to your cousin. Maybe he'll get his head together long enough to actually fix this goddamn thing. All it would take is a phone call."

"Yeah." He's right. Especially given the carrot Jacinto dangled in front of me yesterday. There are contacts he's holding back. Big ones. "I better get up there."

"Yeah, you better."

I'm wiser than to look for Jacinto in the Situation Room. No, when he's hopped up after a "sampling session," there's only one place to find him.

The Arcade.

Sure enough, I can hear the bells of the pinball machine all the way down the hall. I come in, and Jacinto's banging away at the machine with his hips like he's trying to get it pregnant.

"Come on, you bitch," he growls around his cigar. It's never really about winning or losing for him—at least not when he's stoned out of his mind like this. It's about making noise.

"Hola, Jacinto."

"Diego!" He casts a grin over his shoulder, and his pupils are so large his eyes are almost completely black. This guy is gone. Which means this can go one of two ways. He'll either be too loopy to hear the news, or he'll combust.

"How's the latest batch?"

"Estupendo!" Jacinto abandons the machine to face me, spreading his arms wide. The front of his shirt is open, and he's positively drenched in sweat. "We're going to make billions, Diego. *Billions.* As soon as the fleet comes back from this last shipment, I want them loaded and ready. We need this over the border immediately."

Time to bite this bullet.

"If it's as good as you say, maybe we should pull the current load and switch it over. Or do half and half."

"Pull the current load?" All his joy flies out the window, and demons crowd into his face. "Are you telling me it hasn't left?"

"That's right."

He blinks at me for a moment, clenching his jaw so hard I swear I hear one of his teeth crack. Even his sweat starts to sweat.

"So, I have dozens of speedboats, packed with enough cargo to get every man, woman, and child in America high for a calendar year, and they're just sitting in the harbor?"

Perspiration speckles the floor wherever he walks, and his face goes purple. Maybe we won't have to overthrow him after all. Maybe this news will drop him without anyone having to lift a finger.

"I did everything I could, Jacinto."

"Liar," he screams. "If you did *everything* you could, the shipment would be gone." Nobody likes being called a liar—especially by a maniac—but I keep my temper in check.

"The coast guard wouldn't open the gate."

That throws him for another loop.

"The fuck is that supposed to mean?"

"I had Ciges take me out to one of the boats so I could talk with Regina MacManus. She said the American border is closed for the time being."

Jacinto visibly shakes with rage.

"Why?"

"That's what I wanted to know. I called our contact in Austin and he said there are irregularities in the chain. People are spooked."

"That fucking Larry Myer!" Jacinto slams his fist into one of the pinball machines, shattering the glass. Shards stick out of his hand, but he's too hopped up on fentanyl and fury to notice.

"I meant Deke Mulholland." That name stops Jacinto in his tracks.

"You talked to Mulholland?" He approaches me with panther like stillness, and I get the sense I fucked up.

"Larry gave me his number and said to call. I was willing

to do anything if it meant getting the shipment out." Appealing to reason isn't gonna work this time around. Jacinto stops inches from me, glaring up into my face.

"You called Deke Mulholland *behind my back*?"

"Our association with Mulholland isn't a secret, cousin. Larry said to call him, and I did. I thought if I could get answers, we might be able to get things moving, and you'd never even have to worry about it."

"I worry about everything, Dieguito." His lip trembles, and for a split second I think he's going to cry. "I thought I could trust you, my cousin."

"You can," I assure him. "I'm the only one you *can* trust."

"Oh, Diego." He plants that bloody hand on my shirt, flecks of glass sparkling in his skin. "Don't be a viper. I can't have another venomous snake around me. My cousin." He palms my cheek and a coppery smell floods my nostrils. "The blood is thick between us. But if you betray me, your blood will be on the *floor*!"

He snaps his hand away in a sweeping gesture, spattering everything with flecks of crimson. Seeing the stains he's left on my face and shirt jar him back to himself, and he notices his hand for the first time.

"Call Ciges," Jacinto mutters, picking bits of glass out of his hand.

"What for?"

"He's going to take me to the line. And I'm going to kill every last coast guard officer that stands in my way."

Before I can register what he's just said, Jacinto is out the door and down the hallway like a bull on PCP. I run after him like my life depends on it—which it does. All our lives do.

"Jacinto, wait!" We're in the circular drive before I finally catch up with him. "Jacinto!" I grab his shoulders and yank him around, just ducking a haymaker aimed at my head. "You can't kill the coast guard."

"Watch me."

"If you do that, all of this is over."

He pulls up short.

"Over?"

"You think one stalled shipment is bad? Bloody up the gulf and see what happens. The Americans don't give a shit if cartel people kill each other, but if coast guard uniforms start washing up full of bullet holes, the door closes permanently. We could produce the finest product in the world, but it's all for nothing if we can't sell it!" The words cut through the chemicals in his brain, until I can literally see the hamster running inside his skull.

Jacinto lunges for me again, and I'm too unprepared to dodge him. Fortunately, this time it's to pull me into a ferocious hug.

"Diego, my cousin. You're always looking out for me. Thank you for talking sense."

"Of course."

He hangs on too long, squeezing like he wants to crack my spine. Then he turns me loose and paws at my shoulders, a feverish smile on his face.

"Call Don Barrera." Hearing the name of my fellow conspirator on his lips makes my mouth go dry.

"Why?"

"Cocaine," Jacinto cries. "The best he has. We're having a party." The reversal has my head spinning so fast I lose my balance as Jacinto brushes past me, dancing up the steps for the door.

"A party?"

"Yes! Tomorrow night. I'll get a list together and have your father make the invitations."

"But we just had a party," I stammer, trying to get ahead of this one.

"Not like this! This is about *power*. A show of strength. A show of wealth. I want my friends and enemies both to see me as I am—unbreakable and unafraid."

My first impulse is to resist. To talk him out of it. Then I realize what he's doing. Jacinto is handing me the perfect opportunity, and he doesn't even know it.

"Of course, cousin. I'll start making the preparations."

Turning on my heel, I pull out my phone and walk out of the house.

I'm calling Don Barrera alright. He picks up immediately.

"Diego?"

"How soon can you get here?"

"What's happening?"

I look over my shoulder and keep my voice down.

"My cousin has decided to throw a party tomorrow night."

"Another one?"

"This one is different," I say. "He wants *everyone*. Friends, enemies, rivals. Everyone."

"My God," Barrera mutters. "It's perfect."

"It's what we've been waiting for. A public event where everyone can watch Jacinto go down. So they can see the shift in power in real time. The fall of a dictator and the rise of a leader."

"I'll be there within the hour."

"Good. Meet in the usual place. And Don Barrera? My cousin wants your best cocaine."

"Of course," he purrs. "A farewell present."

"Exactly."

I end the call and strut around the perimeter of the house to find Ortega and my father. After all our waiting and planning, it's finally time.

CHAPTER
TWENTY-THREE

One of the most immortal lines in cinema: Don't get high on your own supply.

Evidently Jacinto Osorio never saw the movie. Which is crazy because between his flashy suits and screaming fits, you'd think he suckled on SCARFACE from his diaper days. And just like Tony Montana, Jacinto is perfectly content to get into the official brand and blow it up his nose, between his toes, and anywhere he can find a spot.

Not that I'm complaining. That means that, yet again, by the time he gets back to the room, he's far too wasted to get it up. For a guy so paralyzingly jealous, we've only had sex twice. Two and a half if you count him prematurely ejaculating all over my hands. But who's counting?

And look, don't get me wrong. I had a great time on his merry-go-round. But between him and Diego, it's no contest.

That said, the hot headed second in command is gonna take some handling. And Jackie's incapacity gives me just the opening I need to give Diego another solid dose of medicine.

I shouldn't go.

Should I?

I wouldn't give a shit if it was just Jacinto I was playing around on. But I've got a secret from all of GSIA, and that craves wary walking.

After the little confrontation we had this afternoon, I need a new strategy to handle Diego. If he's suspicious—as well he should be—then it's my job to fuck him until he forgets it, right? Wrap my legs around that guy and don't turn him loose until he doesn't know his ass from a canned ham. Keep him so sexed up he doesn't have time to question anything.

That way I can do all the behind the scenes work I need to, and put this puffer's promised land squarely in my rear view mirror.

"You know what," I mutter to myself. "Fuck it. Let's do this."

The new part of my mission starts right now.

Leaving Jacinto snoring across the foot of the bed with his dick out, I slip into the hallway. Given the schedule I've been able to suss out, it should be shift change time for the guards in this wing. That gives me a little under three minutes to get to Diego's room before the fresh patrol gets going.

Plenty of time.

Stealing through the dim corridors, I do my best to keep a cool head. This isn't the same kind of covert assignation he and I have enjoyed before. This is mission strategy. Sex is just another tool in my belt.

At least that's what I'm telling myself.

I mean, it's not like I'm sneaking to his room because I *want* to fuck him, right? That's crazy talk.

And so what if I enjoy it? Fringe benefits. Who says a spy can't have a little fun along the way? Some have shaken martinis, I get the shaking tinglies. All in support of the mission, of course.

I get to Diego's door undetected, and my heart thumps

my breastbone like it's trying to stage a jailbreak. Placing my palms on the jamb, I steady my breathing and slow my heart rate down. It's a skill that's taken years to master, but it's served me well more times than I can count with my shoes on.

I can't risk taking the time to get back to resting pulse, so I settle for a few beats above and gingerly knock on his door.

Diego opens it like he's been waiting for me. I'm a little taken aback by how immediate his appearance is, but that fades the second we lock eyes. They shine in the low light. A heady mixture of suspicion, mistrust, anger and… is that triumph?

"Expecting company?" I ask.

No answer. At least not verbally.

Diego grabs me by the wrist and whips me into his room, pinning me to the door with his lips.

He's going to make this too easy.

It's a stiff reversal from his attitude this afternoon, but that's not the only thing that's stiff. Here I thought I was going to have to seduce him, and instead he's ready and raring to go.

He kisses me like a starving man tasting food for the first time. I ought to stay in control, but it's so tempting to render myself up to the sweltering crucible of his desire. To melt myself into liquid pleasure just to gratify the animal in his gut.

As his mouth blazes a trail down my throat, I do everything I can to master my discipline.

It's just a mission. It's just a mission. It's just a—

I flash off my feet and land on the bed with one sweep of his arms. Then he plants a hand in the center of my chest, balls up the front of my dress, and yanks me naked.

Goosebumps race over my body and my breath abandons me. I'm all blind, quivering anticipation, and he's all dark power and want.

I shrink back on my elbows, the whole of me open to his gluttonous gaze. Then something terrifying happens.

The fiend in his face evaporates, replaced by something far more dangerous.

Tenderness.

His eyes rove over me, and everything about him softens. Well, not *softens*. He's definitely still mightily, thrillingly, gloriously hard. From the slabs of his pecs down to the dragon in his boxers, everything cries out to be touched.

If I were in control of the situation, I'd do just that. Run my hands over him like I'm slathering butter, drag him onto the bed and obliterate everything else in his world.

But things have spun beyond my control. His perilous, almost *loving* expression robs me of myself, and for the first time in living memory, I'm the one thing I can't afford to be— at least with any man beyond the wounded ex-spy waiting for me back in London.

Vulnerable.

"Lydia…"

"Don't." I put up my hand and avert my eyes, unable to bear another second of it. "Don't use my name."

He takes a step closer to the bed.

"Lydia."

"Don't!" I still can't look at him. "I don't have many rules, Diego, but if you break this one, all of this ends tonight." That brutal promise gives me the strength I need, and I meet his eyes. "All of it."

A flicker of something undefinable dances in his eyes. He puts a knee on the bed, nudging my feet apart so he can ease between them.

"Alana, then?"

Oh, fuck yes.

I bite my lip and nod at him. That simple concession is all I need to bring me back to myself. My code name is the mask that lets me be Lydia.

His shirt comes off, exposing an acre of well-muscled chest to my voracious eyes. Then he plays with his fly, deliberately taking his time undoing his pants. It's torture of the most sublime variety.

I was already slippery with desire for him, but now I'm in danger of soaking the sheets. The whole time, he never takes his gaze off me. That same affectionate smile burns so bright I see it with my eyes closed. It's so captivating that when his trousers slip off, I can't spare a glance for his breathtaking member.

Diego mounts the bed, and I spread my legs to welcome him. As he lowers himself over me, kisses pepper my throat. Not the scorching, livid kisses of a ravisher, but the sensitive brushes of a man who knows what the word *love* means.

It makes me wonder who his heartbreak was.

Who was the woman that left him so utterly broken that he fell headlong into a life so vicious it left nothing in its wake? Thousands of tiny, profound questions flutter through my mind until the brazen fact of his cock parting my lips scatters them.

"Fuck," I mouth, unable to find my voice as I claw at his back. Diego's hips sink slowly, as if really feeling me for the first time. I can sense each catch and shudder of his breath as he delivers himself into me.

Christ he's hard.

And *so* thick.

It's impossible to say what's different, but this time I'm stretched to my limits as he eases deeper.

"Holy shit, Lydia," he whispers when he's all the way in. My name stings like acid in my stomach, and I stiffen under him.

"Don't," I wheeze. "Don't."

"Alright." There's a trick of laughter on his breath. "*Alana.*" More tiny, treacherous kisses dust over my throat on the way to my earlobe. His nose invades my ear, blasting me with the furnace of his breath as his hips roll against my thighs.

I angle my body to meet him, heels pointed at the ceiling so I can take as much of him as possible. Diego takes the cue, resting my calves against his shoulders so high my ass lifts off the mattress. Each probing thrust touches the sparkle at the pit of my body, stoking the itching fire to thundering life.

This isn't fucking. It's something else altogether.

Both Diego and my target have pounded me like brutes and it's been exhilarating in the way only forbidden sex can be. But this is far more forbidden. It's the kind of connection that forces a dangerous word to your lips. Each push threatens to shove it into the open regardless of what it would mean in the cold, sweaty, post-coital light.

I have to bite my lip to keep it back, and just when I'm sure I can't swallow it any longer, Diego's mouth finds mine and drinks every drop.

Don't lose your head, I order myself. *It's a mission. He's an asset.*

I turn my head away to avoid his gaze—his lips—squeezing my eyes shut to become all body. No brain, no mission… no *Lydia*. Just a body, sizzling beneath him.

"Goddamnit, Alana. You feel so…" He lets a searching thrust finish for him and my feet go numb. Toes curled, legs shaking, throat tight, struggling for silence as a whole world pleads to erupt from my throat. Sparks fizz at the edges of my vision and the world spins into darkness.

"Still alive?" he murmurs when I go slack under him. My chest heaves as I rake in massive breaths. Beads of sweat roll down my ribs and over my shoulders, and even though my eyes refuse to focus I can see his lazy, arrogant grin.

"Fuck you," I gasp.

"That's what I'm doing. Fucking *you*."

And boy, is he. I'm barely recovered from the first climax before he's riding another one out of me. Pressing orgasms from my body with devilish glee. My legs break free of his shoulders and I cross my ankles behind his hips, reaching up to meet him.

Our bodies glide in perfect rhythm, and I grip him from the inside like I'm trying to memorize every facet of his cock. If it was like this the first time, the mission would be in real trouble. I'd be a cartel queen for the rest of my days, slinging smack right next to this man.

But the deepest part of my heart knows this is the exception, not the rule. The real Diego is the man who savaged me while I was bound to a chair. The man who pummeled me in a broom closet. Forcing me to scream while demanding silence. Whatever this is can't be trusted. I have to remind myself of that with each delicious drag and shove of our union.

One of his hands finds the small of my back, and he digs into me like he's trying to stab his own palm. The sensation is catastrophic, and I start to shudder all over again.

"Oh my god," I grunt. Shoving a hand between us I fiddle with my clit. Two quick strokes is all it takes. Combined with how flawlessly he fits inside me, I'm powerless beneath the tidal wave crashing over me.

I'm swept up, drowning in pleasure as shock after shock plunges me deeper. My body becomes a thing all its own, and I'm outside myself watching the shivering mess this man makes me.

The next thing I know I'm on top of him, hips jolting at a frenzied gallop. Scrubbing my clit against his body as I claw at his chest. My mouth is locked open, but nothing's coming out. I quit breathing hours ago. There's no room in my body for anything but Diego's cock and my own pounding heart.

Somehow words fall past my lips.

"Diego… I'm… so… close."

"Shit." His voice is thin and tight, and I force my eyes open to see his face contorted in ecstasy. That alone is enough to reduce me to ashes. "Alana, I can't hang on any more. I've got to pull out."

"*No.*" I sink my nails into his shoulders and ride harder. He can't come in Lydia, but Alana is fair game. "Come inside me. Please."

"Fuck."

"Diego, please!"

Like a good soldier, he digs his fingers into my hips and follows orders. The force of his orgasm sends me spinning into my own. We cling to each other and fall into chaos. It lasts for a thousand years, and when the storm breaks, I'm lying in his arms like a baby.

Thank god neither of us has the breath to say anything. Words would only fuck this up.

Words come with the real world, and I'll have to face up to that soon enough. For now, all I want to do is lie on this man's chest and listen to his heartbeat. Mine matches it, and I temper my own pulse to slow along with his.

The thread of his breathing evens out, then ebbs into a low snore. Some women would kill a man for falling asleep right after sex, but I'd say Diego has earned his rest.

I spread myself over him and soak in his strength. Asleep like this, he could be anybody. Not some ruthless, smuggling criminal. Just a man. For now, that's enough.

While I lie basking in the buzzy afterglow, something undefinable creeps over me. I don't recognize it at first, but a nagging feeling won't let me go. Then I let my eyes focus, and realize what I've been looking at.

Diego's phone is on the nightstand.

Not locked up. Not tucked safely out of sight. Out in the open, naked to the world—just like us.

I should grab it.

Nine's ripper is in my bag, right by the door where I dropped it when Diego first kissed me. But I know better than to risk blowing this opportunity. If I move now, I might wake him and the chance slips through my fingers.

Studies show that it takes up to ninety minutes to hit REM sleep. That's when I could hit him with a hammer and he'd stay out.

Ninety minutes is a long time to wait, but I've lingered in less desirable places. So long as I don't drift off myself, I should be golden. Now that Agent Slick is back in charge, there's little chance of sleep cheating me out of this.

Once I've got his phone on the ripper, I'll have every text he's ever sent duplicated in less than an hour. Turns out this tryst might have hit paydirt.

In the meantime, all I have to do is lie here, curled in the arms of the very man I'm betraying.

Don't think about it. Just be here now.

It's enough.

It has to be. Because within days, all this will be a memory. Good or bad, it will be in the past. Like everything else.

CHAPTER
TWENTY-FOUR

Movement in my bed wakes me and my eyes snap open. Sunlight stings them shut again, and I try to sit up but there's something pressing down on my chest. It moves again, then fingertips press into my shoulder.

"Stop," a woman's groggy voice grumbles. "I was comfortable."

Squinting down, I see a tangle of chestnut-colored bedhead. Then an expanse of spotless skin that vanishes under rumpled sheets.

It's Lydia.

"Go back to sleep," she mumbles, nestling her shoulder under my arm. I flop back onto the pillows and blink at the ceiling.

She stayed the night.

She shouldn't have done that. All it would take is one person coming to look for her and we'd both be fed to the crocodiles. But as her breath feathers across my chest, I almost wonder if it would be worth it.

I can't remember the last time I slept this well. Not only that, but waking with her in my arms is one of the most glorious things I've ever felt. I've woken in countless beds with women slung over me, but none of them can compare to this. Every single time I kicked them out as fast as I could—and now I just wish we could stay like this.

Maybe we can. For a while, anyway.

Finding my phone on the nightstand, I look at the screen for the time.

6:07.

The sun's just coming up. Given how hard Jacinto was banging rails last night, I can't imagine he'll peel himself off his mattress before noon.

That means—dangerous or not—Lydia and I should be able to lie like this for a while. Who knows? Maybe we can even get in another round before she has to sneak back to my cousin's room.

There's a perverse delight in sending her back to him still reeking of sex with me. Not that he'd notice. He'd probably just drag her into bed and smear her body with sweat of his own. The thought almost makes me jealous, but I let go of all covetousness.

Who am I to deprive him of one last moment of bliss with Lydia? Especially on his last day on Earth?

"Mm." Lydia stirs, pressing her body against me. "Keep doing that." I've been tracing my fingers up and down her back without realizing it. Grazing from her shoulder to the crest of her ass, scratching little circles there, then trailing upwards again.

"Does that feel good?" I ask. She answers by lifting her head and craning her neck for a kiss. Her leg falls across my thigh and the damp heat of her all but takes my breath away.

Releasing my lips, she gives the point of my jaw a light bite before curling back onto me. My cock shifts, blooming to semi-stiffness and rustling beneath the sheets.

"Ah," Lydia sighs. "Look who's awake." She rests her hand on me, rubbing lightly until I'm all the way extended.

"You're playing with fire." I smirk.

"I know. But I've been burned before." It should be a come on, but there's a sadness in the way she says it that catches me in the chest.

"A checkered past, Agent Slick?"

She doesn't answer for a long moment, but continues her meditative stroking on top of the sheets.

"I never talk about the past," Lydia says at last. "Besides…" Her eyes reach for mine, sparkling pink and purple from the rising sun. "The future is always so much more interesting."

"Isn't it?" I stretch, yawning in all the possibilities today is going to unfold for the Osorio Cartel. With Jacinto gone, maybe we'll even change the name. After all the years my father gave to his brother in law, it would be fitting to erase Esteban and his son Jacinto from memory so that my father's legacy can live on.

My legacy.

"What are you thinking about?" Lydia asks, and I answer without hesitation.

"Changing the name."

Her brow furrows for a second as she studies me.

"The cartel?"

I probably shouldn't talk about this, but the cool comfort of the morning makes it all so easy.

"Yes. My father worked like a dog for my uncle, and never got anything to show for it but his white hair. But with my name, *his* name on the organization, it could signal to the rest of the region that a change is coming."

"What sort of change?"

"A rebirth. A return to loyalty. Duty and honor are more than just words." I catch her eyes so she knows how deeply I mean it. "Even to a criminal organization like this. Alamar is a noble name, and I hope to bring nobility to this enterprise."

Lydia gets up onto her elbow, gazing into my face with a sort of wonder.

"How do you plan to do that?"

"With quality. Purity of product. That's one thing my cousin has done well with his move into the laboratory. We command top prices because our product is unlike any other. No filthy additives, everything is clean. The marijuana has been tending that way as well. But I have to keep that trend moving, and that means paying my workers more. Letting them share in the prosperity."

"Huh." She nods slightly as she takes this in. "Strangely, that *is* noble."

"Jacinto would never dream of it. The only pockets he thinks about are his own. But if he enriches himself while starving out the men who *produce* his product, the quality will fall. And everything falls with it."

"But with you at the helm…" Lydia trails off, leaving the door open for me to spin even more of my fantasy.

"Prosperity. Growing until we're all so rich it's impossible for anyone to get greedy for more." I nod towards the window, and the rising sun beyond it. "This morning is perfect." My arm presses her to me. "In *so many* ways. But tomorrow? Tomorrow will truly be a new dawn."

"Tomorrow?" A hint of trepidation creeps into her voice, and when I look at her, her eyes match it.

"Yes." Pushing back some of her hair with my fingertips, I smooth the crease between her eyebrows with my thumb. "Crazy as he is, Jacinto has handed us a golden opportunity, and everyone concerned agrees. It's time to move forward."

"What opportunity?"

"Oh, Lydia," I chuckle. "Not much of a spy, are you? Didn't you hear about the party?" She shakes her head, and I spread myself in triumph. "Jacinto wants to throw a lavish dinner party tonight. Bigger than the bacchanal a couple nights ago. More *pointed*. This one isn't merely for friends and allies, he's invited rivals. Enemies even."

"Why would he do that?"

"Jacinto has this crazy idea it will keep them in their place. A shameless display of wealth and power so everyone knows who's at the top of the food chain. What he doesn't know is that it's the perfect theatre for us to stage his fall so that I can ascend the throne."

There's a moment of stillness so loud it almost chips the paint. Then Lydia pounces and covers my mouth with hers. She kisses me like she's trying to drink the air from my lungs.

"Oh, my god, Diego," she mutters against my lips. "I can't believe it." Climbing on top of me, she squashes me to the mattress with her body. "Hearing the way you talk about this just makes me…"

Dragging the wetness of her along my shaft, she shows me exactly what I've done to her. Her lips part and she nestles me between them, riding the length of me as she smothers me with her breasts.

"I've never… Diego, I've never… it's just so *brave*. So *courageous*, what you're doing."

Her skin is burning hot to the touch, and I can feel the insistent thump of her heart against my lips as I press them to the center of her chest. Reaching between her legs, she takes my cock and angles it towards her entrance. The head of my dick aches with need to plunge into her, then a voice somewhere in the base of my brain screams like a banshee.

Stop! She's using you.

My eyes flash open, and I grab her shoulders hard to pry her chest off my face. A startled cry slips out of her, and her hand releases my cock.

We stare into each other's faces for a scorching second, and I see what I'm looking for. A tiny sliver of something in the back of her eyes. A sparkle of the mischief she's desperate to hide.

Tossing her aside, I scramble out of bed and stare down at her. It's hard to look intimidating with a rock hard dick, but I'm giving it all I've got. Lydia stares up at me in amazement, her body quivering with sexual arousal.

"Diego," she gasps. "What are you doing?"

"What are *you* doing," I spit back. "What are you up to?"

Lydia gets up on her knees, presenting her body to me in all its supple perfection.

"Trying to have sex with you." She sticks out her lower lip and pouts. "Are you really gonna make me *beg*?"

"Cut it out, I'm serious."

"So am I." Lydia reaches for my cock, but I back away. "Fine." Rocking back on her heels with a groan, she bites her lip. "If you won't have sex with me, will you at least let me blow you?"

"Lydia—"

"*Please*?" Slithering off the bed like the serpent she is, she kneels in front of me and takes me in her hand again. I stare into her face with deadly seriousness.

"Lydia. What are you trying to do?"

"I'm trying to suck you off."

"I'm not falling for that shit," I sneer. "You're going to double cross me."

"You're right." Blinking slowly, she sticks out her tongue and runs the point of it all the way up the underside of my cock. "I was. What are you going to do about it?" That devious tongue traces the crown. "Sell me out to Jacinto? Now that I have all this information about your coup?"

"Tell my cousin? No." I snatch a pistol from my chest of drawers and chamber a round. "I'm going to kill you."

"If you insist." The bitch actually shrugs, then gives my dick another lingering swab with her tongue.

"I mean it," I growl.

"I'm going to blow your fucking brains out." I cram the muzzle against the top of her head, but she looks at me with impish delight.

"No, Diego. I'm going to blow *your* brains out." With that she takes my cock in her mouth and inhales it all the way to the base. Nobody's ever been able to deep throat me before, and the subtle, sloppy gagging sounds as she works me make my head spin.

Somehow I manage to keep the muzzle of my gun in place as she slathers me with her tongue. When she can't take anymore she releases me, gulping in air as strands of saliva stretch from her puffy lips to my cock.

"Jesus Christ, Diego," she pants. "You're so *big*." And she takes me down her throat again. I lean back against the door, groaning as she sucks the orgasm closer and closer to the pulsing head of my dick. The nearer I get to bursting, the more I wonder if I'm really going to go through with it. Once I've painted her tonsils with cum, am I going to paint the floor with her brains?

It seems impossible when she's got me dizzy with pleasure like this. To murder a woman this skilled with her tongue would be a crime.

But that same tongue, that *lying* tongue is why I have no choice.

I have no choice.

I shouldn't come, but I have no choice.

She digs her nails into my legs and drags me from her throat, licking like crazy all the way to the tip.

"Fuck," I groan, letting loose and filling her mouth. She chokes with the first spurt, which only makes me come harder. A blinding tremor rockets through me as I release jets of hot cum. Just as everything reaches its peak, a sharp pain in my thigh cuts through the ecstasy.

Forcing my eyes open, I see Lydia's luminous eyes alight

with victory. She's jabbed something into my leg, and the edges of my vision grow murky as my limbs get stiff. The last thing I see is Lydia waving at me with sticky fingertips.

"Nighty night!"

CHAPTER
TWENTY-FIVE

LYDIA

I f I were anywhere but on a mission, I'd adore an evening like this. A cool breeze wafts in from the east with just a hint of the sea. If I close my eyes, it's almost like being back home.

"My, my. Don't you look enchanting, my diamond?" Jacinto's hands brush over my shoulders, and he plants a kiss on the side of my neck.

"Do I?"

Of fucking course I do. It's my job on an operation like this.

"Enchanting," he whispers, kissing me again. Jacinto's not the only one who thinks so. Plenty of people here are getting an eyeful, and judging from the way all these cartel honchos are licking their chops, I must look like a steak dinner.

I have to admit, Jacinto outdid himself in gifting me this evening's gown. Sleek and midnight blue, with just enough sparkle to turn me into a starlit sky. Cut all the way up to my hip on one side, so underwear is out of the question. A scoop neck gives everyone a solid view of my two scoops, and these jackals are helping themselves.

"Alana, have I introduced you to Don Barrera?" Jacinto spins me like a ballerina, and I get a good look at the face that goes with the voice I've been eavesdropping on.

"Enchanted." I extend my hand to him, and he bows low to kiss it. He's better looking than I expected. Hair just starting to silver, and only a little stout in a richly tailored burgundy suit. Startling blue eyes stand out in such dark company, and I search them for traces of suspicion.

"Easy, my friend," Jacinto chuckles, plucking my hand from Don Barrera's when he deems we've held on too long.

"Forgive me, Jacinto. I was bewitched by your paramour. She's..." He gives me a leisurely once over. "Delicious."

"That she is." Jacinto raises my hand to kiss the inside of my wrist. I let fly with a tinkling laugh and bat at his lapel.

"Stop it, that tickles. Now, Don Barrera—"

"Manuel, please." Everyone around here has bedroom eyes to beat the band.

"Alright, *Manuel*, how long have you and Jacinto been friends?"

"*Friends*?" Jacinto laughs so hard he almost drops his cigar, but succeeds in spilling his drink. "I wouldn't call us friends, would you, Manuel?" He slings his arm around Don Barrera's shoulder, pulling him into an awkward squeeze.

"Would associates be more appropriate?" Manuel asks gamely.

"Rivals," Jacinto exclaims. "Alana, when I was a boy, Don Barrera controlled not just this region, but whole swaths of the gulf coast. But my father was not the visionary I am. He was content in second place, but me?" His smile turns deadly and he blows a slow puff of cigar smoke directly in Barrera's face. "I'm second to none."

The air goes tight as a fiddle string, and for a second I swear Barrera flashes his teeth. I shatter the tension with another laugh, turning up the dial on my pretend drunkenness.

"Oh, Jacinto, you're *terrible*." Then a wink to Don Barrera. "Even if you are right. I can assure you, Jacinto is in a class by himself." That delights the living shit out of Jacinto, but does little to quench the bonfire raging in Barrera's icy stare. "Now, Jacinto, are you going to parade me around all night, or can I have another drink?"

"My pleasure." He leads me away from the steaming cocaine mogul by the crook of his arm, and I survey the scene. Thanks to the peacock beside me, I've made the acquaintance of every major player in the illegal drug trade this side of Mexico City. And a fair number of diplomats as well.

There are repeat players from the other night, some paired off with other members of Jacinto's harem. Frankly, it's unnerving. There but for the grace of God and all that.

Jacinto has orchestrated a brutally fucked up look-but-don't-touch situation. Each one of the women in his harem is clad in the flimsiest gowns that leave *nothing* to the imagination. I could draw topographical maps of half their nipples, and I'm not the only one. It's an open invitation to lechery, but Christ help the man who tries to cash the check.

Just as I'm searching the crowd for signs of danger, Jacinto's eyes are keen for any man who ventures upon his property.

"Urbina!" Jacinto snaps his fingers at the man behind the bar. "Would you please make Alana another drink?"

"Oh." I frown. "Your cousin usually makes my drinks—he's *the best* at it. Where is he, by the way?" I get on my tiptoes and scan the room.

"Diego?" Jacinto laughs around his cigar. "The vain bastard is probably still brushing his suit. Or maybe he's found one of the hookers I brought in to work up an appetite."

"You're so bad." I swat his arm, then turn to the bartender. "Champagne." Now that I've established my distance from Diego, all is well. At least so far as Jacinto is concerned. Every chance I get, I check in between Barrera, Ortega, and Diego's father. They exchange grim looks, but nobody's making a move.

They can't without their leader. And he's indisposed. Ortega makes his way over to Eduardo Alamar, and they have a hushed conversation. The kind where they're smiling just a little too much to try and look innocent.

I call that blood in the water. If only I could get close enough to sneak Nine's microphone onto one of them. It would be a shame to lose the roster of names I've racked up so far this evening, but at this juncture I'd trade that record to know what the conspirators are up to.

"Excuse me my darling," I say to Jacinto once my champagne arrives. "I'm going to swing by the buffet and have a nibble."

"Enjoy." He's set his sights on a politician who came all the way from Ciudad Victoria for tonight.

Weaving my way through the suits, I arc as close as possible to Ortega and Eduardo. Like they can feel me coming, they separate to glad hand other folks. It's worth paying special attention to who they spend their time with. I know who heads the rebellion, but have yet to learn who the allies in the room are. There are just enough winks and nods for me to get a feel for how deep this goes.

Abandoning my initial targets, I amble for the buffet, making a pit stop by a large potted succulent. That poor thing must be wasted from all the drinks I've sloshed into her urn tonight. If it doesn't smell like a distillery come morning, it's not for lack of effort on my part.

I'll say this for Jacinto, he puts out one hell of a spread. Especially if you're into nose candy. Sure, there are elegant arrays of gulf shrimp, king crab, oysters by the dozen, all sorts of exotic meats. But the *real* star of the table are crystal bowls domed with the finest cocaine Mexico has to offer.

Or so I'm led to believe. We've yet to hit the part of Training Day where I have to do a bump to prove my bona fides.

Nobody else has such scruples. Never in my life have I seen so many black tuxedo fronts dusted white. It looks like a powdered donut factory, with an added side of bloodshot eyes and general hysteria.

"Excuse me." A timid voice behind me catches me by surprise, and I paste on a radiant smile to turn and greet it.

"Yes?"

It's one of Jacinto's women. Slender and pale, with large, inquisitive eyes. There's something so meek about her, I wonder how she got swept up into this world in the first place. But then, she's exactly the type of flower Jacinto loves to crush.

She bites her lips, looking both ways as if afraid of being seen speaking to another woman, let alone me. Time to get in the driver's seat.

"I'm sorry, I don't think we've met." I offer my hand. "I'm Alana."

"Ines." The girl damn near curtsies. Again we lapse into silence.

"Was there something you wanted?"

Another stolen glance around, then she leans close.

"Can I speak to you?"

"Of course."

She turns abruptly and heads for the far end of the courtyard, not once looking back to see if I'm following. Everything about her is so furtive, so mysterious I almost wonder if she's another double agent. Someone who slipped in here before me and found herself trapped.

It's a chilling prospect. One I'd fear for myself if I wasn't so ready to blast my way out of here in a hail of explosions and bullets.

Once we're in the shadows, Ines faces me dead on.

"I'm supposed to give you this." She presses a slip of paper into my hand, drawing away as if touching me burns. Those luminous eyes watch me with nervous intensity. I unfold the paper and almost drop it when I see the message inside.

"Watch your step."

"Who gave you this," I hiss. She goes all frightened field mouse, shrinking away.

"Don't ask."

"I have to know."

Her shell cracks and a sheen of tears clouds her.

"Please don't make me say. He said he would kill me if I told you." I advance a step and she cowers from my touch. She turns to flee, then takes one last glance over her shoulder. "Just be careful." And she scampers into the shadows.

My palms sweat as I look at the note again.

"Watch your step."

I have to get rid of this. I can't drop it for fear it would fall into the wrong hands, and needless to say, whoever made my slinky dress forgot to include pockets. With no other options, I take the only route available.

I roll the note into a ball, pray it's not written in poisoned ink, and down the hatch. Lukewarm drops of champagne chase the prickly nugget to my stomach for safe keeping. Then it's roll my shoulders back, toss my hair, and head back into the fray.

A glittering smile, generous laughter, and a swing in my hips. But my eyes are lasers.

I've searched this crowd twenty times over since setting foot on the veranda, but now I scour it with fatal attention. Laughing faces take on a fresh malevolence, and the fever pitch of coke fueled revelry grates beyond measure.

Just what sort of boiling water am I in?

Has Diego revealed my true identity to anyone? Or has someone discovered our affair? With the number of cameras in this place, it's not impossible someone has been getting their jollies watching Diego and I rut like spring pigs.

Or maybe it's just my proximity that puts me in danger. Jacinto Osorio is a dangerous man in the best of times, and whether he knows it or not, these times are far from his best. The man has a king sized target on his broad shoulders, and a girl like me could get caught in the crossfire.

At one side of the crowd, I lock eyes with Don Barrera. He stares at me with preternatural stillness, smoke from his cigar curling around his head. Even at this distance, those piercing blue eyes glitter like a snake.

I smile broadly and lift my empty glass, but he remains unmoved. Suddenly, a real drink becomes a brass tacks imperative and I slink towards the bar. Along the way, I catch sight of Ortega. His stony attention is no less unsettling than his compatriot. Tiny eyes bore into me over the thick pouches that adorn his craggy face.

Eduardo is with him, every bit as stoic. His perpetual frown deeper somehow. They're watching me, alright. I slowly realize everyone is. Whether dead on or from the tail of their eye, every single person is tracking me.

None more rapaciously than the man whose bed I share. By the time I reach the bar, I'm in a full cold sweat.

"Can I help you, miss?"

"Whiskey."

Urbina nods and fetches a glass.

"Is there a particular label the lady prefers?"

I burn him to the ground with my eyes.

"Whiskey."

"As you wish." He pours me a glass and sets it on the marble bar in front of me. I tell him without words that he needs to double up. When he takes the bottle away again, the glass has a goddamn liquor meniscus on the top.

Just what the doctor ordered.

I knock it back so fast Urbina's eyebrows kick his hairline.

"Woah," he gasps before he can catch himself, then recovers with a suave smile. "Thirsty?"

"Parched." I thump the glass with my fingertip and he splashes out another generous round.

"My diamond." Jacinto's voice runs up my back like a spider, immediately followed by his broad, rough hand.

"There you are!" I fling my arms around him. "I've been looking for you everywhere." As if anybody could miss the braying, white suited Napoleon. He puts his lips to the shell of my ear.

"I've been watching you." I stifle the convulsive shudder. "Everyone has. And do you know what they're saying?" My heart is ready to bust out of my chest and make a break for it.

"No," I reply with my best coy smile, taking a demure sip of top shelf bourbon.

"They're all asking how I could get so lucky to have found a woman like you." He takes a handful of my ass, squeezing tightly.

Thank Christ.

"Well, they could say the same thing for me about you." I dab my finger between his pecs, toying with the tiny golden pendant in the thicket of his chest hair. Jacinto's lips part, and his face washes with animal desire.

"Let's go."

"Now?" I toss back my head and laugh, then kiss his cheek. "You were so excited about this party. It would be a shame for the host to leave his guests all alone."

"True. But…" He takes my hand and puts it on the front of his pants, pressing his thick, rooty cock into my grip as he buries his face in my hair. "This won't take long."

Oh, I'm well aware.

Still, there's no getting out of this one. Resigned, I slip my hand off the prick's prick and lay it on his arm.

"In that case, lead the way, tiger."

A new swagger in his step, Jacinto makes sure everyone watches as he leads me into the house. He wants everyone to know what's about to happen, and the bastards almost applaud. For my part, I'm just relieved to get away from the crowd, regardless of how steep the price tag. We ascend the steps, dark eyes trailing my every move.

CHAPTER
TWENTY-SIX

<u>*DIEGO*</u>

She's not going to get away with this!

I should have seen this double cross coming. Who am I kidding? I one-hundred-percent *knew* she was going to betray me at some point. The fact that I laid back and blabbed all my shit just goes to show how my cockiness bites me in the ass.

This is what I get for thinking with my dick.

I saw her pack when she came in, and I knew the kind of shit she keeps in it. At least she had the decency not to zip tie my wrists as tight as she did her own. Mine's gonna leave a mark, but mostly from how hard I've been straining to try and snap it. Tough to get good leverage behind your back.

I don't even know whose fucking closet I'm in. Not mine. That would be too convenient. And it would be a hell of a lot easier to get dressed once I finally get my hands free.

Of course the bitch kept me naked. Insult to injury.

I'll give Lydia one thing, she's a goddamn pro. She taped

my hands into fists so I don't have my fingers free to get at the tape around my ankles.

This is some end-game shit. Because she'd damn well better be gone when I get out of here. I'll flay her alive for this and let the whole world watch.

"Diego?"

Holy shit, it's my father.

He's maybe a few doors down, but he's looking for me.

The way I'm crammed in it's hard to get a lot of leverage, but I writhe like a snake and scream through my gag. Anything to get his attention.

"Diego?"

I'm thrashing so hard when he opens the door, I almost knock him over. Having my dad see me hogtied with my cock out isn't my proudest moment, but I've got other shit to focus right now.

"Oh, my God," dad gasps. "Who did this to you?"

"*I can't answer you with this gag in my fucking mouth,*" I shout through slobbery socks. Dad peels the tape free so I can cough the whole sopping mess onto the floor.

"Lydia fucking Slick, that's who," I roar, working my aching jaw muscles.

"Who?"

"Just get my goddamn hands free!"

Dad snaps out his pocket knife and cuts the tie. Nice as it is to have my arms loose, my hands are still useless as fuck. I hold one out so dad can start peeling back the tape.

"Jesus," he mutters. "Whoever did this knew what he was doing."

"She," I grunt.

"What? A woman did this?"

"I just said," I howl. "And she didn't know what she was doing at all. She left me alive. When I get a hold of her, I'll put a bullet in her brain like I should have this morning."

"Diego, what are you talking about?"

He's got one of my hands free and I scrub it over my face, then stretch my fingers to get the blood flowing again.

"It's that woman—Jacinto's whore."

"Alana?"

"*Alana?*" I snort and get to work on my other hand. "Bullshit. Her name's Lydia Slick. She's a goddamn spy."

"*What?*" Dad's mouth falls open and his eyes almost pop out of his skull.

"That's right. She was sent down here by GSIA to blow up our whole operation. Her mission was to seduce Jacinto, strip whatever information she could find, and relay it all back to headquarters."

"God."

"Yeah." I shake my head with a malicious grin. "And Jacinto was dumb enough to fall for it."

"It looks like Jacinto isn't the only one." A new glint of disapproval sneaks into his eye as he looks at me. There's no hiding the scratches Lydia left all over my body. She's very diligent when it comes to marking her territory.

"What?" I try to bluff it out. "You don't think *I* would get mixed up in something like this?"

He raises an eyebrow and looks me over.

"So, did she scratch your back after she tied you up?"

"Look," I grumble, getting creakily to my feet. "Can we do this later? What time is it?"

"We will do this now!" My father can be awful commanding when he wants to be. "How did she get close enough to tie you up? *Naked?*"

"Fuck." I pinch the bridge of my nose with one hand and cover my balls with the other. "How do you think?"

"Diego." The man knows how to pack an astonishing amount of shame into my name, and it's like I'm a two year old with shitty britches all over again. "You've been sleeping with that woman?"

"Yes."

"Behind Jacinto's back?"

"Keep your voice down," I hiss. "Do you want the whole place to hear you?" A flicker of incandescent rage flashes across his face, but at least he drops his voice.

"You know how volatile your cousin is, and you do something like this?"

"I was seduced."

Boy, he doesn't like that. Dad bares his teeth like he wants to take a bite out of me.

"How long?"

"How long have we been fucking?"

"How long have you *known*," he spits. "That she was a spy?" It's a gut punch of a question, and I know it's gonna get ugly.

"Before she even set foot in Mexico."

My ears are ringing before I even realize I've been slapped. My numb cheek screams to life with a million pin pricks of pain, and I have to check my animal instinct to retaliate.

I deserved that.

When I meet my father's face again, it's turned to granite.

"Diego." His voice is bloody and fierce. "You knew this woman was sent to infiltrate the cartel, and not only are you having an affair with her, but you kept it a secret from us? From *me*?" Pure, cast iron disgust hardens his features.

"I thought I could handle it."

He slaps me again. This time the shame hurts more than the strike.

"Can I at least get dressed if you're going to keep smacking me around?"

"Unbelievable," he scoffs. I turn back to the closet and find a pair of trousers and a shirt. Every joint hurts from being bound and squished into a closet. Not only that, but there's a huge purple bruise on my leg from where she stabbed me with... whatever the fuck that was.

I still have no idea how long I've been out, but when I came to it was clear she'd really done a number on me. Finally dressed, I look to find my dad staring at the floor with his hands on his hips.

After the warning he gave me over the meeting with the Texan, I can feel his misgivings rolling off him like smoke. He's been the hardest one to win over with this whole enterprise, and shit like this isn't doing me any favors to keep him in the game. Without him, our coup loses a key pillar. Someone who has been with the Osorio Cartel since the beginning.

"Listen, Dad…"

"This is poor judgement, Diego." His voice is flat, and he keeps his eyes down. "Foolishness even beyond your cousin. This behavior is reckless, shortsighted, selfish—and you expect me to back you for a takeover?"

"I'll handle it," I snap back. Now that I'm not balls to the wind, I master myself. Dad's not buying it. He pulls his lips tight and exhales hard through his nose.

"Will you?" He finally looks at me, doubt tempering his anger. "Because it looks to me like you've been playing with fire."

"Not anymore. There's fire, alright, but I'm not playing anymore. Where is he?"

"Jacinto?"

"Yes. Is the party still happening? We can do this right now. Topple him and take her out at the same time. This shit ends tonight."

"The party is still going, but Jacinto isn't there. He and that woman left not long ago. That's why I was able to come looking for you. People have noticed your absence."

"Jacinto and Lydia left?"

"Yes."

"Perfect." If Jacinto and Lydia aren't at the party, then I

know right where they are. I make for the door so fast my bare feet squeak on the tile.

"Where are you going?" Dad asks, hot on my heels.

"To finish this." Storming down the hallway, my mind reels with fantasies of plugging them both with one bullet. Or maybe I'll start by exposing her. Tell him just who and what she is and let him rip her to pieces with his bare hands. Beat her to death with her own limbs. It's better than she deserves.

Then when he goes to the party in blood soaked triumph, cut him down.

I get to the door, and it's no secret what's happening in there. The way she's hollering, it's like she wants the whole world to know.

Even if it's obviously fake, the sound of her moaning inflames me even more. To think that the last man to have her won't have been me twists my stomach into barbed wire knots.

Squaring off against the door, I rear back to kick it to splinters. But before I can let loose, Dad gets in the way. He grips the door jamb and glares at me, daring me to kick a hole in him.

"Get out of the way," I growl.

"You can't do this."

"The hell I can't!"

"*Stop shouting!*"

I grit my teeth to bellow back, but another operatic cry from Lydia steals my voice.

"This will only bring disaster," he says. "Whatever you do."

"I'm going to expose her," I hiss.

"And she could do the same to you! How do you think your cousin would react to know you've been fucking his woman? You saw the display in the courtyard. You might win out over her, but I can promise you the victory would be *short lived*." That pulls me up short. Because he's exactly right.

"What do you suggest?"

"Get properly dressed and go to the party. Let's hope Jacinto comes back down when he's through with her. If not, we'll call a meeting."

"Oh, Jacinto," Lydia wails through the door. "You're gonna make me come!" It's enough to make me want to kick the whole house down, not just the door. Carve a path of destruction so wide and so total that nothing's left.

But Dad fixes me with his gaze and gives the smallest shake of his head.

"Fine," I bite out. Turning before I can change my mind, I stomp off for my room. With every step, my heart hardens. Lydia may be safe for now, but the day is fast approaching when I'm going to slit her throat.

And when I do, I want her looking in my face so she knows it was me.

CHAPTER
TWENTY-SEVEN

Everything hurts.

I pant at the ceiling, covered in sweat, trying to get my heart rate back down. My mouth is dry, and I'm so wrung out you'd think I'd been running for my life instead of having sex with a drug lord.

Sex isn't even the word.

Jacinto brutalized me.

I've never been fucked so hard in my entire life—and not in a good way. That man fucked me like I was an object. Like he didn't give a damn whether I lived or died.

Which, of course, he didn't.

The worst part?

I came.

Like, repeatedly.

Jacinto forced orgasms out of me like squeezing an orange, and now I see more plainly than ever it's just a matter of time before he throws away the rind.

And the fucker is _whistling_.

"Still tired, my diamond?" He swaggers over to leer down at me, demonically proud of how hard it is for me to put the pieces back together. Somehow I force a sexy smile.

"Reveling in the afterglow." I stretch my arms and writhe among the sheets, and his lascivious gaze deepens.

"It doesn't have to be *over*..." He stops midway through fastening a cuff link, but the last thing I want is another round.

"Later," I whisper with just enough heat to make his pants bulge. "We should get back out there." Rolling over to hide my tits only earns me a stinging smack on the ass.

"We should. Get dressed."

The stunning dress he bought for me is in tatters, so I brave his boiling eyes to saunter over to the closet. It's crammed with gowns, and I wonder about the other women he's thrown against his headboard. Now that I've seen their haggard faces, it's like they're everywhere. Fixtures at both parties, yet somehow always whispering in corners.

They all have the same broken aura around them. Used to slake Jacinto's thirst then cast aside, yet unable to leave. Prisoners of one man's penis.

I pretend my shudder is a shiver of excitement at all the drop-dead dresses I'm rifling through.

Selecting an emerald cocktail number, I slink into it, inviting him over to do me up the back. My zipper, that is.

"Don't fix your makeup." He breathes into my ear, "I want everyone to see what I did to you."

"Naughty."

I kiss his cheek instead of gnawing it off.

God, I'm going to love killing him when the time comes.

"Well." He smooths his coal dark hair to the side. "Don't take too long." One more pat on the rump and he saunters out. As soon as he's gone my body turns to rubber. It's like someone pulls a plug out of my ass and my intestines fall all over the floor.

"Jesus fucking Christ," I wheeze. It's moments like this that remind me I'm alive. Why is it always misery and exhaustion that do that?

This little no-pants-dance may have forestalled the overthrow plot for tonight, but the clock is ticking. Especially after I jabbed Diego and put him under. We've hit the now or never moment.

Rooting out my phone, I text Zero.

> We need to blow this place now. Things are getting out of control.

It's first thing in the morning in London, and Zero answers like the crack of a gun.

> Negative. Stay the course.

You've got to be fucking kidding me.
There's only so much more of this I can take.

> Things are at an inflection point. Unclear how much longer I can maintain.

Which is putting it Pace Picante Mild when things are actually ghost pepper hot.

> Didn't Diego Alamar's phone rip give us what we need?

> It has opened enough doors for us to see the end of the corridor. But they don't do us any good until we know who's in the locked rooms. The names Jacinto is keeping back. Without them the operation is essentially a failure.

My heart shrivels into a frozen knot.

Even if everyone else goes down?

Yes.

Well, that does it. I'm here until I can get that intel. And the sooner I can fuck it out of Jacinto, the sooner I'm back on my speedboat.

On it.

Which, of course, is the answer she wants.

I stuff my phone in my bag and square myself to the task ahead. Now that I've blown things up with Diego, there's no going back. Even if I can't light the match yet, I can get a lot looser with my info gathering tactics.

Because when Diego's free again, the jig is up.

Shit, I'm tempted to use one of Nine's pellets to blow Jacinto's safe right now. But with the place packed to the gills with coke barons, I'd be full of holes before I could rip the damn phone, let alone forward the files.

Besides, an order's an order.

No, I've got to go down to the party and play nice. Kiss the hands, shake the babies, and memorize every name I come across just in case it's the one that buys my plane ticket.

My hand is on the door knob when a shiver rattles my vertebrae. The fact that he specifically mentioned my makeup gives me the bubble guts. After the Sherman's March of a fuck I just got, I can only imagine the devastation.

When I see myself in the bathroom mirror, I'm such a catastrophe I can barely meet my own eyes. Eyeliner and mascara streak down my cheeks and over my temples. My hair is a positive possum's nest, and my lipstick is everywhere but my lips. It's in full-on Mommy Dearest mode, with Jacinto's mouth prints running down my cheek and all over my neck.

All I can think is how ready I am to paint his throat red. No doubt he'll love his crimson collar every bit as much as I do the one I'm wearing right now.

Forcing all my contempt into the iron box in my stomach, I head back down to the party. As soon as I hit the top of the patio steps there's a goddamn ovation. My blood turns to tar. All eyes are on me, and one pair cuts through the throng blacker than the rest.

Diego.

Fuck.

He's impeccably dressed, which is definitely not how I left him. Deep red lines hide behind his French cuffs, and he chews bile in his mouth like he could spit poisoned darts into the flagstones.

For one bone chilling moment there's no one in the world but us. An eternal universe filled with nothing but barefaced hatred. Then I blink and realize we're not alone. Diego's father is at his side, lip curled in fathomless contempt. Ortega flanks him, his handlebar mustache deepening his scowl. Don Manuel Barrera glares as well, registering who and what I am for the first time.

The word has spread, and my fingers instinctively flit for the stiletto strapped to my thigh. Zero may not want shit to go down tonight, but Zero ain't here. Even she would have to admit an incomplete mission is better than a dead operative, so I steel myself to carve my way out of here if that's what it takes.

And at the center of this family portrait of conspiracy is the object of their revulsion. Jacinto beams up at me with ignorant delight, blissfully unaware of the daggers aimed at his back.

"See," he cries. "What did I tell you?" Throaty chuckles spill in from every side, and I wonder why I bothered getting dressed at all. Everyone's so busy stripping me in their mind's eye, I should have pulled a Lady Godiva and saved them all the trouble.

Jacinto has Diego's neck in the crook of his elbow, jostling him with locker room exaltation. Diego laughs with him, but his mouth is full of butcher knives.

"What are you boys talking about?" I say as I glide up to them. Time to play coy enough to be sexy, and dumb enough not to sniff the gunpowder at my feet.

"Everyone knows where *I've* been," Jacinto smirks. "But Diego here? My cousin is being far more cryptic about why he's late to the party."

"Interesting, isn't it?" Diego stares through me. He hasn't blinked since we locked eyes. "What do you say, *Alana*? Shall I tell him where I've been?"

"Please," I reply with a twinkling smile. "I'm so curious what could keep anyone away from an event like this."

Eduardo's fists are clenched so tight the veins in the back of his hands look ready to pop. He knows what I did to his son alright. And I'd bet my body weight in pesos he knows what his son has been doing to me.

After a long beat, Diego licks his lips and curls them back into a sneering smile. I ball up the hip of my dress in my fingers, ready to hike it up and bury my blade in every chest I can reach.

"Let's just say I overslept," Diego says at last.

A reprieve. Unfortunately, in my line of work, I know an inch of rope now means a tight noose down the road.

"Overslept?" Jacinto cackles like crazy, but the others remain stone faced. "Do you hear that, Alana? My cousin is being shy, but I know him." He claps his hand on Diego's neck. "If all of my women hadn't been out here all night, I'd think you were playing with one of them instead of joining us."

"You know I'd never do that to you." Diego's voice is low

and flat, his eyes never leaving my face. "Betrayal of that kind is unforgivable."

Not only is the bridge burned, but the whole river is on fire. I'm on my own now. Which, thankfully, is how I like to work. No alliances means no compromises. It doesn't matter who I hurt now—all the real damage has been done.

Unfortunately, that also means there's nothing to stop their secret schemes from coming to a head. Treachery is ripe for the plucking, and Jacinto is the sweetest berry on the tree.

"A toast," Eduardo says as a tray of glasses skates past. They equip themselves with drinks, and as Don Barrera passes one to Jacinto I swear it glows. "To loyalty."

"I love it!" Jacinto raises the radioactive glass, balls-out unaware of the shark tank he's swimming in.

"To loyalty," they all proclaim, but before Jacinto can take a sip I lift the glass from his fingers.

"Thank goodness. I'm so parched." I place a hand on the astonished Jacinto's lapel and take a sip while the others glare. "After what *you* just put me through…" I give Jacinto a wink that dissolves any ire. "I'm more than ready for a drink."

"Do you hear that?" He tips his head back and laughs while my tongue does an inventory on the glass before swallowing. No trace of poison. At least none I know, and I've got a palate for them all.

Now that it's established, I lift the glass to Jacinto's lips, tipping it back so the liquor spills down his face and onto his clothes. Jacinto burbles with hedonistic delight, and the conspirators scald me with furious eyes. If nothing else, I've told them just how far I'm ready to go to keep things as they are.

If I'm willing to take a mouthful of poison to keep their quarry alive, their plans for the night are well and truly fucked. They know exactly how things are going to go tonight, and there's not a damn thing they can do about it.

"Jacinto," I coo, snaking my arm through his. "Weren't there people you wanted to introduce me to?"

"Of course." He nibbles my neck and I lock eyes with Diego.

How do you like it?

Open warfare now, motherfucker.

Jacinto steers me away, and I scan the crowd with keen attention. I know the cabal of four, but how deep the roots go is still a mystery. Every hand Jacinto shakes could be holding a knife, and I'm ready to crack knuckles.

The whole place turns into a snake pit and I realize the only safe place in the whole compound is between my legs. Locked safely in his room, I can defend Jacinto against an army if I need to. As long as his skull contains the info I need to get out of here, his head is staying right where it is.

"Lover," I whisper hot and husky into his ear. "Do we really have to stay down here when there's a comfortable bed upstairs? This is all so *boring* after what you did to me." My words catch in his chest like a grappling hook and those pointed eyebrows knit together.

"My diamond…" He fetches a kiss across my knuckles. "A bed is the only throne for a queen like you."

We sweep up the stairs with a flourish, and he spins to present me in triumph to his toadies.

"My friends! Much as I would love to spend my evening with you, my little kitten is just *insatiable*." Lewd laughter oozes from the crowd as a hundred eyes rake over me. Not that I give a damn. I'm resolved to fuck him so good he passes out for three days. Maybe by then I'll have gotten the intel Zero needs to get me outta here.

We turn to go, and even though I can't see them, I can feel Diego's eyes burning into my spine.

Get a good look, asshole. As far as your dick is concerned, this road is closed.

CHAPTER
TWENTY-EIGHT

<u>Diego</u>

Leave it to my fucking father to crush opportunity in the shell. If he'd just let me batter down the door and start swinging, this whole thing would be over by now.

Would it have been messy? Sure. What's life without a rocky launch here and there? Nothing like a little turbulence to make you kiss the runway when you land. Dragging Jacinto's head out to a dinner party would have made a statement if nothing else.

Now it looks like the window of opportunity is painted shut, and there's no telling when we'll be able to pry the fucker open again.

And I don't just mean in public. Jacinto hasn't come out of his room for two solid days. For that matter, neither has Lydia. And I know goddamn good and well what's been keeping them so busy.

Every time I walk past they're either fucking or sleeping. When the afternoon is still, the whole house can hear them. I keep going out to the growing fields just so I don't have to hear her screaming his name at the ceiling. It burns my ass to admit it, but I hate my cousin for it. There's no doubt the sex she and I had was better, but she never got to howl like that for me.

Maybe I can make it happen after my cousin is gone. Just before I put her down for good.

Making yet another pass by their door, I spot Ortega skulking around the corner. When he sees me catch him he tries to duck back, giving clean away that he's been spying.

For a head of security, Lope Ortega is about as subtle as a kick in the teeth. But then, he's not paid to eavesdrop. His checks are cut for his bloody knuckles and ruthless nature. All Rottweiler and no puma.

It's why Jacinto keeps him so close—they're cut from the same cloth. Graceless, shallow-skulled killers. Both have their talents, but neither of them are winning any prizes in the brains department.

"You know I can see you, right?"

"Okay." Ortega steps out into the open. "You got me. But it's not what it looks like."

"Really? Because it looks like you're spying on me." Those heavy eyes flicker and it's clear he's been caught.

"Your father told me to." A resentful sizzle races up my backbone.

"Oh, did he?"

"Don Barrera too. Eduardo told us how close you came to blowing this whole thing the other night. We can't have you busting in on them just because you're scared your cousin is better in the sack than you are."

"The fuck is that supposed to mean?" I storm over, struggling to keep my voice down so Jacinto can't hear me over Lydia's wailing. Ortega instinctively takes a step back and puts up his hands. He's a scrapper from way back, but I'm a solid thirty years younger. His right hook is no joke, but I'd have him on the floor before he could lock and load.

"I'm just saying you're letting your prick cloud your judgement. Listen to that, man." He cocks his head to the side and we both stand in silence as Jacinto grunts his way closer to a nut. "Really listen. *That's* what she's here for. Not you."

"She's here to bring us all down!"

"Maybe. So far the only person she's brought down is you." Leveling a stout finger in my face, his words hit home. "Do you know how much shame you brought on your father being found like that? He said you were trussed up like a pig, your dick out and everything."

"Don't remind me."

"Somebody has to! Because if you let your pride get in the way, all of this is fucked."

He's got a point. Standing there while my father caught Ortega and Barrera up to speed was the most humiliating moment of my life. They don't need to know how foolish I was over some piece of tail.

And then I had to stand next to them when she came back out to the party looking like a freshly fucked ten peso whore —which is exactly what she is. These men put their trust in me, and they got a good look at what I was willing to risk it all for. Don't misunderstand, every one of them would have cut off his little finger for a shot with her, but that didn't make it any easier.

"Yeah, well..." A shudder runs over me as my cousin's groans rattle through the hallway. "Fuck it. I'm getting out of here."

"Where are you going?" he calls as I brush past him.

"To talk to the Americans. Somebody's got to worry about this shipment. Jacinto can stay balls deep all he wants. I'm getting this shipment moving come hell or high water!" It may be bravado, but I hope that sunburnt cockroach scuttles back to my dad and Don Barrera with the news.

I may have missed a few steps, but my eyes are still on the prize.

Climbing in the jeep, I zigzag to the front gate and set off for the coast. Along the way I dial up Larry Myer to see what's moving.

The son of a bitch lets me go to voicemail. Gritting my teeth, I call again immediately. I don't give a damn if the son of a bitch is in church, he's picking up my call. Nobody ignores Diego Alamar.

"What do you want?" The irritation in his voice riles me right the fuck up.

"It's not about what I want, *asshole*. It's about what you don't want."

"Meaning?"

"I don't know if you've forgotten, *Representative Myer*," I throw his title in his face. "But we've got a hefty shipment of contraband down here, and a long history of payloads just like it. If we don't get shit moving soon, an anonymous source might just start feeding names to the media."

There's a long silence.

"You're bluffing," he says at last.

"Try me."

"Diego, you and I both know half the news desks in Texas are getting a cut."

"And imagine how happy they'll be to get an even bigger cut, and the pleasure of a media blitz when a whole bunch of politicians get their cover blown." I'm breaking all kinds of rules, but fuck it. I'm tired of riding back seat, and putting the screws to some cowardly, limp-dicked rich guy feels awful sweet.

When he speaks again, it's nearly a whisper.

"We're working on it."

It dawns on me why he didn't pick up right away. They're getting into primary season and his smarmy face has been all over TV. I probably spooked the dumb bastard out of a makeup chair.

"Not fast enough," I snarl, delighted to imagine him

quaking in his ostrich skin boots. "Just because you and your cronies are content to leave money on the table doesn't mean production has stopped. Run it up the chain that if we can pull this cork, we're looking at a shipment and a half."

I can hear the cash register ring in his skull.

"Say that again."

"Larry." I lean over the phone, pulling to a stop at the edge of the beach. "Say the word and we'll have a metric goddamn *ton* of narcotics ready to melt into greenback dollars. Call whoever you need to, but this shit needs to move."

"What about Jacinto?"

"If he's still breathing by breakfast on Sunday, I'll give you my personal cut. That's a promise."

The guy licks his lips so hard I'm surprised his tongue doesn't come through the phone to tickle my ear.

"Let me see what I can do."

"Make it happen." I end the call and my breath is high. This is exactly the kind of thing my dad gets furious about, and with good reason. Shooting from the hip like this is dangerous as hell, but I'm in a reckless mood.

Besides, all this product doesn't mean shit if it just sits by the coast getting dusty.

There's a wooden plank shack on the dunes, the sounds of cheap porn echoing up the shoreline to me. I head straight over, stopping in the doorway to look over Ciges' shoulder at the heavy bosomed Latina getting nailed.

"Nice."

Ciges' phone flies out of his hand and he sputters around in his chair. His chub is obvious, but at least it's still in his pants.

"Diego," he gasps. "What are you doing here? Nobody radioed."

"Just checking on you," I smirk. "Good to see you're *hard* at work."

"What the hell am I supposed to do?" He frowns, picking up his phone and wiping the sand off the flesh covered screen. "Until word comes to load up and move out, I'm out here twiddling my thumbs."

"Twiddling something." He shoots me another shame-faced look and shuts the video off. "Listen," I say. "Get the team together and load."

"*Now?*"

"That's right. And not just the scheduled shipment. I want everything that's ready for packaging on these boats. Anything that doesn't fit can go in the autos to drive over the border."

"Yeah?" Suspicion plays on his features and he shies away from me. "Do you know something I don't?"

"Ciges." I put a hand on his shoulder. "I know so many things you don't, it's a wonder we're the same species. Now, get the word out. I just talked to one of our US contacts, and I expect things to open up again by noon tomorrow."

"Yes, sir."

Driving back towards the compound, I can't stop myself from humming a little tune. This feels good. This is what I've been missing.

Before Lydia's pussy scrambled my brains, this was the trajectory I was on. This momentary taste of what it's like to run things only makes me hungry for more. No more of Jacinto's commands coming out of my mouth. Whatever I say goes, and it's on everyone else to get it done.

A swell of certainty expands in my chest. This is how things are supposed to go. My father's throat got stepped on so I could breathe free. And let me tell you, the air is sweet.

Skidding to a halt in the circular drive, I hop out and toss the keys to one of the security men.

"Park it." He looks at me with his chin on his chest, but does as he's told. It's sublime to give orders instead of taking them. No wonder my cousin lost his head. This kind of power is intoxicating.

But there's one big difference between us.

My mother's son has a brain. So what if my dad and the others don't see the future the way I do? They're playing checkers, and I'm not even playing chess. It's all Monopoly for me. And I don't just own every square on the board, I own the bank.

Hell, when this shit is all over, I'll be the one printing the money.

CHAPTER
TWENTY-NINE

LYDIA

After three days on me, under me, or unconscious, Jacinto has decided it's time to rejoin the outside world. My legs are jelly, and that's saying something coming from someone who free dives at least two hours a day when she's home.

Kicking under the Adriatic is child's play next to trying to get a stubborn bull like Jacinto to come for the billionth time in a row. Seriously, I was astonished how fierce he was for having only plowed me twice, but he's been making up for lost time.

Keeping him in here has been tactical protection, but he should be good to patrol the grounds for a bit. I'd be lying if I said I'm not breathing easier with a few moments to myself.

A hot shower helps me scrub away the aches, along with all kinds of crusty reminders of his dedicated attention. It's a miracle the guy isn't completely dehydrated. All he drinks is liquor, and it all pours out of him in sweat and ejaculate. By last night, his dick was dry heaving at my tits. So, you take the blessings where you can get them.

Between fragments of sleep I've been able to keep Zero up to date. Even she's getting antsy for this whole thing to be over. Glad I'm not alone in that.

Toweling off, I tiptoe back into the room half expecting to find Diego. He's not shy about inviting himself into Jacinto's room, and we've got a score to settle. No doubt he's driven himself crazy listening at the door. Between jealousy and vengeance, his brains should be so fried I could take him out in a heartbeat.

One thing I've learned in this business—these guys love to get the last word. He'll launch into some tirade, and I'll pitch him over the balcony.

Strange as it is, I get no joy out of imagining his head cracking on the paving stones. We had some good times— some *very* good times—but dealing death is my business. And baby, business is about to be *booming*.

Literally.

My phone buzzes on the nightstand just as I'm slipping into a tank top, and a heavy breath falls out of me.

"Calm your tits, Zero," I grumble. "There's nothing to report."

But it's not Zero at all. Sir John's name gazes up at me from the lock screen, bringing a tearful smile to my face.

My port in any storm.

Worrying over you.

Three simple words rob me of my knees, and I plump down on the edge of the bed. I know I shouldn't but my thumbs type out my forbidden request anyway. Stolen moments are all we have, and I've more than earned one.

Time for a chat?

The message barely goes through before the phone rings.

"Hello?"

"Hullo, darlin'," he drawls. That voice pours into my chest, warm honey soothing. "How you making out?"

"Ugh. If only it was *just* making out."

"Turning into a chore, is it?"

"You could say that." I flick some cigar ash off the sheets and onto the lion skin rug. "I don't know if Jacinto is aware how close he came to being rubbed out, but he sure has invested in living recently."

"Zero and I spoke in depth about the assassination you thwarted."

"Please tell me she's changed her mind about waiting?"

The sympathetic quiet on the other end of the line tells me everything I need to know. Sir John wants me out of here every bit as badly as I do.

"Tell you what," he says. "When you get back to London, we'll open a bottle of Chateau Lafite to wash the tequila off your tongue. How's that?"

"Yes, please," I groan. "I've had enough agave to last the rest of my life. If I never taste another drop, I'll count myself doubly blessed."

Sir John chuckles softly, and my shoulders drop.

"Where is Señor Osorio, by the way?"

"Out at the labs, I think. He's blown through his private stash, so it's time to replenish."

"He sounds delightful," Sir John says in that dry British way that makes every compliment an insult.

"You have no idea."

"Much though I hate to ask…"

"I know, I know." Scrunching my eyes shut, I pinch the bridge of my nose hard. "I should be with him."

"It wouldn't do if he caught a bullet before Zero gets her names."

"Wouldn't do for anybody." If the cabal decides to cut him

down, I'd be next in the crosshairs. Every one of them wants to put me under the ground, but I've no doubt Diego would make the trip as unpleasant as possible.

"Do me a favor, Lydia." His voice is low, and the sound of my name on his lips is so vulnerable it makes me tremble.

"Yes?"

"Come back alive."

God, I wish I could wrap my arms around him.

"Don't tell me what to do," I snip, trying to hide the tears in my throat.

"Lydia." How can he sound stern and fearful at the same time? "Please?" Water rushes to my eyes, and I clench my jaw to keep it from breaking free.

"Fine," I fake a put-upon sigh. "Just for you."

His, "Thank you," is so faint my whole body goes tight. I screw my eyes shut and clutch the phone, telling myself it's his hand.

Then something buzzes in the sheets.

My eyes snap open, every professional instinct taking over. It continues, and I dig through the cummy bedding to ferret out my prize. When my fingers finally find it, a thousand stars explode in my chest.

It's Jacinto's phone.

He left it behind.

"Son of a bitch," I whisper.

"What?" I'm too stunned to answer right away. "Lydia, what is it?"

"I just found the motherlode."

"Have you?" Hope soars in his voice, rocketing me to the moon.

"Sir John, I'll have to call you back. Tell Zero to fire up the jet."

"Gladly."

As soon as the call ends, I take a picture of Jacinto's screen.

The call is obviously coming from a code name, but that's a start.

Caviar.

Sure. Why not?

I shoot the photo to Zero and grab my bag. Nine's ripper is in it, and I clap Jacinto's phone to it and stare with my heart in my throat until the little light goes green. As soon as it does, my whole body breaks into an excited sweat.

Download initiated.

Trouble is, I don't know how long I have. If Jacinto comes back looking for his phone, I'm going to have one hell of a time explaining why it's in my kit bag.

I need to move.

Dangerous as it is to head into the open with the ripper and phone, I opt to leave my bag on the floor by the door. A clutch left behind is the international women's signal for be-right-back.

Instead, I stuff the booty in my waistband and pull on a loose top to billow around it. Then it's into the hallway to find a place to hole up until I've got everything.

Tiptoeing down the corridor hits different when there's sunlight streaming through all the windows. There's no need to sneak, right? That would just make me look guilty. So, I straighten my shoulders, adopting a languid pace as I saunter along. Anybody would think I was just another well-fucked concubine reveling in the luxury of an opioid palace.

I could stroll around like this and wait for the rip to complete, but being in the open only increases my chances of bumping into someone. Most notably Diego. No doubt he's on the prowl for me, and I'm about as red handed as they come. Ortega and Eduardo Alamar are bound to be knocking around as well—along with who knows how many security goons?

Best to find a secluded spot to hide out.

My lazy steps guide me right to the Situation Room. If Jacinto's not in there, it's an ideal spot to post up and wait.

Reaching the door, I strain my ear against it. Nothing. Taking another quick scan of the corridor—studiously avoiding looking directly at any of the cameras—I pop the door open and slip inside. It's empty, but voices waft through the open window. I inch over, keeping my face in shadow as I peer out.

It's Jacinto, along with Diego, Ortega, and a couple of Americans in well-cut suits. Even if I didn't know he was mixed up in things, I'd recognize Texas politician Larry Myer. Typical greasy fucker with a bad tan and capped teeth. A woman is with him, and even at this distance, I can see Jacinto ogling her cleavage. She's doing a heroic job of pretending not to notice.

Then Diego runs his fingers through his hair and lifts his eyes. I jolt back from the window, but can't tell whether or not I've been spotted. I'll be goddamned if I stick my nose out again to check, so there's only one option.

I've gotta bounce.

Going back to Jacinto's room is out of the question, and I steal a look at the ripper to see how things are coming along.

Less than a quarter cloned. Ditching now isn't going to do me much good. A partial rip would be better than nothing, but having this little would leave me all haystacks and no needles.

I need time.

Assuming Diego saw me, it's best to keep on the run. It's always harder to hit a moving target. I don't have to escape them, I just need to stay ahead of them. Once I have something worth sending, I can fall into their clutches all I want. A struggling captive is a great distraction while Zero and the team pick through the intel.

Back in the hallway, I do my best to keep a cool head. Stay the course and wait it out. At least that's the plan before I hear voices coming up the stairs. It's Jacinto and Diego, speaking in hushed, hurried tones.

Welp. All my studied calm goes right out the fucking window. A full-on sprint would draw the eye of every camera in the pace, so I settle for a brisk strut.

Best to look like a bad bitch on her way to the pool. If I wasn't hiding equipment I'd strip. Leave a trail of clothes like breadcrumbs, then book it bare assed in a different direction. But that's not an option.

Their voices get louder, and I can tell they're closing fast. Time to get serious.

Bolting around the corner into a corridor I haven't visited before, I break and start trying doorknobs. Something I can lock. But someone else beat me to the punch because every damn handle is a non-starter.

Which is a big problem because the hallway dead ends. The further down I move, the deeper into a pinch point I get. I've knuckled my way out of tighter spots, but I'd rather not crack heads unless it's absolutely necessary. On the other hand, if kicking the dookie out of these two men is what it takes to put a button on his mission, so fucking be it.

But then I find an unlocked room and thank my fucking stars. I'm through in a twinkling, locking myself in before I even turn around to case the joint.

When I do, I find a dozen sets of eyes leveled at me.

As luck would have it, I've stumbled into the goddamn harem. Beds line the walls, and apart from an overstuffed armoire at the far end of the room, that's it for furniture. It's a pretty spartan setup, which goes partway to explaining all the hard looks I've been catching.

"Hey," I say by way of introduction. "Um." There's no time to explain, and I doubt they'd give a damn if I tried.

Mistrust fills the room like a smoke bomb, and I get the sinking feeling I'm on my own. Every single one of these women has been in my position—the favorite. And they've all fallen from grace. The bitch of it is, they can't leave. It's a harrowing thought. Truly a fate worse than death, and I half wonder if getting caught and mutilated by Jacinto won't be the easier way out.

Among all the faces, there's only one with a trace of sympathy. The girl who snuck me the note at the party.

"Ines," I say, rushing over to her. "I need your help, and I don't have time to explain." She cowers back, and a tall, sturdily built brunette interposes.

"Leave her alone," she commands in heavily accented English. "You're not welcome here."

"Please. They're coming for me. Ines, I need to know who gave you that note." She winces away, right into the arms of one of the other girls. No allies here. Not for me, anyway.

Brushing through them, I throw open the window and look down, hoping for something to break my fall if I jumped.

All I find are paving stones and the promise of a broken ankle.

"Shit." I lift my shirt and glance down, grateful to find the rip is ninety eight percent complete. I pull out the apparatus and every eye in the place widens in shock.

"Is that Jacinto's phone," one woman asks, voice brimming with fear.

"It is," another replies. "How did you get it?"

"There isn't time. I'm—" The knob rattles, and my pulse skyrockets. I wheel around, looking for anything like a friend. Telling them who and what I am would be a colossal risk. One I can't afford right now.

A key slips into the lock and my eyes flash back down to the ripper, and the light pings off.

Rip complete.

I snatch Jacinto's phone off it just as the door swings open. Holding the phone in front of me, I tuck the ripper behind my back. Fumbling with my shirt would only draw attention, so I wind up standing like some dumb toddler with an ice cream sandwich melting down my arm.

"Alana?" Jacinto's pointed brows slam together over his nose. "What are you doing in here, my diamond?"

The air in the room changes the second he crosses the threshold. A collective sigh goes up, each woman breathing his name with blind, honeyed adoration. It's an astonishing shift, and they all advance on him, dripping with manufactured worship. For a split second, I'm grateful, then I realize they aren't protecting me. They're saving their own skins.

Diego sneers his way through the door, eyes gleaming with unholy pride.

"Jacinto." He grins. "Did you see what she has?" He points at the phone, and Jacinto's eyes widen as I press it to my chest. Confusion gives way to blistering rage. I inch backwards, hoping to at least be able to drop the ripper onto one of the beds. Anything so it can survive, even if I get the worst of things.

But a hand greets the small of my back and another plucks the ripper from my grasp. The dark flower of defeat blooms in my chest, but when I glance back, I'm greeted by Ines' large, watchful eyes. Something in them tells me she's not going to give me up.

"Alana…" My name passes like a dagger through Jacinto's clenched teeth, snapping my attention back to him. "What are you doing with that?"

"It's just like I told you." Diego's evil grin spreads faster than an oil spill. "Why don't you ask *your diamond* what her real name is?"

A blast of suspicion blows up the room, and I'm dead at the epicenter. This is it. The moment has come.

And here I am without a weapon to my name.

CHAPTER
THIRTY

<u>*Diego*</u>

Deer in the headlights doesn't even begin to describe Lydia. Besides, deer are innocent creatures and the spider in front of me is guilty as mortal sin. And I've got her right in my crosshairs.

"Real name?" My cousin flashes a glance my way, then advances on Lydia. "What's he talking about?" All the affection has drained out of his voice, leaving only blood behind. Lydia clutches his phone tighter and backs away a step. It's the retreat of the guilty, and the whole room reeks with it.

"Jacinto, what's gotten into you?"

"Answer me!" His shout peels the paint off the walls and every bitch in the joint clears away. I swear to God, Lydia trembles. She's in the hot seat now, and there's no way out.

"I told you she was deceiving you." The words taste rich on my tongue, and I pour them on thick. "Your precious *Alana* isn't what you thought she was at all. A club girl for you to dabble and play with?" I snort a laugh. "She's a GISA operative."

"GSIA," Jacinto parrots, dumbly looking back at me. It's all I can do not to roll my eyes at the stupid son of a bitch.

"Global Secret Intelligence Agency, Jacinto. She's a goddamn spy." That does the trick. Jacinto damn near doubles in size, his skin ready to split as the devil in him struggles to get free.

"A *spy*?" He spits the word between tight, furious lips. The rest of his harem quake in their nighties, wishing like hell they could all vanish in a puff of smoke. Not me, though. Having an audience to this shitshow is making my dick hard.

Well, harder.

"Watch this." I shoulder past him to tower over her. "What's your name?"

"Alana McCormick. I came to Matamoros on vacation—"

"Bullshit," I cut her off, plucking my cousin's phone from her hands. "You'd have to be some kind of party girl to hop in bed with the head of the most powerful cartel in Mexico without giving a damn about going home. Strange, isn't it?" I glance back at Jacinto. "I bet she hasn't asked once when she can head back to the states."

The drug lord's face darkens.

"Didn't think so. And what kind of club girl is so goddamn interested in the operation? She wants to see every inch of this place, and hasn't so much as asked for a bump of coke, has she?"

"No." Jacinto's in full glower, and his fists balled up into iron hammers. Lydia's in for a world of hurt.

"That's because it's not part of her core mission. She's here to fuck you so blind you can't see her learning everything about you." I toss him his phone and he catches it awkwardly. "*Everything*. Isn't that right..." I look back at her, my body vibrating with victory, "Lydia Slick?"

"A spy," Jacinto mutters, looking at his phone as he turns all this over in his pea brain. "Diego?" There's something treacherous in his voice, and when he lifts his gaze it's brimming with menace. "How long have you known this?"

Shit.

When I started this dance, I didn't expect the target to be on my back. Time to do what I do best—lie my ass off.

"I just found out." Even Lydia's jaw drops at that one. "Actually, that's why I was late to your party. A contact reached out to me saying he had urgent information. I told him I had plans, but he said it couldn't wait. Turns out he was right." Smirking at Lydia, I can't resist throwing it all in her face. "Good old Nando Rivera. I can always count on him."

Hearing a familiar name is all Jacinto needs. He rears up, ready to spit nails into the lid of Lydia's coffin.

"That's a lie," Lydia wails, somewhere between fury and despair. "Why would you tell him that? Jacinto, honey…" She reaches for him, but he evades her like her touch would scald him.

"Get away from me, you *whore*." She reels back as if struck. Hell, every girl in the room does. That's a ruthless word to throw around in a room full of women who live and die to suck his cock.

"He's lying to you," she pleads. "You have to believe me."

"Do I?" A bitter smile crosses his face. "Why? Why would my cousin lie to me?" The question hangs in the air, then she turns to me with boiling anger.

"Because he's been fucking me behind your back. And he's scared what will happen if he gets caught."

Jacinto shits his pants on the spot. Wheeling on me with a barely controlled wrath, I can tell it's all he can do not to pull me apart joint by joint.

"That's right," Lydia snarls. "Every time you weren't looking, every time you were out of the room, Diego stuffed his dick in me and made me his. And Jacinto?" She waits for his eyes, devious malice coloring her face. "He was better than you."

A fifteen megaton bomb detonates in the room. It's one of history's greatest miracles that the whole place doesn't crumble to ashes.

Jacinto raises his fists, chest heaving with scorching breaths. So I do the only thing I can think of.

I start laughing.

Cackling until I'm doubled over red in the face. Nobody moves until I'm upright again, wiping tears from my eyes.

"Diego." He's ready to combust. "*Are you laughing at me?*"

"At you?" Another fresh bray trips up my throat. "Don't be fucking stupid, Jacinto. I'm laughing at her. You don't really believe that horseshit, do you?"

He blinks like the idiot he is, looking back and forth between Lydia and I in utter confusion.

"Look at her," he stutters at last. "Look at her face. She's telling the truth."

"Oh, come on! You can't be serious?" Putting my hand on his shoulder is basically taking my life in my hands, but I've got to sell this pony. "Get a good look at her. I told you she's a spy, and she hasn't even denied it. Just started shouting all kinds of nonsense. Isn't that right?"

Lydia blanches. The machinery behind her eyes whirrs like crazy, and I can see clear as day she wishes she could go back and deny it when I spilled her identity.

Too late now, babe.

"I'm telling you, cousin." I give his shoulder an extra squeeze, shaking him slightly. "This woman lies for a living. It's not just how she butters her bread, it's how she buys it. And now that she's caught, she'll say anything to save her neck. Even something as crazy as having an affair with me. I mean, really?" I lean closer, putting my mouth right next to his ear. "Do you really think I'd do something like that to you?"

Lydia's sailing through the air before I realize he's slapped her. Jacinto breaks free from me, driving her across the room with one punishing smack after another.

And she just takes it.

The rest of the girls clear out of the way as he beats her like a rented mule, shoving her around the room with his fists. Muffled cries and grunts slip past her busted lips with each fresh blow.

None of it is enough for Jacinto.

The more he hits her, the crueler it becomes. Filth pours from his mouth, raining down on Lydia's bloodied face.

To see a woman so beautiful slick with crimson—those captivating eyes swelling shut—turns my stomach. It's better than she deserves, but the part of me that yearns for her hates this.

Why isn't she fighting back?

I don't know the full extent of Agent Slick's reputation, but I know enough that I wouldn't lay the odds in Jacinto's favor. That bitch eats men like him for breakfast and shits them into open graves. So what if she doesn't have a weapon? She's lethal enough to lay him out with her bare hands.

Which would be perfect. She could gut him like a fish right here, and I'd have a dozen Brides of Jacinto who would swear as witnesses on any stand in the free world. It'd be as clean an end as anybody could hope for. Then I'd use his body to fertilize the growing fields and ascend the throne as smooth as butter. Piece of cake. Hell, it wouldn't even look like a coup.

Shit, I wish I'd thought of that before dragging my cousin up here. Then I'd just have to plug Lydia, dust off my hands, and get down to counting money.

"Stop," Ines screams, and the whole room goes whisper still. Jacinto stops pummeling Lydia long enough to snarl at the mousiest of his concubines, but she pleads the spy's case with tears in her eyes. "You're going to kill her."

An angry beat hangs in the air, then a wicked smile dances on Jacinto's face.

"Good idea." He gets a fistful of Lydia's hair, wrenching her head back so she can gaze up at him with puffy, bleary eyes. "But not yet." And he drags her towards the door like a doll.

The floor is speckled with Lydia's blood, and streaks of it trail behind as he hauls her along. Passing me, Jacinto thumps a bloody hand on my shoulder, then runs it up to rest on my cheek.

"Thank you, cousin. Who knows what would have happened if you hadn't found out her secret?"

What, indeed?

"It was my duty, Jacinto."

"This was more than duty. This was loyalty. The kind that can only come from love and deep trust. A heart like yours deserves to be rewarded, and you will be. Once I've dealt with *her*." He tightens his grip, jerking her around until she winces in agony. "Come to me and we can talk about what matters most." His eyes shine. "The future."

Then he lugs her into the hall. As soon as they're gone, the room goes freezing cold. Even the hot afternoon sun spilling through the windows, you could hang meat in this place.

Looking around, I see that every one of Jacinto's women has turned into solid fucking granite. They stare at me with undisguised hatred, and I grace them with a breezy smile. After all, what the hell are they gonna do?

I pity whichever one of them gets to share Jacinto's bed tonight. After working up a sweat like that, there's no doubt he'll want to vent the flip side of his savagery between the sheets.

Better you than me, I think.

With one last wink, I head out into the hallway. Bright red smears stain the tiles, and I find Ortega looking down at them, his lips pulled into a thin line.

"Looks like you finally told him, huh?"

"It had to happen eventually."

"So? What happened?"

"Justice." It's not clear whether or not he likes the answer, but I don't give a shit. Right now I'm flying too high. Images of Lydia's brutalized face try to shove their way into my brain, tugging at whatever attraction I once felt for her.

Too bad. That shit is over.

"Everything's pointed in the right direction," I tell Ortega. "Now all we need is the perfect opportunity to strike."

"Yeah." He nods, looking at the streaks on the floor again. "I may have something in mind. We should call Don Barrera and set up a meeting."

"Do it. I'll talk to my father."

Striding down the hallway, every inch of my skin is electric. We're right on the brink. And after selling Lydia down the river, my cousin and I are closer than ever.

The perfect distance to stick in a knife.

CHAPTER
THIRTY-ONE

LYDIA

None of my bones are broken, so I guess that's something. The last time I was in this basement, it was under very different circumstances. Shit, I can see the chair where Diego pounded the shit out of me less than a week ago.

Right now I'm recovering from a very different kind of pounding.

No orgasms for this girl.

Jacinto has left me alive for the time being, but somehow I can't manage any gratitude. If he'd had the simple human decency to turn out the lights for me, at least I wouldn't be lying here like this. Naked as hell, covered with grit, and aching all over.

I wonder why I didn't notice this row of cages bolted to the floor when Diego dragged me down here to fuck the living daylights out of me. Who am I kidding? I was too chewed up with lust, that's why. My naughty bits were so wet, it was hard to see anything past his belt buckle. Just another example of how I've let this whole mission go to shit in pursuit of a stiff dick.

I'd say I've learned my lesson if I was able to kid myself I'm getting out of here alive. No chance of that, I'm afraid.

To make matters worse, Jacinto is straight-up dedicated to making sure what remains of my short ass life is as uncomfortable as possible. The cage is too low to sit upright in, and too narrow to lay all the way down in. The rough bars are covered with nicks and barbs, so no matter how I lean up against them, they bite into my skin. There are even bloodstains from whatever unlucky son of a bitch last shacked up here.

And not a drop of water. Even a mad dog gets a dish to drink from, but I'm left praying for one of the pipes on the ceiling to spring a leak. My lips are swollen from thirst as much as from the whipping I endured.

A door opens somewhere overhead, and I recognize Jacinto's footsteps on the stairs. He's alone, which means I'm probably alive for the time being. There's no way he's going to kill me without an audience. And I know Diego will be right beside him to watch the show. Maybe I'll blow him a kiss right before the end, just to try and screw him over on the way out.

"I'm coming for you, my diamond…" His singsong tune is about as malignant as anything I've ever heard. A billion times more unsettling than his bull-faced threats.

Creaking onto my side, I drag myself to my knees and crouch to face him. Caked with blood and smeared with dirt, I must be one hell of a sight. Especially contrasted with him.

Jacinto sidles up wearing the same white linen suit he had on the night we met. Slick as an eel and beaming with macho pride. The kind that can only come from smacking a woman around.

"Look at you." He rolls his cigar to the corner of his mouth, contempt and lust blazing in his eyes. "I should have known what you were the moment I saw you. You have deceit printed on your skin."

Only if it was written on your knuckles.

"You've failed, you know that, Alana?" Leaning closer, he huffs a billow of acrid cigar stink right in my face. "Or should I say, *Lydia*? I have to say, once Diego told us your real name, Ortega was able to cook up quite a file on you. You're a very impressive girl, you know that?" That sour grin deepens. "There's just one thing you didn't count on."

He lets the words linger, and I dutifully play my part.

"What's that?" I ask, my voice raw from chewing back screams. Jacinto puffs out his chest and hooks his thumbs through his belt.

"Me."

Of course he's one of those.

"You see, my diamond, *nobody* fools me. At least not for long. I'll admit, I let your tits distract me for a while, but they've lost their appeal now that I've figured out the truth." Big words, but they don't stop him from ogling the goods. Even bruised and battered, the girls don't disappoint.

His shirt is unbuttoned halfway down his brawny chest, and I catch sight of something glinting amidst the hair. It hasn't been there before, and I squint up at it to try and focus. Jacinto notices and chuckles, twirling it between his fingers.

"You like my new necklace? I hoped you'd recognize it." He brandishes the bauble in my face. "It's the key to your little prison. I want to keep it next to my heart."

Just seeing it makes the underside of my skin itch. He's so fucking close. If I could just coax him a little closer—even a step—I might be able to get my mitts on it. Then I'd stomp a mudhole in this piece of shit and it'd be high-ho, silver, away!

But he hangs back and I know luck's not going to break in my favor.

"Is that what you came down here for?" I ask. "To gloat?"

"Mostly." Another one of his greasy smiles fouls my stomach. "But there's more." He draws near, dropping into a crouch so we're eye to eye. "I have a shipment loading as we speak. The biggest in the history of the cartel, maybe even the whole gulf coast. Every boat in our fleet is packed tight. We even commandeered some from Don Barrera to meet the supply."

Don Barrera. Boy, I could tell you about him.

The only thing stopping me is the fact that Barrera and the boys are gonna slit this bastard's throat. Too bad I won't be here to see it.

"It's beautiful," Jacinto rattles on, standing up again. "Hundreds of speedboats shining in the sun, each one so full of product water laps over the sides. Cars, jeeps, trucks, all waiting to cross the border. Texas has thrown its arms open wide, and before long all of America will be in the palm of my hand. I'm going to make so much money I'll have to hire people to spend it for me."

He chews his cigar, smug triumph crashing off him in waves. God, I hate it when guys like this decide to make speeches.

"Why are you telling me this?" I don't even try to mask my boredom. Not that he notices.

"Why? Oh, Lydia." He leans over the top of my cage, and the key swings like a pendulum over my pit. "So you'll know how much you've failed."

In spite of all my defenses, that cuts so deep nothing could ever close the wound up again. I rock back on my ass, a convulsive shudder racing up my bare back. Biting my lip hard is the only thing keeping tears from welling up.

Much as I hate it, Jacinto sees this. But instead of drinking it in, a bit of the nastiness ebbs from his face.

"Oh, Alana. It should have been different. If only you weren't a spy, you could have ruled by my side. Jewels, gowns, peasants to do your bidding. Nothing would have been too good for you. But now?"

All the sympathy vanishes, replaced by demonic loathing. He straightens, undoes his belt, and unzips his fly. Out comes that dick that searched my insides more times than I care to remember. But this time it's not hard. He aims his flaccid, rubbery member at me and a steaming stream of piss blasts onto my naked skin.

It's hot and pungent, and it's all I can do not to retch. But I'm too good for that.

Then it occurs to me. If his cock is out, there's still a chance I can turn this to my advantage.

"Oh, my *god*," I groan. Arching my back, I present myself to him, smashing my tits together so that they're soaked in his urine. "Yes. Jacinto, *yes*!" The stream sputters, and he looks down at me aghast. All the same, there's a glint of intrigue in the back of his black eyes. Nobody's ever done this for him before, and forbidden things are catnip to fuckers like him.

"Christ," he mutters, starting to get hard in spite of himself.

"More," I beg, breathless. "Please, Jacinto, more!" Snaking a hand between the bars, I reach for his bulbous cock. If I can just get a grip on it, I'm free.

But he knows better than to let me get the best of him that way. Dodging back with his hips, he tucks himself away and zips up the front of his piss speckled pants.

"Nice try," he smirks. "I'm not falling for that again. Look at you. Just like I suspected." I must be one hell of a sight. Crouching like the wounded animal I am, soaked in cold, reeking pee. "Dirty whore. If I'd known how filthy you really were, I would never have soiled my sheets with you."

It's hard to argue. With him out of arm's reach, I'm fresh out of tricks. The inevitability of my situation settles over me like a shroud.

"What's going to happen to me?"

"I'm going to kill you." He says it like a prediction of rain. Just a plain fact, as sure as sunrise in the morning. "But it won't be easy, my diamond." That venomous shift in his tone makes my chest constrict. "What I did to you this afternoon? It's nothing—*nothing* compared to what's waiting for you. I'll make you beg me for death. You'll pray to God to take you, but he won't. The God hasn't been born who can save you from me."

The ugliest part is I know he's right. Because if there was a God, he would strike down a devil like this.

Jacinto leaves without another word, and I slump down in defeat. My line of work has put me in some perilous positions. There have been times where I've been at the brink of despair, but nothing could touch this. It's the absolute nadir of my life, which is rapidly drawing to a close.

Naked, caged in the basement of a drug cartel, shivering under a sheen of piss. I'm no expert, but this looks like the end of the line.

Against all odds, I start to cry. It's been so long since I've done it I almost forgot how freeing it can be.

Great, fat tears roll down my face, mixing with the fetid fluid I'm steeped in. But they aren't tears of self-pity, or even fear. I can't remember a time in my life when I was afraid of dying. These tears are for the only thing I wish I could live for.

I wish I could have spent the night with Sir John one last time. For both our sakes. Maybe I'd even say something we'd both have to pretend I didn't in the morning.

The door at the top of the stairs opens again, and I struggle to put myself back together. I can stomach all kinds of things—*clearly*—but if anyone on this godforsaken property saw me cry, that would be the end of it.

Straining my ears, I can't detect a footfall on the stairs. Not Jacinto's, not Diego's. If someone's coming, they have a featherlight step.

"Miss?" The voice comes from the shadows, and even

though I've only heard it say a handful of words, I know exactly who it belongs to.

Ines.

"It's alright," I say. "He's gone."

"I know. I waited." She inches into the light, and my heart blossoms to see what she's brought. In one hand is a bundle of rags, and in the other is a pitcher of water.

I slam against the bars, sticking my greedy arms through to coax her closer. She approaches like a feral cat. Skittish, watchful, and feverishly hungry for a friendly touch.

As soon as it's in reach, I grab the pitcher and glug down mouthfuls of water.

Not too much, I caution myself. *Not too fast. You don't want to get sick.*

As if it fucking matters anymore.

"Thank you," I gasp, water spilling down my chin. Dipping rags in, I start to swab myself down, clearing away as much urine and grime as I can manage. It's cold comfort, but I'll take what I can get. What's most important is that I might just have an ally.

For her part, Ines watches in almost perfect stillness, her eyes darting as she catalogues every bruise and bump her master meted out for me. No doubt she's known beatings of her own in her time.

"Why did you come down here?" I ask, looking at her sideways. "It's risky."

"I know. We all do. But..." With a furtive look over her shoulder, she unfolds something wrapped up in her skirt. "The way you acted, I thought this was important." She holds up a black rectangle, and I damn near faint.

The Ripper.

I could kiss the girl.

Moving slowly and deliberately for fear of breaking it now, I take the proffered equipment and turn it over in my hands.

"How did you manage to keep this?"

"Oh." Something between sorrow and a smile flits across her face. "No one pays attention to the women."

"I bet." I smirk. Looking at the tiny monitor, I see that Jacinto's phone is still uploaded. Saying a little prayer to the God I don't believe in, I ready the files to send to Zero.

"Is that all you needed?" she asks timidly. "We can get our hands on almost anything."

"We?" After all the granite looks I've gotten from the women in this place, it's hard to picture them rallying behind me. Ines tucks her chin, a dash of... is that *pride* creeping into her face?

"You had Jacinto's phone. And when he beat you, you didn't break. You're one of us."

A wave crashes over me, drowning me in something perilously like hope.

"You can get just about anything, huh?" I can't help chuckling when I add, "Like the key to this cage?" Look, I mean it as a joke, but her silence arrests my attention. Looking up from the device, it's clear she just might be able to.

"I'm sorry." She shrinks back on her heels. "I don't know where it is."

"Funny thing about that." I hit send, and every secret Jacinto Osorio ever tried to keep goes sailing off to headquarters. "I do. I know *exactly* where the key is."

CHAPTER
THIRTY-TWO

Diego

Things are quiet, so I figure I'll trip downstairs and see how the bitch is doing. For old time's sake.

It'll be a good excuse to get away from all these prying eyes. I can go days, sometimes weeks without catching a glimpse of a single woman in Jacinto's keep. But after this afternoon, they seem to be everywhere. Hovering in corners or glaring across the patio. Shooting silent daggers my way.

I can tell you one thing for sure—once Jacinto's gone, it's gonna be open season on these bitches. Fuck 'em or hunt 'em, I'm cleaning this place out. I'm opting for the latter. I've had enough of Jacinto's sloppy seconds to last me a fucking lifetime.

So why am I sneaking to the basement? Lydia Slick has been the sloppiest second I've ever tangled with, but I just can't seem to quit her.

It was something else watching my cousin lock her up. He ripped her clothes off so violently her skin was covered in welts. Which is saying something because he'd already slapped her around so much it's a wonder there was a part of her left that wasn't black and blue.

But all my eyes saw were the white bits.

And the pink ones.

Even thrashed like crazy, that woman is something to behold. Which I guess is why I'm heading down again. Might as well get an eyeful to remember her by before that delectable body is dumped in a gutter up in Matamoros. That'll be one hell of a treat for GSIA to find. Maybe they'll think twice before trying the same trick on me.

Lydia doesn't even move when I approach the cage. She's always been lithe and lean, but it's like all the life has gone out of her. Curled on her side, she looks more like a wounded bird or whipped dog than an international super spy.

It's almost enough to make me pity her.

Almost.

She's wet all over, and I've smelled enough of Jacinto's piss to have a pretty good idea what went down. This bitch has had one hell of a lousy afternoon.

"Hey." I kick the corner of her cage. "How's life going down here?"

"Short." She doesn't even roll over. There's a grim resignation in her voice that ruffles my feathers.

"Yeah, well. That's what you get. If you play with snakes, don't complain when you get bit." No reply. She just scrunches into a tighter ball. Beaten up as she is, I still find myself wishing I could trace my fingers along the line of her backbone. Maybe get a handful of her ass for good measure.

I have to look away.

If I keep staring at her like this, I might even start to feel a little pity. Problem is when I avoid staring at her, the first thing I see is fraught all on its own.

That sturdy wooden office chair stares right back at me.

Ten days ago I wouldn't give it a second look, but now the goddamn thing is pregnant with meaning. I swear I can almost make out the sweat stains where her body heaved against it. There are bits of tape clinging to the arms where I cinched her legs in place. Shit, the zip ties from her wrists are still on the floor. Good thing my cousin doesn't know what they're from. Otherwise I'd be locked up right next to her. Or worse.

"Don't take it so hard," I tell her, ambling over to nudge the chair with my toe. "It wasn't a total loss. We had some good times if I remember correctly."

"What difference does it make? The party's over."

"But it was a party though, right?" I don't know why I need her validation so badly. Maybe because she's going to die, so there's no need to save face with her. I need to know that the times she melted on the end of my dick weren't an act. They have to be real.

Lydia rolls onto her back and fixes her eyes on me. Even with every bit of her glorious body spread out in front of me, all I can see is those luminous eyes gone flat with desolation.

"I'm going to die." The blunt statement makes me squirm, and I shrug away from her.

"Yeah? Are you saying it's my fault or something?"

"No. A rabid dog is never at fault. All it knows how to do is bite, so that's what it does." It comes off like such a dismissal, a prickle of anger flushes over me.

"So now I'm a dog?"

Lydia closes her eyes, mouths a few words I can't quite decipher, and then something shocking happens. A tear rolls down her face. And then another one. This battle hardened black widow is actually *crying*. Silent sobs bob her chest, and she grimaces as more and more water rushes towards her temples.

"What the hell are you doing?" I ask, incredulous. "Are you crying?" I'd think it was another tactic if it wasn't so wholly out of character.

"Please." The word barely croaks out, her voice choked

and thin. "Diego..." Her eyes open, imploring me before she can get out another word. My heart shatters for her, but I catch myself and back up a step.

"Oh, no. Don't even ask." This is slippery fucking ground.

My outright refusal sparks something in her because she rolls onto all fours and painfully pushes herself up. Those flashing eyes never leave mine.

"Diego, *please*. Don't let me die."

"Keep that shit up and I'm walking out of here."

"*Please*," she wails, completely calling my bluff. The bleak misery in her voice spikes my feet to the concrete. "It doesn't have to be like this. You know it doesn't. You're going to kill him anyway—"

"Keep your fucking voice down," I hiss, but she keeps going.

"What difference does it make? You've been planning this forever. Why not take Jacinto out before he tortures me to death?"

"Stop it!"

"I've failed," she cries, and my throat slams shut. "Don't you get it? Nothing I did here matters. The mission fell apart the second you told him who I was. It's over. I wasn't able to give the agency the information they wanted, and without that, they're paralyzed."

"Then what do you want?"

"I want to *live*." She grabs the bars and rattles them with everything she's got. "Fuck the mission, fuck the agency, fuck everything. Diego?" Her eyes lock on mine, overflowing with ferocious terror. "Everything's over but my life. Let me at least have that." This sudden vitality sends a rush of pink to her cheeks, setting off the bits of her that are still ivory white.

I rock back on my heel to look at this caged woman. This muzzled siren exposed totally for my eyes to feast on.

"In exchange for what?" That catches her up, and her breath comes in short sips. "Lydia," I lean closer to the cage, the demon in my shorts stirring to life. "What will you give me to set you free?"

If tears were a shock, then the coy smile on her bruised lips is a goddamn revelation.

"Diego," Lydia says, almost shyly. "We both know the answer to that."

Sitting up as tall as she can in the cramped pen, she runs her hands from her hips up along her ribs, smoothing them over her breasts. Her eyes bore into mine, daring me to look down as she twists her nipples to stiff beads.

Goddamnit, I'm already so hard it stings.

"Do you miss it?" She pivots on her knees, raising her ass and presenting herself to me. There's nothing to hide behind, and her rosy slit has me throbbing. "Don't tell me you don't."

"Fuck," I grunt, and she settles back to press her ass against the bars.

"Let me out. Let me out and you can have me as often and as hard as you want. I'll be *yours*."

"God fucking damnit." I rub my cock over the outside of my pants, stiffening even more. "You know I can't do that."

"Says who? Jacinto? If you're as good as your word, he'll be dead by the end of the week." Her hand slips between her legs and she toys with her clit. The damp squelch of her fingers is all it takes and I rip my fly open to work my cock in my hand.

Lydia's eyes widen when she sees me, her fingers working faster, delving into herself until she whimpers.

"Jesus, Diego," she pants, her hooded eyes devouring my cock. "I need you. I need you so badly."

Before I know what I'm doing, I'm right next to the cage, gripping the top edge with one hand while I jerk myself off at her ass. Her thighs start to quiver, and I can tell she's getting close.

"Let me out," she whimpers. "Open this thing up and take me. Now."

"I don't have the key."

"Fuck," she screams, but I can't tell if it's from frustration or the orgasm rippling over her. If it ain't the climax, it will be in a second. I hit my knees, jam my hips against the bars, and push my cock past her fingers and into her sweet cunt. She shoves back against me, taking me as deep as she can with this barrier between us. Her slippery inner walls flutter around me as she clamps down hard. It's almost enough to make me fill her up right now.

"Oh, my god," she cries. "Thank you. Even if this is all I get. It might just be enough." Lydia rocks back and forth, gliding along my shaft all the way to the tip, then sinking over me again. I reach between the bars and grab her haunches, bucking into her with quick, devastating thrusts. Moans pour out of her throat and onto the concrete, echoing back at us from the walls.

"You like that?" I grunt.

"*Yes*. You know I do. Christ, Diego…" She pushes back to meet me again, opening herself up as much as she can. "I can't tell you how much I've *loved* fucking you. No other man could ever hope to compare. Especially that limp-dicked fool Jacinto. He could never make me scream like this. Not really."

"Scream for me," I command her. Until now, we've stifled the sounds of our passion, but now she's right – there's nothing to lose. And I want her to howl so loud they hear her in Texas. Her voice rises higher and higher, but not that phony bullshit I heard through the door while my cousin humped her. This is different. This is *real*. As real as the fountain of cum mounting inside me.

"I knew it!" Jacinto's voice shatters everything, reverberating through the low basement like a cannon blast. I spring backwards, but it's no good. My pants are around my knees, and I topple over myself, tangling up as I try to hide my rock hard dick.

Lydia crouches in the corner of her cage, cowering away as Jacinto advances on me with cold, deliberate steps.

"Cousin," I babble. "It's not what it looks like." Which is the stupidest thing anybody could possibly say when getting caught with my dick literally inside the enemy. "Fuck." I manage to get my boxers up, hiding at least some of my shame. "I can explain."

"No need. Ortega?"

Ortega steps from the shadows, holding my father by the scruff of his jacket. The open disgrace on my father's face is enough to make me wish I was dead. Then Jacinto draws his pistol, and I get the awful feeling he's in the mood to start granting wishes like mine.

"Wait." I put a hand in front of me. Like that would actually stop a bullet. "You have to listen. She tricked me. You know how she is."

"That's true. I do *now*. But I know a lot more than that, Dieguito. You're an easy man to fool, it seems. Not as savvy as you like to believe." There's such cunning in his face my insides turn to ice.

"What does that mean?"

"Oh, Diego." My father hangs his head, his cheeks ashen.

"Quiet!" Ortega kicks my father in the back of his legs and dad goes down hard, his knees landing with an ugly smack on the unforgiving floor.

"That's right, Ortega," Jacinto grins. "Your day in the sun has finally come. You've been waiting for this, haven't you?"

"Yes, sir," Ortega nods. "It feels like forever."

"Waiting for what?" I ask, sensing the walls closing in.

"A day of reckoning." Jacinto stretches to his full height, radiant in his terrible triumph. "You're such an idiot, Dieguito. But don't feel too bad. All the Alamars are." He pats my father on the cheek. "I'm surprised you didn't figure it out sooner. Tell me—who planted the first seed of treason? Who dreamed up your little coup?"

Me, I want to say, but an admission like that would seal my fate for good. Not that it matters. Jacinto can see it on my face, and shakes his head with a knowing smile.

"Think harder, cousin," he coaxes me. "Who came to you and grumbled about me? Who told you he wished you were head of the cartel?"

It flashes over me in an instant, and Ortega's name is out of my mouth before I can catch it. And just like that, my guilt is proven.

"Why?" It's stupid, but it's all I can think to say. "Why entrap me like that?"

"It wouldn't have been a trap if you weren't already a rat, Diego."

The truth settles in my bones like lead poisoning. There they stand, Jacinto, Ortega, and my father, all watching me with gallows attention. There was a conspiracy alright, but it was against *me* the whole time.

"Dad," I say, my voice shaking. "Did… Did you…?"

"Uncle Eduardo?" Jacinto laughs. "Not a chance. Like I said, no Alamar would have the stomach for this, let alone the brains."

"I don't understand. Then what is my father doing here?"

"Oh, him?" Jacinto shrugs casually, pointing at my father with his thumb. "Nothing. Just collateral damage." With one swift move, he levels the muzzle of his gun at my father's temple and pulls the trigger.

Dad probably never saw it coming. His head bursts open in a spray of horrible crimson and he drops over in a heap.

My voice shreds my throat as I scramble to his body, screaming like I'm on the wrong side of Judgement Day. Which I am. Reason flies out the window and I cup my hands over my father's skull, doing everything I can to piece it back together. As if he would suddenly be alive again if I could just stuff enough of his brains back together. But all I get for the effort is a pair of bloody hands and a mouth full of vomit.

Lurching to the side, I spew so hard it almost gets on Jacinto's shoes. He has to back up as I gasp hard and let out another rush of bile.

"Too bad," Jacinto sighs. "Just think. If you hadn't dragged your father into this conspiracy, this would never have happened. See? Just like I said." Reaching out with his shoe, he nudges some of the pink matter globbed on the cement. "Barely any brains."

I'm on my feet in an instant, grief and rage surging through every part of my body. But before I can get a hand on Jacinto, Ortega's fist catches me in the jaw and sends me sprawling. I smack on my back, knocking the wind out of me. And there's no hope of getting it back with Ortega's boot slammed down on my chest.

All I can do is stare across the floor at my father's body, misery hollowing out my bones and filling them with ice.

Jacinto sees the tears on my face and chortles gleefully. Then he gestures to the stairs, and between the stars in my eyes, I see a willowy figure step forward. It's one of his harem. Ines, I think. Jacinto snakes an arm around her, pulling her close so he can lick her ear. "Good girl. Time to reward you for coming to get me so quickly."

Coming to get him? What the hell is he talking about?

I try to sit up, but Ortega's boot catches me in the temple and everything cuts out.

CHAPTER
THIRTY-THREE

JACINTO

God, I love the smell of gunpowder and blood. So coppery. So clean. So rich with wasted life. And it always gets my dick *so* fucking hard.

It's the smell of goddamn victory. I've never been on the losing side of it, and my cock is ready to cut a fucking diamond mine. But my *diamond* turns out to be dogshit, so I'll have to drill someone else.

"You like that?" I grind against Ines' hip. The bitch is all skin and bones, so I have to work myself around to find some softness. Why the fuck doesn't she just turn her ass towards me? She knows what I like. "Here." I grab her wrist and put her palm on my dick, humping into her hand. "Feel."

Jesus. A bolt of liquid fire runs all the way down to my fucking balls.

She's so fragile. Her fingers are so fine, so delicate, so *easily broken* it makes the head of my cock throb for more. I grip the back of her neck, and lick from her collarbone to her earlobe. Jesus, her skin tastes just right. Salty. Tender. A hint of perfume. The one I bought for her when she first came here. Lapping at her earlobe gets a breath out of her, so I take it between my teeth and pinch hard.

She still hasn't answered me.

"I asked you a question. *Do. You. Like. That*?"

"I do," she murmurs, gliding her hand over the outside of my pants like she's afraid to touch me. "You know I do."

Goddamn right you do.

I *love* the way her fear feels on the underside of my rock hard dick.

"Jefe?" Ortega's bullfrog voice breaks up the party.

"What the fuck do you want, Lope? Can't you see we're trying to celebrate?"

"Forgive me, Jefe, but what do you want me to do with him?" Ortega gives Diego a nudge with the toe of his combat boot, keeping him flat on the cement.

Winning feels so good I almost forgot about that traitor Diego. I turn Ines loose and strut over to tower over my cousin.

There's blood on his chin from a split lip, and his eye is puffy from Ortega's boot. I wish it had been mine. After what he's done, I should be the one to punish him.

It's alright. I will in the end.

Diego's shirt is soaked with his father's blood, bits of brain stuck all over the fucking place. I want to stomp him to death right here. Crush his ribs under my heel, splintering his bones to puncture his lungs, his heart. All the organs that keep his worthless life going. But not while he's asleep. I want him awake for every second of it.

"Lock him up next to his whore," I tell Ortega, making sure to spit on the lying cunt. She doesn't even flinch, so I kick the side of her cage as hard as I can. "Don't think I forgot about you, *my diamond*. You two?" I look at the unconscious Diego with all the hatred in my heart. "You deserve each other."

Ortega's got the cage open and stuffs my cousin inside, then slams the door. He locks it up, and I grab the key out of his hand and stuff it in my pocket. Seeing the two of them trapped like rats is just too perfect.

"Come," I say, seizing Ines by the wrist and pulling her to the stairs. "Follow me, Ortega!"

The night air is so sweet. Too sweet. It needs my favorite blend of herbs and spices to really mark the occasion.

So, it's out with my pistol, and I empty a clip into the air, crowing in like the prize cock I am. Frightened fuckers take off in every direction hoping to Christ I don't decide to start dropping bodies. Believe me, it's tempting.

"Ortega!" God, I love the way my throat feels when I howl like this.

"Jefe?"

"Tell them to load the boats! The shipment leaves at dawn."

"Yes, sir." He takes off across the courtyard, and I shout after him, "And have someone bring me Don Manuel. He's going to get what's coming to him!" Ortega sticks his thumb in the air without even breaking his stride. That's the kind of attitude that's kept him in my good graces. He deserves a reward.

Maybe I'll let him fuck Lydia before I kill her.

Speaking of fucking…

"Now." My fingers close around Ines' throat until little gagging sounds are all she can make. Soon she'll be gagging from something else. "Are you ready for your present?" Tears rim the underside of her frightened eyes, and her mouth opens and closes as she struggles to breathe. So I tighten my grip. "I can't hear you."

She tries to swallow, but can't. So she nods.

"Good girl."

I'm off for my room like a rocket, towing her behind so hard she can't keep her feet. Not even on the stairs. I drag her up by force as she staggers to try and get up. Ines has always been so goddamn vulnerable.

It's impossible to be anything other than cruel to a creature like that.

We get to my room and I don't even kick the door shut behind us. Swinging her around, I grab her shoulders and give her a good shake.

"Stop crying," I growl. "Tell me you love me."

"I love you," she chokes.

"Tell me you need me."

"I need you."

"How badly?" Instead of answering she sobs, so I slap her across the face.

"Badly," she wails. "Jacinto, so, *so badly*." Lucky for her, that's just what she's going to get—the worst of me.

Grabbing the front of her blouse in both hands, I rip it right down the middle. Flat girls were never my favorite, but her tiny tits make me crazy. Just ribs and two large dark circles begging to be bitten.

And that's just what I do.

Jerking the rags of her dress down to her elbows, I pin her arms to her sides with the fabric and savage her with my teeth and tongue. The effect on her is electric. Ines is a live wire, slithering and whimpering as I tease her nipples to raw, aching points.

The taste of her is all it takes for my cock to start leaking. But my balls are full of victory, all the way to the head of my dick. I'm not wasting a load like this on the inside of my pants.

I fling Ines onto the bed and lash off my belt. The feel of the buckle in my hand makes me itch to start whipping her, but I hold back. Not yet. I've got other things to do first.

My dick twitches as soon as air touches it, and I almost trip over my trousers rushing to the bed to bury it in the scrawny girl waiting there. Fuck, she's dutiful. By the time I hit the edge of the mattress, her dress is up.

None of my women wear panties. They need to be ready at a moment's notice. If any of them are caught with underwear at any time, it's an automatic beating. So all that's waiting for me on the bed is warm, slick heaven.

Well, it should be slick. Hard as I am, she's dry as the desert. No matter how I try to push in, it's no use.

"Spit on my hand," I command her, laying my palm by her cheek. She looks at me confused, so I hock one right in her face. "Spit in my hand." This time she does as she's told. I clap it to her bits and grease them up before wedging myself inside.

Fuck, she's tight.

I guess that's what happens when it's been a while. Not that I mind. Three pumps and she's already got me ready to blow. If only she weren't dead-fishing it.

"Come on!" I shove into her so hard the whole bed creaks. "Come on or I'll get someone who wants it."

That does the trick. The thought of losing me must be overwhelming because she snaps her legs around my ass and cinches me in place. Stuffing her hands under my jacket, she claws at my back and kisses my neck.

"Take this off," she moans. "I need to feel you."

Stripping off my jacket while pinning her down isn't easy, but I've done it with enough women to be a master in the craft. Ines grabs my shoulders and fucks up into me, groaning and wriggling with pleasure.

"Oh, Jacinto," she cries. "*Jacinto!* Your shirt too. *Please.*"

The jacket was easy, but the tiny fucking buttons on this shirt are too much. Especially when all my hands want is her smooth, tight flesh. Grabbing her by the ass, I roll both of us over until I'm on my back.

"If you want it so bad, you take it off for me."

Her fingers are calm at first, so I grit down to make it hard for her. Every time she's got her composure, I cram myself up into her, stabbing out a scream and robbing her of her hands. But she's determined, and in less than a minute she spreads my shirt back and claws at my chest. Grabbing her hips, I pummel her. Using her little body to stroke my dick until I'm on the brink.

"Fuck me," I shout. "Fuck me, you whore!"

Ines rides me like the stallion I am, digging her nails in my shoulders and leaning over me to lick my neck. Each groan she makes is higher and more frantic than the last.

She's going to come. I can feel it.

Suddenly she sits up, staring down at me with fire in her eyes. Her fingers grab the chain around my neck and hold on like a bridle as I gallop underneath her. We're close to the finish line, and the sight of those brown sand dollar nipples bouncing drives me even closer to the edge.

So lean and perfect. Screaming and wincing like it's her first time. I might just have to bring her back into rotation.

Careful thinking like that, Jacinto.

Letting myself get wrapped up in one woman almost got me killed. What I really need is to fuck my way through the whole harem again. Rank them so I know who to keep and who to kill.

The ones at the bottom of the list I can fuck to death.

Just thinking it tips me past the brink. A hot prickle races up my shaft, ready to spill in blistering spurts.

With a mighty roar, I fling her off me so fast the chain at my throat snaps. Taking Ines by the hair, I force her to her knees and stand on the mattress, gripping my pulsing cock in the other hand. Giving her hair one final twist, the cringe of pain and tears in the corners of her eyes sends me off to oblivion.

Rattling the whole compound with my animal cries, I plaster her face with thick, hot cum.

Her reward for a job well done.

CHAPTER
THIRTY-FOUR

DIEGO

I t's all over. Everything.

And the fucker didn't even have the decency to take my father's body away.

For the first half hour I tried not to look at it, but now I can't stop myself. He's like a rag doll, lying jumbled in a glossy pool of deep purple blood. His head scattered everywhere, with just one eye glaring at me from what's left of his face.

Accusing me. All my sins sit so heavy on me I can hardly breathe. My pride, my hatred, my greed… my lust. That last one was my real undoing. If I hadn't gotten snared by Lydia Slick, we might've gone through with the plan. Ortega or not. With Jacinto gone it would have been easy to take him out.

But I let a piece of ass blind me.

At least she's being quiet. Huddled up in her little cell next to mine. The only bright spot in my whole shitty universe is that she's as miserable as I am. I just hope Jacinto does me the favor of letting me watch him torture her before he puts me down like the dog I am.

I know she's naked over there, but I can't bring myself to look at her. That perfect body I was so desperate to see in all its glory would only make me want to retch if I looked at it now.

Betrayal like hers is the most despicable kind. Luring me into a false sense of security. Complicity even. Flattering me enough to believe we might actually be on the same page—linked somehow—only to use it against me at the first opportunity.

Staring at what's left of my dad, an even darker revelation looms up to greet me.

She and I are the same. I can hate her as much as I want, but we're two sides of a single coin. Lydia Slick ruined me, but I was perpetrating the exact same thing. Diego Romero Alamar, traitor to the Osorio Cartel. My whole life for the last six months has been spent bringing Jacinto ever closer into my confidence, looking for a place to slip the knife.

If she hadn't come along, I'd have done it.

Her arrival was so fucking *convenient*. Just thinking that word pulls me up short so fast I almost lose my breath.

Convenient.

Her arrival wasn't the only one with treacherously pinpoint accuracy. My cousin sure was in the cellar biding his time when I showed up.

The whole world was a loaded gun, hammer back with a hair trigger. And I just *had* to come down here and gloat over her downfall. Just like she knew I would.

And she pleaded with me. Begged me to let her live. An agent with her cold blooded reputation would never debase herself to grovel in front of a man like me. No matter how many orgasms I forced out of her, she'd meet whatever was coming head on.

But no, even through the bars she managed to twist me

around her little finger. And the second I was dumb enough to slip my dick into her one last time, the trap springs to snap my cock off. And my head along with it.

"You did this, didn't you?" I ask. There's a long beat where I can hear her deciding whether or not to answer me.

"Did what?"

"You planned this. This whole plot to get me down here. Trick me into fucking you so Jacinto could catch us together."

"You think a lot of me, Diego."

"Bullshit," I snort. "I think you're worse than the lowest trash in the filthiest gutter. But I still believe you orchestrated all this."

"Diego, I'm naked in a cage. How could I possibly do that?"

"You're sneaky. And resourceful. It's your life's work to pull shit like this. Whatever you may think about the nobility of your profession—international espionage—you're nothing more than a poisonous snake, always looking for ways to strike."

The bitch laughs.

Low and sarcastic, but a laugh just the same. It's enough to reignite the dynamite lodged in my guts.

"Let me tell you something, Diego. Are you listening?" She waits, and I force myself to look at her. When I do, her eyes gleam and a smug smile teases her lips. "You're right." Lydia gives a low, percussive whistle, then something moves in the darkness of the far reaches of the cellar.

A figure inches towards us, then another. And another. All those faces I've seen skulking around corners for the last twenty four hours creep to us from the shadows, and my body goes numb with shock.

It's Jacinto's harem.

The-fuck weary faces of all the women he's used up and thrown away. Disregarded and unwatched, they make the perfect instrument for a crafty bitch like Lydia. My impulse seeing them is to hunker against the back of my cage, but Lydia lunges forward, grabbing the bars until her knuckles are white.

"Ines," Lydia hisses. "Did you get it?"

There's a suspended beat where the girls stand warily, then they part and Ines walks forward. Wrapped in a robe, her face puffy from being smacked around. Her hair's a mess, and bruises are already starting to show. Telltale signs of Jacinto's 'affection.' Someone like Lydia might be able to shoulder such a load, but it an ugly weight for a waif like Ines.

"Did you get it?" Lydia asks again, anxiety rising in her voice.

Ines has both hands clasped in front of her chest, like an icon in one of those rural chapels along the coast. Then her hands part and something slips into view. It's the chain Jacinto always wears around his neck. And at the bottom is a key. It swings back and forth, glinting in the low light.

At the sight of it, Lydia exhales in utter relief, and I realize how deep this whole conspiracy runs. As soon as the key is in the open, everything springs into motion. Ines turns the lock on Lydia's cage while the others rush forward with clothes and her tool kit. The same one she pulled tape and ties out of when I bound her to the chair.

"Shit!" I kick the door of my cage, growling in fury. "Fuck!"

"Careful," Lydia smirks, slipping into a pair of tight, black pants. "Someone will hear you."

"You fucking *bitch*!" Grappling with my door, I shake it with everything I've got. The girls cower away from me, but Lydia is cool as the other side of the pillow. She zips up a form fitting tactical top, then takes her kit bag from one of the girls.

"It's all here." Lydia smiles broadly and lays a comforting

hand on the woman's shoulder. All this feminine camaraderie has me ready to burst into flames.

"You can't do this," I growl.

"It's already done." Fuck, her arrogance riles me.

"I'll kill you! I swear on a stack of holy fucking bibles, Lydia Slick, I'm going to kill you. I'll murder every last one of you!" Shaking the door again, my whole cage rattles. "Let me out of here!"

"Oh, Diego." The most patronizing laugh since the dawn of time trips past Lydia's treacherous lips. "You'd be such a terrible spy." Coming closer, she drops into a crouch in front of my cage to look me in the face. "If you wanted out, you wouldn't say you were going to kill us. You'd promise to help us. Beg forgiveness and tell us what an ally you'd be. But words are just words." The bitch *winks* at me. "You'd have to make it convincing."

"Fuck," I yowl. All my human parts vanish and I turn into a wild animal. Thrashing around in my cage, desperate to break free. I finally understand my cousin's feral need for blood on his hands. I'll never sleep until I'm slick with the gore of every woman in this room.

"Look at him." The women have grouped around Lydia, each of their faces molded into the same haughty pride of their new goddess. Well, I'm here to burn down their church. Jamming myself against the bars nearest the cellar door, I open up and pour all my hatred at the steps.

"Help! Someone get down here! There's still time to stop them!" I scream until my throat is raw and I'm coughing blood. None of the women move. They just watch in self-satisfied silence.

"Who are you hoping will hear you?" Lydia asks as I try to catch my breath. "Ortega?" At the mention of his name one of the girls steps forward. A tall, dark haired woman with full hips and pitch black eyes. Marisol, I think. There's something in her hands, and only when she passes it to Lydia do I realize it's a stiletto knife. And the blade is painted red.

Lydia takes a white handkerchief from her bag and wipes the blade clean again. As she does, her eyes never leave my face. The meaning is perfectly clear.

I can scream all I want to, Ortega ain't coming.

My mouth goes dry, and all the blood drains from my face. Looking from whore to whore, I realize that every one of them has a weapon in her hands. Some small, some improvised, but all lethal.

Swallowing hard, I press my back to the far side of the cage and glare up at them. If this is it, I'm damn well going to make them fight for it.

"Wait. Are you going to kill me?" A bone cold silence follows, not a single slut in the bunch blinking.

"No," Lydia says at last.

"Then what are you going to do?"

"Leave you here." Her voice is cryptic, and I look at her out of the corner of my eye, waiting for the trick.

"You're not going to kill me?"

"Not me." For a second I'm almost relieved, but then a fearsome grin paints all their faces. "Don't get me wrong," Lydia goes on. "You're going to die. I just won't be here to see it." The truth of it hits like a bucket of freezing water.

"Wait." It's too late. Lydia heads for the stairs, and the whole harem follows in silence. "Wait! You need me. You'll die out there without me." Rearing back, I kick the door as hard as I can. "Let me out! I'm telling you, you'll need me!"

Lydia stops halfway up the steps, her face half lit from the world above.

"See? Now you're getting the idea. Keep it up and you might be a spy after all." And she's gone, trailing her coven of soiled witches like a chilly smoke.

CHAPTER
THIRTY-FIVE

Things are so hectic when we get out in the open, it's not hard to blend in. It helps that being women renders us virtually invisible in this testosterone fueled world. Men hoof it on all sides, loaded to the gills with guns, drugs, the whole schmear. Judging by the scrambling security guys, nobody's found Ortega's body yet. Oh, they miss him, sure—they just haven't found the bastard.

"Come on," I whisper, waving my cabal of women to the rear of the compound. That's where the weak spots are, along with the motorcycles we'll need to get things moving.

The drug runners are way ahead of us. Jeeps zip around from the front of the mansion and head for the growing fields and labs. If it's go-time for them, that means it's go-time-thirty for me.

We need a distraction to get this show on the road, and fortunately, I have the best distraction in the business right in my tool belt. Turning to the women who have been my saviors, I hate that I have to treat them like meat just like everyone else does. But in my line of work, you use anything and everything you've got to your advantage.

Sneaking around behind a row of cabanas at the rear of the house, we circle up behind the exact one Diego and I made out against. The irony of it isn't lost on me as we lay plans to bring the whole place down around our ears.

"I'm sorry to have to ask this, but we need a diversion. I need three of you willing to get naked and run for the pool." Nudity is cheap with this crowd, so every hand in the bunch goes up.

Looks like it's up to me not only to assess who's going to draw the most eyes in their altogethers, but who's the best asset when it comes to kicking ass.

Ines has already done her nudie-duty for the night, so she gets a pass. It comes down to a slender siren with smoky eyes, a black goddess with an ass for days, and a shortstack with a great rack.

I don't need to tell them twice. Off come the clothes, and they frolic towards the pool whooping with every step. As they weave between the flunkies humping cargo, it's clear the men get ideas about humping something else. The beehive of activity slows to a halt while my three decoys cavort around, giggling and playing hide-and-seek among the men.

It has exactly the effect I'm after. These saps are so titmerized I could set fire to their shoes and they'd be toast before they noticed the smell.

At least I hope so.

"Alright," I say as the first girl dives into the pool. "This is where shit gets real. You see this?" Holding up one of Nine's explosive tablets, I make sure I've got everyone's full attention. "Get one of these bitches wet and it blows up more than a stick of dynamite. Instant firebomb. I need people willing to plant these in key spots under the sprinkler system. As close to the security offices as you can get, Jacinto's room, the armory, that kind of thing. Who's in?"

Again, all hands go up.

"You have to understand," I caution them. "These are some serious shit. One drop of water and it's New Year's Eve without the countdown." That gives them pause.

"Even sweat?"

Pulling my lips in a tight line, I sigh through my nose.

"Honestly? I don't know. But I can guarantee you don't want one of these in your bra when you jump in the pool."

Stillness.

They exchange wary glances, unsure if they're willing to take this kind of risk. Which I get a thousand percent. Then, mousy Ines—a girl who has more than proved her mettle—nods firmly.

"I haven't come this far to back out now." She sticks out her palm, and I drop two tablets into it. More hands follow, and I dole out the Christmas candy, making damn sure to keep plenty for my own stocking.

"Next we have these." Out with those handy little knock-out needles. "Just take off the cap, jab, and squeeze. It's instant night-night for anybody on the wrong end of these little bad boys. Any takers?" As expected, they're all eager to take them off my hands. Given their lack of experience in hand to hand combat, I'm more than happy to deplete my supply.

If I wind up in a spot I can't karate chop my way out of, that's on me. But these gals deserve every fighting chance I can give them. After the life they've had, I'm sure they're eager to get a bit of their own back.

"Here's what we're going to do. I want as many of these explosives planted as we can get. Once you've hit the key spots, put them under jeeps, in guy's pockets, whatever you can think of. If you see somebody who might be trouble, give 'em a jab and keep moving. We'll call this the rendezvous point. When you're empty handed, come back here and wait for me. Understood?"

"Si," they say almost in unison. Just then a familiar laugh ruptures the night, and even I involuntarily flinch.

Jacinto.

"What have we here?" he shouts. "Are my flowers thirsty?" Peering out around the edge of the cabana, I spot him standing astride the top of the steps, gazing down on the women in the pool and beaming with pride.

The trio call his name and splash even more, displaying their glistening bodies to him. All the foot soldiers surrounding the pool have averted their eyes, fearful of the wrath of the shirtless demon grinning down over the scene.

"What's the matter with you?" Jacinto hectors his men. "Did you turn queer? Look at them!" Relief breaks out, and every swinging dick on the scene gets back to ogling. "That's right, my jewels. Give my men a show! They're loyal enough to deserve it." It's crass, hedonistic, and exactly what I need.

"We move on my signal." I hold up a hand and all the girls go taut, poised for action. One flick of the wrist, and they scatter for their duties.

I'd be lying if I said their lives weren't in danger. Any one of them could wind up dead with a single false move. But I've saved the most perilous mission for myself.

Skirting in a wide arc just at the edge of the shadows, I sprint for the far portico where the motorcycles are. If I have any luck at all—and that's a dubious prospect under the circumstances—there'll be one waiting.

To my delight, there's a whole bank. So I get the pick of the litter, settling on a Lightning LS. God knows what this beauty is doing out here. Toys like this weren't made for field work. It doesn't even have a sidecar.

Kicking her to life here would only bring the wrong kind of attention, so I walk her down the path a good hundred yards before slinging my leg over the top and turning the key. She thunders to life like a greyhound in the slip, straining upon the start. Fortunately for the bike, I'm ready to cry God for Harry, and we're off like a shot.

A cloud of dust is all I leave behind as I carve my way to the far end of the growing fields. To my surprise, there's still a scattering of men working. I guess three pairs of tits aren't enough to spread word of a pool party back this far. Looks like I'm gonna have to be strategic. Which isn't as delicate as it sounds under the circumstances.

It's a rip and run affair.

So it's the fentanyl labs first to plant explosives and make a couple of good old fashioned fire bombs for the growing fields.

It's a tense ride under the cover of dark, and when that unassuming shed comes into view, my breath is coming in high and thick in my chest. Nice as it would be to ditch the bike, I'm going to need her for the next leg of the evening. Besides, she's too pretty to be thrown in the dirt.

My memory is like a steel trap, so it's nothing to punch in the code. The spiral staircase greets me, but without a pistol, it's not so simple to go in ready to rain fire.

All that meets me is mushroom loam and silence. Not bad for starters, but I keep my guard up as I wind my way down into the deserted cultivation hall. It's so damp that I'd be a fool to plant a tablet in here right now. Save it for the way out—if then. Lord knows this place will be primed to blow before I'm done.

After the blacklight glow of the psilocybin rooms, the fluorescents humming in the stark white lab sting my eyes. Too bad there's no time to adjust. I just have to skitter around and make do.

The sprinkler system is exposed along the ceiling, so it's easy work to drop a tab or two in each workstation and keep moving. As soon as the lever is pulled, it'll be curtains for this joint.

"Ey!"

Fuck. I thought this place was empty.

Front zipper down, hands up.

"What are you doing in here?" It's one of the scientists. Unfortunately, not one of the glasses-pushing variety. No, this is a hardened manufacturer of illicit pharmaceuticals. Every bit as comfortable wielding a handgun as a test tube. Bad news for me, it's the former in his paw at the moment.

But I've got something he hasn't got—a killer pair of tits and no scruples.

"Excuse me," I say, raising my hands higher as I turn to face him. That parts the front of my top so that the girls really get some air. "I must've gotten lost."

"Nice try." He smirks, keeping the gun trained on me as he closes in. "I know better than to mess with one of Jacinto's girls. Especially a troublemaker like you."

"My reputation precedes me." I pull a mocking half bow, then dive forward and catch him around the waist. He's so surprised the gun goes off, and I get the feeling this isn't the first time he's shot early with a woman around. We grapple for a second, rolling on the floor before I manage to straddle him.

The fucker has both hands on the butt of the gun, doing everything in his power to point the barrel my way. He's strong, and it drags a tortuous line closer and closer to my face. A vicious smile jags across his lips as he sees he's gaining the upper hand.

At the last minute, I release one of my hands and wrap my forearm under his elbows. All it takes is one quick tug and his arms give way. The barrel swings back and his eyes go wide as it damn near hits him in the nose. Slipping my pinkie around his finger on the trigger I clench my fist and blast his brains across the pristine floor.

Getting the pistol out of his limp hands is a snap, and I tuck it in the back of my waistband before zipping up my top again. To be honest, I'm almost grateful to the guy. I didn't have a gun before coming down here.

But cracking off a round in the lab is bound to get some attention, so there's no time to waste. The back wall is loaded with enough chemicals to make Nine drool on his lab coat. Shame I can't go shopping for his Christmas present.

Instead, I gather up all the flammables I can find and stuff their necks with gauze. Makeshift wicks are all the moment calls for. A handy cardboard box is perfect for loading up my arsenal, and just before I turn tail and head for the motorcycle idling overhead, I catch a glimpse of a jar with an old fashioned skull and crossbones on it.

It thought that shit was just in the cartoons.

Picking it up to read the label, it's even more bonkers than I thought.

Hydrochloric Acid.

You know what? Why not? It's too perfect of a cliché to pass up.

CHAPTER
THIRTY-SIX

Tempting as it is to yank the fire alarm and start tossing Molotov cocktails, I need to get back to the rendezvous point. Too many people have left these women in the lurch for me to go and join the list. They're putting their lives in jeopardy. The least I can do is give them the best fighting chance I can.

I'll zip back out here and pull the rip cord on my way out.

By the time the mansion is in sight again, a party is in full swing. The music is so loud I don't even have to cut the engine before getting close. Hell, there are bikes fishtailing across the lawn as it is, so all I have to do is join in.

Would-be guards pop wheelies while swilling tequila right from the bottle. Men from the growing fields romp around like it's the second coming, laughing and hitting joints the size of baseball bats. Everybody's having such a good time, it's almost a shame to bust up the party.

Unfortunately for them, I'm a girl on a mission. And we've just hit my favorite part.

As expected, a cluster of women is waiting for me behind the cabana. I know they've done their jobs perfectly without even having to ask. If only every team I worked with was this dedicated.

Maybe I should try to reach Zero to see if she needs a dozen trusty foot soldiers.

"How did it go?" I ask as I jog up with my box of handmade bombs.

"Everything is planted." The tall brunette is clearly their de facto leader, all hard edges and harder eyes. I'd bet my eye teeth she's been here the longest.

"Well done. What's your name?"

"Raya." Her chin is high and proud.

"Raya, I wish I had time to thank you for your help. All of you. But we've got to keep things moving." Time to play Santa Clause with the Molotovs. Each girl gets a jar of alcohol and a book of matches. But I run out of girls before I'm out of bombs. I counted perfectly, and a quick head count tells me we're missing a few. Unfortunately, I have neither the names nor the grip on their faces to know exactly who. "Where are the others?" A tiny, curvy woman speaks up.

"Luisa and Sasha went into the pool to help the others. I don't know where Ines is."

Ines!

How did I not notice she was missing? Of all of them, that girl is the one I've come to rely on the most, and missing her puts me on high alert. She's so vulnerable just thinking of her in peril sends adrenaline screaming through my veins.

"We need to get eyes on her fast."

As if on cue, someone starts hollering from around the front of the house. Along comes a walking side of beef in a black tee shirt, his hand like a vise around the back of Ines' neck.

"Jefe! I caught one of your girls sneaking around!" The look of pain and terror on her face stirs up every sympathetic feeling I've got, swirling them into a tornado of ill-advised affection.

I'm gonna save that girl.

Creeping to the edge of the cabana, I peek out to see how far the news has traveled. So far it's nothing but deaf ears. Every man in the joint is too focused on pleasure to give one lone dickhead a second thought. Thank Christ, I've got the best kind of weapon at my disposal to keep that shit rolling.

"Change in plan," I tell the girls. "Get naked and head for the pool."

"What about these?" Raya asks, turning her bomb over in her hands.

"Half of them back in the box, keep the other half here for when shit starts. For now, get out there and shake what your mama gave you. When the time comes, keep low. Being in the water might be just the protection you need."

"Jefe," the guy shouts again. It's do or die time, and I'm not in the dying mood right now. So it's jackrabbit out into the open.

Stay low, run hard.

The dumb fucker never sees me coming. The nastiest tool in my pack is a string of piano wire, and nobody deserves it more than the guy manhandling Ines. I hit him mid-step, catching him around the neck with a rodeo superstar lasso. One sharp pull and his throat squelches open, cutting his words to a tortured gurgle. Both his hands fly to his neck as he tries desperately to keep the life in his body.

But today's not his day.

Ines reels around breathless, mouth wide at the sight of her erstwhile captor juddering in the grass. Then she sees who rescued her and clings to me for dear life.

"Alana," she murmurs. "I was so scared."

"You're not out of the woods yet. The others are in the pool. Take your clothes off and don't stop splashing until shit starts exploding. Go!" Ines has seen so much rough treatment it pains me to give her an ugly shove. But it might just be the thing to save this little bird's neck.

She takes off, and I watch her for a moment. So much courage in such an unassuming package. Without her I'd be dead. Life has taught me God doesn't exist, but Ines is almost enough to make a believer out of me.

Hope she gets out of this alive.

I hope a lot of us do. But if that's going to happen, I need to make get hoofing.

Taking to my heels, I bolt back to the far side of the cabana. Plan is, once I've pitched the first fireball at the mansion, it's back on the bike to torch the growing fields.

Tearing around the corner, I'm pulled up short by a shadowy figure with an unlit Molotov cocktail in his hands. He gazes down on it, a smile of dark admiration on his face. My heart skids to a halt as Jacinto turns those gleaming, werewolf eyes on me.

"I admire your handiwork," he says. "Reminds me of when I was young and reckless."

"Not young anymore, huh?"

"No." A thin chuckle slips through the corner of his smirk. "But tonight I'm not the one who's reckless."

"You don't think?"

"At first I didn't suspect anything," he says. "I called for celebration, so why wouldn't my jewels come cavorting to please me?" Shifting the bomb to one hand, he draws a cigar from his pocket with the other. He bites the end, then pulls out his lighter and sparks it to life. But he doesn't extinguish the lighter. Just leaves it going as he puffs and grins at me.

"What gave it away?" I ask. "Just out of curiosity."

"They all kept coming from the same spot. So, I thought I'd come over and see why." The lighter snaps off, but I don't breathe any easier. Once it's in his pocket, he sucks the end of the Cubano until the cherry glows a vicious red. Then he plucks it from his lips, keeping it casually close to the improvised wick as he speaks. "You've done very well. I didn't even miss my key at first."

"What makes you think I've got it?"

"You're free. Though I imagine Diego is still in his kennel?" I nod, and he shakes his head approvingly. "Vicious. I admire that. Oh, my diamond." The tip of his cigar kisses the alcohol soaked gauze, orange flame dancing to life. "We could have been perfect. Just know that when you're dead, I'll warm my hands over what's left of you."

"Ever the romantic, Jacinto."

Just when I think he might ask for one last kiss, a joyous shout goes up by the pool. Jacinto looks over his shoulder, and that's just the opening I need.

Lashing out, I kick the fire bomb right out of his hands. It sails through the air and the rotten son of a bitch can't help watching its arc. Which gives me plenty of time to shoot a hand into the box of goodies I brought from the lab.

The jar I'm looking for comes perfectly to hand.

Alright, hydrochloric acid. Do your shit.

Jacinto looks back at me, equal parts stunned and delighted by my little gambit. But any mirth fades as I smash the bottle against his head. Hard. The glass cracks, and I jerk my hand back in hopes of sparing myself from the corrosive sting.

My buddy Jack ain't so lucky.

"Puta," he howls, tipping backward to scramble in the grass clawing at his face.

The bomb I kicked lands on the flagstones at the nearest corner of the patio, sending up a deafening boom and a blazing mushroom cloud. Say what you will about the damn things, their theatricality is hard to beat.

"You bitch," Jacinto hisses, still squirming in the grass. His pulpy face sends up curls of fetid smoke. I've always hated the smell of burning flesh, and the metallic stink of acid only heightens things.

"Enjoy your party," I chirp before scooping up the rest of my ammunition and charging for the motorcycle. Turning the tires for the growing fields, I get the jars ready and break my lighter out.

Funnily enough, when shit gets crazy is when my head is the coolest. Calm, focused, and razor sharp. Which is just what I'm going to need.

The road isn't dark for long. A cataclysmic roar goes up as all those little tablets Nine gave me go off at once. The mansion cracks as fire belches through the windows, scattering shards of glass into onlookers' faces and lighting the path ahead of me brilliant orange.

I hope at least some of the girls survived. But hope is all I can do.

Because I'm not looking back.

CHAPTER
THIRTY-SEVEN

<u>*DIEGO*</u>

Dust chokes the air until I can't stop coughing. The blast knocked most of the plaster off the ceiling and I'm covered with grime and flecks of grit. My ears ring so bad I'm amazed they're not bleeding. Swiping my hands over my cheeks, I'm grateful to see my palms are just covered with sweat, soot, and dirt.

No blood.

At least not yet.

The bad news is my cage is completely undamaged. At least the top kept some of the bigger hunks from hitting me.

My dad isn't so lucky. A floor joist came loose and crunched down over him, along with enough construction dust to powder him like Jacinto's upper lip.

My father was as honorable a man as can be found in this awful trade. He deserved better than this. At the same time, it's probably the closest thing to a burial he's going to get. At least until the house comes down on top of us.

That bitch got her way.

I should have put a bullet in her the second she stepped out of Jacinto's SUV. Dropped her dead on the spot. My cousin would have hit the fucking sky, but I doubt he would have killed me over some random bar bitch. Probably slapped me around, but I could deal with that.

Shit, I'd have let him do it. God knows I let him get away with worse indignities. All because I could see the light at the end of the tunnel. That glorious day when all of this would be mine.

And all I've got to show for damn near a decade of boot licking is a set of bars in the basement. I've looked through them before, but always from the other side. It was so easy to tower over someone begging for their life when I knew it was pointless. Shit, sometimes the pleading was the best part.

But I can tell you now, it tastes like shit when the words are coming out of your own mouth.

Another explosion shakes the world, sending more stinging filth hailing down on me. The floor overhead groans like a dying man, and I brace for the end.

Nothing.

A few seconds of awful splintering to promise the inevitable, but then it stops. Prolonging my cockroach life waiting to be squished.

Evil as he is, even my cousin couldn't devise a torture like this. He's done plenty of heinous things, and I've stood right at his side and watched. Jacinto has always been a master of pushing the limits of physical pain, but psychological agony like this is beyond him. It requires a level of empathy to know how to ruin someone from the inside out.

More explosions sound in the distance, faint enough I can't even tell which direction they're coming from. Like it matters. I've breathed fresh air for the last time.

A new roar goes up over head, and I roll on my back to squint through the swirling dust. Orange threads stretch above me, lined up parallel. Growing brighter. Closer. For a second I'm not sure what I'm looking at. Then the truth screams through my brain like the fire truck that ain't coming.

It's the floorboards. They're on fire. And that fire is eating its way between them.

On its way to me.

Something breaks free at the far end of the cellar and another joist comes down. This one brings some planks with it and a tongue of fire lashes down. First orange, then blue as it grabs ahold of the underside of the floor and starts to crawl my way. Like a demon on the ceiling billowing closer and closer.

The orange takes over again, along with crackling pops. Dry wood burns best, and this basement is dry as a bone. It had to be. This is where the drugs were stored back in the earliest days of the cartel, so it had to be watertight.

Good for weed, bad for me.

An air pocket breaks loose and the flames roar to life. A blast of heat singes me so hard I flatten against the floor to try and escape it. In a few minutes, the bars of my cell will be a fucking barbecue grill. Part of me hopes I'm dead before that happens. Maybe I'll have the good fortune to suffocate.

My brain may be willing to buy the idea, but my body says *fuck that*. Survival instinct is a son of a bitch, and I batter the bars with everything I've got. Kicking and punching, pushing myself against them until I'm blue in the face. Who gives a fuck about broken bones if it means saving my skin?

A punishing crash over by the steps seizes my attention and I scuttle around to look. Raging flames shoot down the steps as the door surfs down over them as if kicked from above. A second of pure inferno, then it subsides.

To my astonishment, a figure thumps down the steps. Then it reaches down and flings the door out of the way so it can continue its descent.

Who the fuck would come down here? It's not like this is

some kind of refuge. It's the oven in hell's kitchen, and the heat just keeps cranking up.

But the figure keeps coming. Step by pitiless step. The man is so impervious to the flames I half wonder if it's the Devil himself, come to drag me down to hell in person. I'm not up on my Dante, but I seem to remember that the deepest circle is reserved for those who specialized in betrayal.

I wonder if just planning betrayal counts…

I wonder if Lydia Slick will be waiting when I get there.

Then the smoke swirls away, and I recognize the figure.

It's Jacinto.

Firelight flickers across what's left of his face, and tiny flames dance along the fringes of his clothes, rising from his shoulders to make him even more demonic than he already is.

He comes to stand in front of my cage, glaring down on me with the only eye he's got left. The other is a putrid, milky ball in a bloodied, ruined mash of flesh. One side of his head is bald and blistered to the top of his scalp, his ear sliding down towards his slimy neck. Like something out of a nightmare—his external appearance finally catching up to his horrid, remorseless soul.

"Have you come to kill me?" I ask, but he just shakes his head. "Then what? To watch me die?"

Jacinto doesn't move. He just stares at me with the horrible intensity of the damned. Then his lips part, one side of his mouth sticking together with gooey threads as he talks.

"Do you hate her?"

Lydia?

I lunge forward, grabbing the bars. They're steaming hot, searing my flesh, but I don't give a good goddamn.

"Yes," I reply.

"Do you want to kill her?" he asks, unblinking.

"Yes!"

"Say it again," he commands, that cruel voice roaring louder than the flames. "Do you want to kill her?"

"YES!"

It's a howl of boundless, quivering rage. If I could, I'd rip her to bits. Tiny shreds of deceitful woman to scatter to the bloody winds.

Jacinto keeps on staring. Motionless. Utterly still, yet quaking with wrath. Then his eye glows hotter than the flames swelling higher around us each second.

"The enemy of the enemy is my friend," he says flatly. "Get away from the door." At first I don't know what he's talking about, but when his pistol comes out, I get the hint real quick. Huddling hard to one side of the cramped cell, I watch as Jacinto takes aim. At first he closes his eye, then laughs at himself remembering he doesn't have to squint anymore. His shooting eye is long gone.

I just hope it doesn't impact his aim too much.

He pulls the trigger and the lock snaps with a metallic crunch. Two solid kicks and the door swings open, and I crawl to freedom.

When I stand, Jacinto holds his ground, looking up at me with iron determination.

"You are not forgiven, Diego. But I need you. Is that understood?"

I swallow hard and nod. There's still a bullet in his clip with my name on it.

That's a bridge I'll have to burn when I get to it. Right now I need to get out of this deathtrap.

Jacinto leads the way, turning without another word and walking back to the stairs. They're fully on fire now, but he mounts them as easily as if out for a Sunday stroll. It's a picture straight out of a horror movie, but if I'm going to make it I have to follow.

To finish this means I'll literally have to walk through fire. But if I get to take my revenge on Lydia Slick on the other side, it's a walk worth taking.

THE CLOSER

LYDIA

The world is one big tinder box, and I'm a bitch with a fistful of matches. There's enough burning weed to keep the whole continent high for a calendar year.

It's gonna rain bong resin come monsoon season.

Man, there's nothing like fire to bring the chaos. The compound is full-on pants-shitting festival before I've even reached the labs to yank the fire alarm. By the time I'm done, the whole operation is a ring of fire big enough to make Johnny Cash smile down from cowboy heaven.

Fun as all this is, at a certain point I've got to let the flames spread themselves and get the hell out of here. All hanging around is going to do is put a target on my back. Hell, I've already got one, but it gets bigger with each second I'm not hightailing it for home.

It's just a shame I can't bring this Lightning-LS with me. She'd purr like a kitten from one end of the Dalmatian Coast to the other and love every red hot minute. Maybe I'll get Zero to buy me one as a reward for this dogshit mission. It looked like trash from jump, and only lived down to my expectations.

Well, if all I get out of this bike is a ride to the coast, I'm gonna run the wheels off this bitch. So, it's set a course for the beach and don't take no for an answer.

This beauty goes from fast to faster in half a heartbeat. The shocks are for shit, but then again, she wasn't built for off-road adventures. Good thing I am. It's gotta be ass up high in the saddle while I'm thundering over the open plains.

I'm in the midst of a crow-flies situation, which means blacktop is in short supply. Whatever gets me to the coast fastest.

Anything to get me off base before any of those jackasses gets their heads together enough to come looking for me. Because they're gonna. That's a brass tacks fact. Best to be out on the gulf where trails are harder to follow.

Not knowing where their launch point is, I'm taking a hip shot and banging the shortest route to the gulf. From there I'll head north until I either hit their boats or the border.

My tires are eating sand in short order, which slows things down a bit. The Lightning rumbles between my thighs like an angry lover, and I push that bad bitch to the brink. Sorry, girl —mama's got bigger issues than whether or not you blow a gasket.

A bank of headlights swell over the dunes ahead of me, all pointed directly my way. My chest gets tight and I lean low over the motor. If they've called in the cavalry, I don't exactly have the firepower to fight my way out. We're talking full-on Custer, which would suck after getting this close.

Gritting my teeth, I cut my headlight, steer straight into the eye of the hurricane, and hope for the best. Maybe I can break through and leave them spinning. In a matter of seconds, it's a maelstrom of jeeps and motorcycles, each one bringing its own personal sandstorm.

Narrowing my eyes as much as I can, I fire right down the middle.

They blow past without a second look. Maybe it's the squawking radios, or the orange glow on the horizon. One way or the other, they're too obsessed with getting back to base to pay me a lick of attention.

Which means I'm home free.

The coast spills out ahead of me, about a thousand different names for salvation bobbing in the surf. Shrink wrapped bundles of illicit vein snacks pockmark the sand, right where the mooks dropped them when the SOS came through. It'd be poetic justice if the locals swarmed this place for some freebies.

Anything to take the edge off a generation of having a boot on your neck.

I drive until sand turns to mud, then salute the Lightning for her duty and ditch her in the short surf.

"Hey," a frantic voice hollers at me. "Hey, you! Stop!" Looking over my shoulder, I see a short, reedy man running for me and waving his arms. He's fifty if he's a minute, with a face weathered like a coastal stump. If it wasn't for the captain's hat perched on his head, he might have a chance. But that marks him as one of Jacinto's flunkies, so he's about to have a shitty night.

"Stop," he cries again. The gun I stole from the scientist flies out of my waistband, cracking off a bullet that chases the word right back down his throat. Captain crunches down in place, and after a quick pocket check to make sure none of Nine's pesky pellets are loitering in my clothes, I slosh out up to my knees.

This is always the hardest part. Fighting the surf when it's still shallow enough to yank your feet around. The second it's deep enough, I'm under the surface like an otter.

It's a cold kiss, and salty as shit. But the sea is the least fickle lover I've ever known, so I let her hug me and carry me along. Easy as it would be to grab one of the nearer boats, I'd just wind up having to weave through the others to break free. Best to kick my way to something closer to the front.

All my training pays off, and I hit the vanguard in no time. Grabbing the stern, I haul myself out of the briny and pitch over into the boat.

Say what I will about Jacinto—and I will—the man knows how to buy the best of everything. Up until tonight, he could afford it.

This is a sleek little number with an outboard built for speed. Oversized in the way that only the most expert among us can handle. Thank goodness I've spent half my life on the verge of capsizing.

In every possible way.

The fleet must have been ready to roll because the keys are in the ignition. Rather than kiss my finger up to God, I crank the bitch to life and boogie out into the gulf. No sense in thanking Sky Daddy until I know I'm free and clear. Counting chickens and all.

Gunning the engine like hell, the front of the boat lifts out of the water so high it damn near pulls a backflip. Which is exactly the kind of speed I'm after. But once that first burst passes things slow down a bit. She's loaded and sluggish, which means I'm about to make a bunch of junkies really pissed.

Throwing open the hold, I'm greeted by a king's ransom in dope.

"Sorry, kids. This is a solo ride." One by one, I chuck those bitches into the drink. It's a trail fit for a tweaker Hansel and Gretel, and I wonder for a second if my pursuers will stop to try and salvage any of the bunk. It'd sure gain me some time. But that's not exactly my luck, so I double down and fling poppy babies overboard until I'm sweating to beat the band.

Once the hold is empty, I hit the wheel again to check my speed.

Fast. But not fast enough.

A glance back to shore doesn't reveal much. Under cover of dark there's not much I could hope to see anyway. That doesn't mean they're not mobilizing. Best to assume the worst and go from there.

Digging in my pack, I come up with my multi tool and get down to the nitty gritty work of stripping this bad bitch down to the essentials. Everything that's not structural is fish food. We're talking seats, floaties, hatches, the works. All the way down to the chrome. Shit, I even yank the rigging and toss it.

I'm not tying up anytime soon. And if the opportunity came, I'd probably abandon ship and swim for it. I can trust my arms more than a fiberglass hull six days a week and twice on Sundays.

By the time I'm done it's just me, the throttle, and the steering wheel. The speed and fuel gauges survived by a whisper. Good news is now we're talking. This stolen rocket and I skip over the waves at breakneck pace, due west.

Which is nice and all, but there ain't much chance of hitting Florida. Time to cut north for Texas. Who knows? If I'm lucky I'll run into some Coast Guard. True, I don't have my credentials on me, but I can call Zero from the clink if I have to. The Coast Guard may be in on things, but a holding cell might not be the worst place to wait this one out. At least my death will be on the official record.

No use worrying about that now. The sun is down, and there's hardly any land in sight.

Son of a bitch, I might just have gotten away with this one.

"Lydia." A man's voice skitters down my spine like a rat, telling me I spoke too soon. "Lydia," it taunts again, riding a wave of static. All the blood drains out of my face as I look at the radio, its red light blazing like a bloodshot eye in the growing dark.

"I know you can hear me…"

Holy fuck.

It's Diego.

"Fine, fuck you," he snarls. "You don't have to respond—Just listen. That was a cute trick cutting a sharp north. It just tells us how to close the triangle to find you."

How the fuck did he know I just banked north?

Then it hits me.

There's a tracking device on this thing.

But how is that possible? Everything above the water line is long gone. Well, almost.

My stomach is in my shoes as I unscrew the comm unit and drop it overboard. It sinks out of view along with any hope of contacting land. Now it's just me and the gulf.

I even unscrew the knob on top of the throttle and pitch it over for good measure. No use taking chances.

Digging my phone out of my pack, I strip it out of its water bag and hold it up to the sky. No signal. I wave it from side to side like some dumb bitch in a commercial, to exactly zero effect. My first impulse is to pitch it too, but I think better of it. That wouldn't help anybody but my enemies.

So, I slip behind the wheel, gun the throttle and stick my nose in the air, filling my nostrils with salt air. If I close my eyes just right, I can picture myself back home in Croatia. The wind in my hair, the Adriatic lapping at the hull, and grilled squid for dinner.

Who knows? Maybe someday, right?

If I live that long.

ACKNOWLEDGMENTS

A book is a village, and I have to acknowledge all the butchers, bakers, and candlestick makers who populated this little world.

First, always to Kay and John - my parents. The ones who have my back, even when smut is the order of the day. Also to my incredible network of friends who never stop laughing and goading me on. You know who you are, and I'll always be grateful to you.

Special notice to my incredible editor Aimee Ferro (aimee ferroedits@gmail.com). She's the best editor on the planet, and the ideal partner in crime.

Finally, love to the folks at Trashcan Publishing for having the nerve to put this thing in front of the public. It's not for the faint of heart, but neither are you. I can't wait to see what else we get up to. Thanks to Sharp Levarius for green lighting publication, and to Dan Hodge—without whom literally none of this would be possible.

ABOUT DIDI POUNDER

—"I could never write those books. The pen would catch fire."

Didi Pounder has been a professional ghostwriter since 2019, authoring or co-authoring dozens of novels. Not only is she ready to have her own work out in the open, she thinks it's about damn time.

When not writing, she enjoys taking long walks along the Dalmatian Coast, eating oysters, sipping wine, and living a life she never dreamed of.

— "We only get one shot at this, so why not use both barrels?"

ALSO FROM TRASHCAN PUBLISHING

- **RED HOT BLACKTOP** by Didi Pounder
- **BOOKMARK FOR THE HEART** by Charlotte Northeast - Small Town Talk, Book 1
- **SABINE AND THE SILVER HAMMER** by Charlotte Northeast - Assisted Sinning, Book 1
- **DOWN FOR THE COUNT** by Ailis Elliot